D1527360

PRAISE FOR JAMES W. HALL

"James Hall's prose runs clean and fast as Gulf Stream waters."
Marilyn Stasio, *The New York Times Book Review*

"The real pleasures in Jim Hall's books are the sensual ones of place and people. It's the honest feel of South Florida, with all its menacing rhythms and contagious lassitude, that Hall nails down so well." - **Carl Hiaasen.**

"Mr. Hall's lyrical passion for the Florida Keys, his spare language and unusual images haunt us long after the story has faded."
Sara Paretsky, *The New York Times Book Review*

"James Hall is a writer I have learned from over the years. His people and places have more brush strokes than a van Gogh. He delivers taut and muscular stories about a place where evil always lurks below the surface." - **Michael Connelly**

"An expert creator of grotesque villains and fast action, former poet Hall raises the crossbar with his sensitive insights into the human condition." *Publishers Weekly*

"Like top-drawer Dutch Leonard turned inside out..smart, observant, richly grotesque."
James Ellroy.

"Highly original and entertaining." - **Elmore Leonard**

"James Hall's writing is astringent, penetrating, and unfailingly gripping long after you read the last page...The story and the characters crackle like lingering currents of electricity in your mind." - **Dean Koontz.**

"Not to be missed! James Hall started fast and gets better and better." - **Tony Hillerman**.

"Hall nails you to the page until the suspense-laden climax." - **Clive Cussler**.

"If you don't know the fine suspense novels of James W. Hall, this will get you off to a rousing start." - **Scott Turow**.

"...a cold eye for detail and a passionate commitment to justice." **Sue Grafton**

ALSO BY JAMES W. HALL

Novels

1987 *Under Cover of Daylight*
1990 *Tropical Freeze*
1992 *Bones of Coral*
1993 *Hard Aground*
1994 *Mean High Tide*
1995 *Gone Wild*
1996 *Buzz Cut*
1997 *Red Sky at Night*
1998 *Body Language*
2000 *Rough Draft*
2002 *Blackwater Sound*
2003 *Off the Chart*
2004 *Forests of the Night*
2007 *Magic City*
2010 *Silencer*
2011 *Dead Last*
2013 *Going Dark*
2014 *The Big Finish*
2017 *When They Come For You*
2018 *When You Can't Stop*

Short Story Collections

2014 *Over Exposure*

1991 *Paper Products*

Poetry

1976 *The Lady From The Dark Green Hills*

1980 *Mating Reflex*

1986 *False Statements*

1980 *Ham Operator*

2011 *All My Pwoblems (collected poems)*

Non-fiction

2001 *Hot Damn*

2012 *Hit Lit*

CHARLESTON COUNTY LIBRARY

BAD AXE

JAMES W. HALL

Copyright © 2020 JAMES W. HALL

All rights reserved.

ISBN: 9798655823051

Cover Design by Lon Shapiro
Guttman Shapiro Creative Group

Heat not a furnace for your foe so hot/ That it do singe yourself

SHAKESPEARE— HENRY VIII

DEDICATION

Always and forever to Evelyn

And deep thanks to Doug Teel for his inspiration

PART ONE

ONE

September 1

Marco drove the panel van slowly past Savannah's house, checking it out.

Ingrid said, "Don't go so damn slow, one of them will notice."

"They're gone, I told you. No one's home."

"You can't be sure."

"I'm sure."

He kept rolling down that deserted strip of road. Nothing but woods and empty fields along the way. Ingrid raked her fingers through her scarlet hair, jittery.

"First time back in Bad Axe since we were kids. Feels weird."

"Does it?"

"If you had feelings, you'd know."

He looked over at her and shrugged. Always looking for a chance to ding him.

Marco kept rolling the three miles down Taggart Road to make sure their old place was still standing. He stopped in the drive, didn't get out.

"Man, it's rundown," Ingrid said. "Whole house is sagging left."

"Foundation must be cracking," he said. "What do you expect, twenty years away. Houses don't take care of themselves. Anyway, the house isn't important. It's the barn that matters."

"It looks just as dilapidated as it always did," she said.

"It'll work fine," Marco said.

He circled back to Savannah's.

"Well, okay, it does look deserted."

"Told you," he said. "They won't be back till late tomorrow. Let's get this done and get out of here."

"Sure this isn't a trap?"

"I double-checked, found the death notice online. They're picking up the body like she said on the phone. Dover Air Force Base, military honors bullshit."

"Where's that, Dover?"

"Delaware, a long way off from here."

"You kept that goddamn phone number active all this time, that's crazy, Marco. Twenty years paying the bill for a phone number you never use."

"I did it for one reason, and this is it. Her calling me, letting me know they'd be out of town for four days. How else would she have gotten in touch? All in all, I'd say it's paying off pretty well."

"Hasn't yet."

"It will, you'll see."

"I don't trust her. Calling out of the blue, she could be setting us up."

"You don't trust her because you don't know her. Not like I do."

He backed the van to the front of the shed, opened the rear doors. Ingrid got out and stood nearby, nervous, scanning the area, brushing her hand across her blouse, touching the .38 revolver tucked in her waistband.

"Savannah must be heartbroken losing her grandbaby."

"I don't believe that woman has a heart."

"Well, if this works out, hell, we can travel. I always wanted to see some of the world. Like Italy, especially Florence. Stay in five star hotels, up high where you could see all the cathedrals and turrets and shit. When I was little, I cut out magazine pictures. Never thought you and me would have enough cash to take that trip. Or maybe Fiji, that would be nice too. What do you think, Fiji or Florence?"

"Maybe we'll do both. Go in alphabetical order."

"Really, you're serious?"

"We'll figure it out when we've got the cash."

"All I say, coming this far, taking this kind of risk, it damn well better be worth it. Savannah's going to know it was you and me stole them."

"No, she won't. It could be anybody. Lot of crazies would kill for one of these bad boys, much less two dozen."

"She's not stupid. She'll guess it was you."

"So? What's she going to do, call the feds, turn me in? Get her own ass thrown in jail."

He used the bolt cutter on the padlock and rolled open the shed doors.

Big Blue was still in her cage. Still alive after all these years.

"We ought to get a macaw," Ingrid said. "I'd like a bird for a pet."

"That bird's worthless," he said. "Does nothing but eat and shit."

"It talks, doesn't it? I remember it cussing like a trucker."

They loaded the crates into the van. Heavier than he'd expected. Both of them sweating through their clothes in the late summer heat. Big Blue watched the whole time, head turning back and forth like a tennis match. Never making a sound.

"Maybe it got old and doesn't talk anymore," Ingrid said.

He loaded the last three crates. With all twenty-four of them stacked inside, the van's suspension was sagging, but he was pretty sure it was still drivable. They didn't need to go far.

He slammed the rear door and went back to the shed and looked at the empty shelves. Big Blue fluffed up her wings and croaked so loud it made him jump.

"Marco, Marco, Marco, Marco."

"Jesus," Ingrid said. "After all this time she remembers your name."

"Stupid bird just signed her death warrant."

TWO

Five weeks later.

"Where the hell you disappear to, Thorn?"

On the upstairs deck of Thorn's stilt house, Sugarman leaned against the railing, his back to Blackwater Sound. The bay gleamed in the morning sun, its surface as bright and flawlessly flat as a silver platter. Overnight the first cool front of the fall swept through, bathing Key Largo in dense, chilly Canadian air that flushed away the October humidity and officially brought to a close six months of summer doldrums.

"I've been out on the water. Where've you been?"

"For a whole week?"

"Is there a problem?"

"And that music," Sugar said. "What's that?"

"'Hey Jude,'" Thorn said. "It's a Beatles song."

"I <u>know</u> that. You buy a stereo or something?"

"It's a portable," Thorn said. "She likes having a sound track."

"She?"

Thorn nodded at the screen door.

Sugar tilted his head to see past Thorn into the living room. Sofia Mendoza was perched at the workbench, focused like a brain surgeon on the bonefish fly pinched in Thorn's custom vice.

Sofia was naked, her face, shoulders and breasts radiant from a week's unremitting exposure to the sun. She looked up and trilled her fingers at Sugar.

Sugar ducked his eyes and turned away.

"Sorry," he said. "I interrupted something."

"It's okay. She's not shy. Sofia's a naturist."

"Like a nudist?"

"Different word, same thing, yeah."

"All the time? Everywhere?"

"Just about, though she dresses for work."

"Well," Sugar drew a quick breath. "I guess you get used to being around her like that."

"Haven't yet," Thorn said.

"Where'd you meet her? You been hanging out at nudist camps?"

"She tends bar at the Lorelei. You've seen her a few hundred times."

"Oh, Sofia Mendoza," he said. "I didn't recognize her."

"Yeah," said Thorn. "Cause you didn't notice her face."

"What can I say?" Sugar said. "I'm human."

"One of your better qualities.

Hanging loose down her back, Sofia's black hair glistened like the iridescent wings of a crow. She one-handed a thick strand away from her face and bent close to the fly, and snipped an end of the GSP thread with Thorn's micro-tip scissors, looked up and smiled at him then bent back to her work.

"Must be true love," Sugarman said. "Letting her use your tools."

"She's got better eyesight than I do and steadier hands."

"Has she like moved in with you?"

"Getting close."

"Thought you were too damn independent for the shacking-up thing."

"People change," Thorn said.

"Well, good for you. Another Rubicon crossed."

"We enjoy each other's company. It seems natural."

"How long's this been going on?"

"We been seeing each other, I don't know, a few weeks."

"And I'm just finding out about it?"

"It wasn't serious enough to mention."

"But it is now."

Thorn shrugged in the affirmative.

"Where'd you cruise?"

"Took the Chris Craft to Key West," Thorn said. "Sofia's family owns a hotel down there. They were *balseros*, came over on a homemade raft, inner tubes and plywood. Sofia's little sister nearly died of thirst, spent a month in the hospital. Now her parents run an inn on Caroline Street, place is packed all year. You'd like her family. They're loud and funny and make their own spiced rum."

"They nudists too?"

"Yep, the whole clan. Brown as coffee beans, nose to toes. Hotel has high walls and thick hedges, so the place is clothing optional."

"And you? Did you keep your pants on?"

"When in Rome."

Sugarman looked down at his loafers and shook his head as if to clear away the image. He was outfitted in khaki slacks and a red and yellow flowered shirt.

Sugar was a handsome fellow, a striking blend of his hard-partying Jamaican dad and his svelte milky-blond mom. His skin tone was café con leche, a double shot of leche. Arm against arm, Thorn's tan was darker. Sugar inherited his mom's delicate features and long lashes and got the rangy physique of his Rastafarian dad as well as his rawboned tensile strength that fooled some people into thinking he was merely lanky.

Something about the combination of his skin color, elegant looks and his carefree style was a provocation to certain bully boys. They sniffed Sugar out, spotted him across a bar room, a restaurant. That guy. Too pretty, too calm, his tranquil smile causing the assholes to mistake him for an easy mark. Let's go slap the shit out of that prissy son-of-a-bitch.

It was such a moment that brought Thorn and Sugar together back in grade school before Thorn even knew Sugarman's name. Spotting an after-school four-against-Sugar brawl on the playground, Thorn waded in, and after he and Sugar sent those four shit-stains running off bloody and blubbering, Sugarman and Thorn began a lifelong alliance, brothers-in-arms for the duration.

Sugar's Jamaican father disappeared shortly after his birth and his Norwegian mother, a fragile teenager, stayed around Key Largo a year or two more before she too vanished. There was a single overexposed photo of her hanging in Sugarman's office. Not more than eighteen at the time, his mother sat on a ratty sofa, a cigarette in one hand, a can of Schlitz in the other, laughing at someone's joke. An attractive young woman whose eyes seemed filled with an insatiable yearning.

After she disappeared, Sugar was raised by two church ladies in Hibiscus Park, Key Largo's black district that abutted the Overseas

Highway—a collection of tumbledown shacks and lopsided mobile homes where roadside entrepreneurs sold fresh mangos and hubcaps off their front porches. Growing up under the watchful care of those elderly sisters, Sugar absorbed their modesty and devotion to the rules of fair play and as an adult, he turned out as serene, steady and trustworthy as Thorn was the polar opposite.

Thorn liked to think their yin and yang friendship endured because Thorn's recklessness was the poetry to Sugar's prose, the jalapeno in the guacamole. Though the truth was more complicated. Sugar's methodical and disciplined approach had more than once saved Thorn's ass, and Thorn, despite his all too frequent rash outbursts had a few times returned the favor.

"You got that look," Thorn said.

"Which look is that?"

"Man on a mission."

Sugar took a lengthy breath as if steeling himself for what came next, then said, "You know Bobby Tennyson, right?"

"Bobby Tennyson?"

Sugar nodded.

Ten years earlier Tennyson had saved Thorn's life. Thorn was fishing in the backcountry, anchored up on a shoal near Nine Mile Bank. Bobby arrived, waved hello, then picked a spot a courteous distance away. Close enough to see each other, but too far to hear a cry for help.

For the next half hour a few schools of bonefish ghosted by, but all snubbed Thorn's flies. He was climbing down from his poling platform to reposition the skiff when he snagged the leather lace on his boat shoe on a gap in the aluminum frame. A freakish mishap. He lost his balance, tumbled headfirst and clipped his skull on the upraised prop. Knocked unconscious, face under water, shoe still trapped in the poling frame, inhaling seawater.

Bobby was there in less than a minute, hauled Thorn out, gave him CPR till Thorn spit up all he'd swallowed, then Bobby patched up the gash from his first aid kit.

Afterwards he brushed off Thorn's gratitude. Nothing heroic about it, Bobby claimed, just right-place-right-time, what anybody would've done. And sure, Bobby was probably right about that, but it still left an indelible memory that had replayed a hundred times since, especially when Thorn was fishing alone in a remote backcountry spot. No one around to save his ass if he got clumsy a second time.

"What's Bobby's problem?"

"You knew he was a pilot in the Air Force?"

"Sure. But he's not a big talker, so not much beyond that."

"Nothing about Johnston Atoll?"

Thorn shook his head. He wasn't sure why, but the special bond he had with Bobby had never turned into friendship. Bobby always seemed to shy away whenever Thorn took the bar stool next to him and tried to chat.

"Go on, Sugar. What's this about?"

"I need your opinion. I can't decide if Bobby's story is terrifying or nuts."

"I may not be the best judge of what's nuts."

"You willing to hear him out?"

"Sure, tell him to come over."

"He's downstairs in my car."

"Oh, this is serious."

Sugar nodded.

"Mind if Sofia listens in? A woman's perspective."

"Does she own any clothes?"

"They're around here somewhere. Give us five minutes then

bring him up."

When Thorn explained the situation to Sofia she said, "Sure, I know Bobby. Never thought he was a prude."

"I think you misjudge the arousing effect your bare flesh has on some guys."

"Like it does on you."

"I'm not complaining."

"You're cute, Thorn. You come across all worldly and cool, but you're as bashful and straight as the next guy."

"Is that bad?"

"Not at all. Worldly guys, cool guys, they usually turn out to be schmucks."

Sofia went to the bedroom, returning in jeans and a long sleeve T-shirt.

"Better? Or am I still too arousing?"

"You're just right," Thorn said.

Sugarman tapped on the screen door, staring self-consciously up at the sky.

"It's safe," Sofia called out. "Come on in."

Bobby Tennyson was in his mid-seventies. His thatch of hair had turned silver, and the beginning of a gut stretched his Caribbean Club T-shirt. He had pale blue eyes, a whimsical smile and ruddy cheeks. He walked over to Sofia and took her hand and brought her knuckles to his lips. A courtly gent.

"Hi there, mister vodka and tonic with an extra slice of lime."

"Miss Sofia, good to see you out from behind that bar."

Bobby shook Thorn's hand and took a seat in one of the sculptured wood chairs that Thorn's adoptive father had fashioned from local hardwoods. They appeared rigid and uncomfortable, much like their creator, but those chairs never failed to draw a sigh of surprise and contentment from first-time sitters. Some magic blend of contour and art that seemed to de-stress any anatomy they held. Thorn, who'd done his share of woodworking, had studied those chairs for years but had never managed to decode their mystery.

Under his arm Bobby Tennyson carried a leather-bound volume that he set on the side table. It looked like a photo album bulging with snapshots.

"All right, Bobby, the floor's yours." Thorn took a perch on the edge of the footlocker that served as a coffee table. Sofia sat close beside him. "Something about Johnston Atoll?"

For most of the next hour he told his yarn, going into such graphic detail it was clear that for Bobby Tennyson those long ago moments were still vividly alive.

THREE

It was 1971, early June, 1130 hours. In the dazzle of mid-day sun with a silky breeze off the Pacific rattling the palm fronds overhead, Captain Bobby Tennyson was relishing the fine island vibe, utterly oblivious to the hatchet-blow of fate about to sever his first twenty-seven years from all that followed.

"I'll be damned, Captain. I found one." Tech sergeant Kervin was aiming the wand of the Geiger counter at the downspout on a corner of the mess hall, the instrument clicking faster than a terrified heartbeat.

"You sure?" Bobby said.

Kervin moved the wand away from the spot then brought it back. The clicks faded then resumed.

"Yes, sir, it's the real deal."

"Well, okay," Bobby said. "You know the drill."

Kervin set down the Geiger counter and picked up the paint can. While he dabbed the spot with brown house paint, Bobby edged out of range, still a little spooked by this whole exercise. Painting over traces of plutonium seemed like a half-assed fix, but those were his orders, the way things had been done on Johnston Atoll for the last ten years, ever since the Thor missile blew up on the launch pad a few hundred yards from where Tennyson and Kervin were standing.

On the tip of that doomed Thor rocket was a W50 nuclear warhead. The explosion destroyed the missile's atomic payload before it could detonate, but in the fire and windblown smoke that followed, the launch pad was contaminated, and a shitload of plutonium and god knows what else was sprayed far and wide over the island and surrounding waters.

Army cleanup teams bulldozed up a layer of soil and dumped the radioactive mess into the nearby lagoon. The following year, some brilliant military minds ordered crews to dredge that same lagoon and use the coral and muck to expand Johnston Atoll from 220 acres to three times that size, and in the process they recontaminated the whole damn island.

But what the hell. Even if the atoll was bristling with hazardous isotopes and gamma rays, Bobby would still rather be serving his hitch on Johnston than the alternative: fighting in the bloody mire of Vietnam a few thousand miles west.

Bobby was a pilot, a good one, though it still surprised him to acknowledge it. To avoid the draft he'd enrolled in college, wound up earning a B.A. at Wichita State, and after graduation, with the U.S. Army circling in on him, Bobby joined the Air Force which seemed a safer route even though he was scared shitless of heights and was certain he'd wash out of flight training.

He did OTS at Lackland in San Antonio where he was required to take a ride beside an instructor in a Cessna 172 twin-engine trainer. To his everlasting surprise he discovered he loved flying. It was the most damn fun he'd ever had with his pants on.

A year later he shipped out to Laughlin and moved up to jets, the T-37 Tweet, a slow and forgiving trainer, then two years later he shifted to the big birds, the Lockheed C-141 Starlifter. A workhorse that could airlift combat forces long distances, insert them into war zones, re-supply ground troops, extract the wounded from hostile territories, carry tanks or Jeeps or pallets of food or armaments or whatever the hell was needed. All of which he did during a six month tour in Nam before he got the dream transfer to this island in the north Pacific, a two hour flight west of Hawaii.

Only downside of the Johnston deployment was that Bobby had no flying duties. His official title was Operations Officer, second in command under Colonel Joshua Snyder. The workload was low stress. Three times a week he met the incoming Air Micronesia flights, supervised the off loading of food and other supplies for the five hundred men stationed on the island, then oversaw the outgoing loads of garbage, mail and an occasional serviceman or civilian contractor taking R&R in Hawaii. He ran safety drills: fire, tsunami, power loss. And it fell to him to direct the plutonium sweeps which until today had been uneventful.

When Kervin finished painting over the speck of plutonium on the drain pipe, the kid checked his watch, nodded at the mess hall and said, "I been smelling that pot roast for hours. You coming, Captain?"

"Go eat," Bobby said. "Swim time for me."

"More painting this afternoon?"

"Back here at two, we'll work south."

"I'm wondering, sir. How come these spots weren't found already, all these years later."

Bobby patted Kervin on the shoulder.

"Apparently nobody's ever been as gifted with the Geiger as you, Kervin."

The airman grinned, snapped a salute and jogged off to lunch.

Bobby returned to his quarters, changed into swim trunks, got his snorkeling gear out of his locker and headed down to the beach on the west shore where the current was mild. On the opposite side of the island, if you were crazy, you could wade out ten feet into waist high surf, an hour later you'd be halfway to Hawaii.

Standing on the scrap of beach, Bobby watched the unceasing line of swells follow one another toward land as if some tempest beyond the horizon was roiling the Pacific, sending out its agitated heartbeat in all directions.

All that blue water was enough to make a Kansas boy swoon. Bobby had served his childhood in a suburb south of Wichita where any direction you looked all you'd see was dreary flatlands. He never connected to that terrain, always hungered to reconnoiter beyond those empty prairies.

Now, after months of charmed duty on this oasis, he was still spellbound by the blue expanse of sea, its restless churn, and my god, what he'd seen while diving beneath the surface, the showy fish lacing between the twists of coral, bursts of flickering neon in every direction, vast schools of fish juking left and right in synchronized dances, it was all too hallucinatory to absorb, such an abundance it might take him the rest of his days to process.

When Kervin called out, Bobby was knee-high in the surf, about to dive in.

"Sorry to bother you, sir."

Kervin stood atop the seawall, his mouth clenched.

Bobby asked him what was up.

"A Red Hatter said come fetch you. One of their rabbits died."

"Oh, Jesus."

As if that island wasn't already polluted enough with radioactive residue, two years earlier Johnston Atoll had been chosen by the Department of Defense as the primary collection point for America's recently banned chemical arsenal.

Months before Bobby arrived on Johnston, Operation Red Hat had removed a huge stockpile of biological agents stored in Okinawa, Japan, loaded them on Navy transports and brought them to Johnston where they were slated to remain until an incinerator was constructed to safely destroy them. Till then an Army contingent had been deployed to guard the stash.

Stored in a half dozen Quonset huts on the southeast end of the island were 150 tons of mustard gas munitions and twenty-four thousand pounds of landmines, mortar shells and assorted armaments, all of which contained either Sarin or VX nerve gas. Enough poison to kill every human being on earth and all the animal life as well.

That's where rabbits came in. The Army guys kept a warren of the critters near their quarters. A single caged rabbit was left in each bunker at all times to monitor leakage. If a rabbit croaked, you had a problem. In the months Bobby had been on the island, not a single creature had died and the whole cottontail exercise had struck him as a silly joke. Until now.

"Couple of technicians are suited up and going inside to track down the leak. With Colonel Snyder away, they wanted you to know what was going down."

Wearing only his swim trunks, Captain Bobby Tennyson hustled over to the Red Hat area, and was halted by an Army corporal standing guard at the chain-link gate. The corporal looked Bobby up and down, stepped back and gave the half-naked officer a half-hearted salute.

Bobby knew about the rule of threes—a principle that seemed to apply to everything from jokes to fairy tales and advertising copy. Three wise men, Scrooge's three ghosts, third time's the charm. There were always three curtains on the game show. Every storybook hero had three tests, three monsters to battle. And of course the third ogre was always bigger, more fierce and deadly than the two before.

As Bobby watched the Red Hat team in their rubber suits and gas masks exit the Quonset hut and stand under the decontamination shower, he was thinking: plutonium, nerve gas leak, good Lord, what next?

He hung back, waiting, until one of the Army techs came over to tell him all was well. They'd found the leak—a dried out seal—and repaired it. When the storage hut had been sufficiently aired out, it would be business as usual.

Minutes later as Bobby was exiting the Red Hat area, Kervin came trotting across the airfield. Bobby smiled to himself. Cue up number three.

Kervin caught his breath and said, "Radio room got a distress call."

"What kind of distress?"

"Civilian sailing vessel lost its rudder."

"Foundering?"

"No, sir, calm seas. But you know, without a rudder they're

adrift."

"They give coordinates?"

"Seven miles south southwest."

"Number aboard?"

"A man and woman."

"Nationality?"

"Schoen said they sounded American."

"Okay, get Fredal and Troseth, and have them take the Mike boat out and tow the party in. But the civilians stay aboard till repairs are made. They should be informed of this on first contact."

"Stay aboard?"

Bobby nodded toward the Red Hat guys peeling out of their rubber suits.

"For the civilians' safety," Bobby said. "They stay on their ship for the duration. Have Fredal inform our guests of the rules before arrival."

"Yes, sir."

Hours later, with no sign of the disabled ship, Bobby was indulging in his daily ritual—watching the unfolding of another astonishing sunset. Today the western sky had erupted in outlandish shades of red and gold, and clouds along the horizon were swirled and twisted into airy peaks that reminded Bobby of the sugary scallops of a meringue topping. Higher in the sky red puffs of cumulus resembled small explosions, and long contrails of darker reds and brighter golds crosshatched like the bars of a heavenly prison. It was a sky so immense and so busy Bobby almost missed the sailboat gliding toward the island at the end of the Mike boat's tow line.

With its boxy hull and twin masts with elliptical curved sails, that vessel might have just sailed out of Shanghai harbor in the Han Dynasty. A Chinese junk maybe forty feet long with a wide beam.

Bobby hiked across the island and met the ship at the boat basin. The two newcomers were standing out on deck gazing at the growing crowd of airmen and soldiers. The sailors were in their twenties, their flesh roasted to a dark mahogany, and both had shoulder-length hair bleached shades of blond. The guy was tall and powerfully built and naked except for a red bandana wrapped around his privates in a makeshift loincloth. The woman was topless, wearing only cut-off jeans. Hippies at sea.

A few of the airmen wolf-whistled. It had been a long time since some had seen a woman and even longer since they'd seen one in such a state of undress.

When the tow line was unfastened, the woman heaved the dock lines ashore to a cluster of airmen who'd hopped down onto the cement dock for a closer look. It took considerable grunting and several minutes of sweaty work with two guys on each dock line before they got that squat Chinese junk snug against the pier.

"Thanks, fellas," the woman called down.

She brought her fingertips to her mouth and blew the horny guys a kiss.

She had a long mane of coppery hair and her body was as sinewy as a distance runner's. A pair of ragged denim shorts hung loose on her narrow hips. But it was her black, cutting eyes that held him. After a second or two Bobby was lost in their smoky depths and it wasn't until Kervin nudged him in the arm that he resurfaced.

"You okay, Captain?"

Bobby blinked and looked at Kervin's knowing smile.

"Troseth says the bodybuilder's name is Judson, the skinny girl you were checking out is Savannah, like the town."

Bobby nodded.

"They asked permission to come ashore. Their shower isn't working, haven't had a bath in a couple of weeks. Might be the polite thing to do. "

Bobby pulled away from Kervin, and stepped closer to the junk.

"Young lady, you need to get some clothes on," he said. "This is a military installation. We have rules."

Behind him the guys grumbled until Bobby turned, gave them a cautioning look, and they fell silent.

"All right, gentlemen," he said. "Fun time's over. Thanks for your help. See you at dinner."

Bobby turned his attention to the vessel which was painted red and gold in shades even more garish than the sunset he'd witnessed minutes earlier. *Flying Dragon* was emblazoned on its hull in a florid script and below that was a gold bas-relief carving of a dragon with its wings folded to its sides. The ship had a pointed prow and a high squared-off stern with four glass windows facing aft.

For the next week that ship would stay docked at Johnston Atoll while waiting for a rudder to be fashioned in a certain marine specialty shop in Hong Kong. The rudder had to be custom-carved from teak and fenestrated with diamond-shaped cutouts. Only historically accurate parts were suitable for the crew of the *Flying Dragon*.

Around midnight on that first evening after the junk arrived, Bobby lay in the dark and listened to the wails rising from the sailboat. Male and female voices floated across the island, first it was drunken singing, then when that died down, there were yips and squeals of passion that persisted so long into the night that the next morning the men trooped into breakfast in a state of stupefied exhaustion.

Three days later, Colonel Snyder returned from his leave in Honolulu. The Colonel was a taciturn man with a habitual grimace. Ignoring Bobby's repeated attempts at banter, Snyder had always kept a gruff distance, so Bobby had learned not even the most innocent detail of the man's personal life.

The Colonel was tall and gaunt and wore his thick silver hair in a crew-cut with the forehead bristles waxed to rigid attention. His face was craggy and full of harsh angles and his eyes had dark, wounded depths as if he had witnessed acts so vile and inexcusable, they would have crippled a lesser man.

When the Colonel's flight landed, Bobby met him on the tarmac and informed him of the visiting ship.

"And does this vessel have a name?"

"*Flying Dragon*. A Chinese junk. And quite the crew."

The Colonel drew a careful breath then by slow degrees his perpetual scowl melted and his mouth widened into the first smile Bobby had seen from him.

"Well, I'll be goddamned."

"What is it, sir?"

"She's come for a visit."

The Colonel fixed his eyes on Bobby and in that instant, Bobby saw the truth in the Colonel's dark and fathomless eyes and in the broad mouth and hard cheekbones. He also had the same arch of eyebrow, the identical contour of jaw. As close to a carbon copy as genetics would permit.

"That girl's your daughter? Savannah?"

The Colonel continued to smile as he hitched his duffel over his shoulder and strode toward the docks.

That evening the crew of the *Flying Dragon* moved into the Colonel's house on the northwest point. The bright yellow edifice had two bedrooms, two baths, a grassy backyard and a view of endless blue and was, by Johnston standards, palatial.

Bobby's quarters were a distant second—a two room suite with a tiny kitchen and a private entrance and a view of the back of the mess hall.

Over the coming few days, while the visitors waited for their rudder to arrive, they spent their daylight hours exploring the neighboring waters on one of the island's two pontoon boats. They usually left the docks around noon and headed out to one of the reefs to dive and spearfish. Probably following the Colonel's orders, they didn't associate with the airmen or soldiers, keeping an aloof distance.

Once when Bobby happened by their docks as the boat was departing, Savannah eyed him as she cast off their lines, giving him a secret smile while they motored away.

"I smelled marijuana coming from the Colonel's house," Kervin told Bobby that afternoon as they finished up the day's Geiger counter duty—once again finding a single plutonium spot.

"No way. They're probably just cooking something exotic."

"No, sir, it's pot. I spent a month in Frisco. I know what weed smells like."

"Snyder would never permit it."

Kervin shrugged.

"Looks to me like the Colonel can't say no to anything that girl does. She's got the old man knotted around her little finger."

Late that evening, Bobby was in his bunk reading a paperback novel. Travis McGee on his houseboat in Ft. Lauderdale was once again coming to the aid of a beautiful, damaged woman. It was a book Bobby had read twice before but it was holding his interest—seeing things he'd missed on the previous journey. With the bedside lamp still lit, Bobby dozed off. Not the book's fault. The steady trade winds were whispering outside his open window, easing him into slumber as they did most nights.

When he opened his eyes, Savannah Snyder was perched on the side of his bed holding a roach clip to her lips and blowing sweet pungent smoke toward the darkened window. She was naked, her clothes piled in a heap beside her.

Bobby lay still for a minute waiting for the mirage to fade.

"You don't snore," she said. "I like that in a man."

She offered him the joint, but Bobby waved it away.

"Suit yourself, but it's good shit. Very sensual."

"You shouldn't be here."

"I know," she said. "That's what makes it so delicious."

She tapped a finger against the paperback that was splayed on his chest.

"You go for this he-man stuff. Brawny guy on the cover, sultry vixen in the background. You fantasize about sultry ladies, do you?"

Bobby didn't answer. Savannah rose and prowled his room, studying the items on his dresser as if taking an inventory of his personality.

"Are you a true believer?" she said.

Bobby asked her what she meant.

"Like my Daddy, live and breathe the military code, all that jazz."

"I believe in most of it."

She turned and faced him. Her luxurious bush glittering in the soft light.

"And the war? Burning villages, murdering babies? You believe in that?"

"You need to get dressed."

"You keep telling me that. Since the first time we met.'"

"Nobody believes in shooting babies, or burning villages."

"But they do it anyway, right? Old people, women, children. They're gooks, so it's fine. Gooks don't value life the way Americans do. Makes it all okay."

"It's not okay," he said. "Not fine."

"We have a connection, you and me. You know that, right? An electric charge flickering between us. You've felt it too. The way you look at me. The way you're looking at me right now. You've felt it. Don't lie."

"I've felt it."

"What're we going to do about it, Captain Bobby?"

Bobby's breath had deserted him.

She came back to the bed and sat near him. She held his eyes and lifted the edge of the spread and snaked her hand below the sheet and touched his thigh.

Bobby shook his head but didn't pull away.

Her fingers slipped beneath the elastic band of his briefs, her nails raking through his pubic hair, gripping a handful and tugging lightly. He wanted to pull away, and he wanted to roll toward her and drag her down on top of him.

But he did neither.

She cupped his balls, rolled them in her hand as if weighing their contents. He was firm. Firmer than he'd ever been. Achingly rigid.

"You need to go," he said. A croak.

"No, Bobby, I need to stay. I need to make you happy. And you need to make me happy. I think you can. I think you can make me very happy."

She clasped his cock, squeezed it until he gasped, then relaxed her grip and moved up the shaft with a feathery touch, and when she reached the tip she trickled her fingers down again.

"You feel it, don't you, Bobby?"

God, did he ever.

But all he managed was a grunt.

"My father doesn't think much of you. Says you're too tenderhearted, a poet type. But I think being a poet is a good thing. Much better than the alternative."

"What's that? The alternative?"

"A robot. Blindly obeying commands."

Bobby wanted to respond, to say maybe it was possible to be both. To be a good soldier who was also sensitive. But her hand was moving faster up and down his length and his breath was trapped in his lungs.

"Tell me, Bobby," she said. "Am I as desirable as the woman in your book?"

"More," he said. "She's just words."

"Does the hero in your book save the woman in distress?"

"He does, yes."

"Would you save me?"

"Are you in distress?"

"We all are, Bobby. Every one of us is in distress. Especially now, the way the world is. We're all in grave trouble."

Her hands were oily slick, milking him expertly. He held back. Held on.

"Would your book hero do anything in the world to save his lady fair?"

Bobby nodded.

"And you, Bobby? Would you be that brave and daring? Would you do anything? Risk anything? Overcome all odds."

"Sail away with you?"

She laughed.

"Riskier than that."

He hesitated then said, "I don't know what you're asking."

It was as if she'd bumped a tripwire in his psyche that jolted him out of the trance. A cold detachment took hold, a sudden distance from her heat and her hand. She'd pushed too far, too fast.

Savannah sensed it too. Her hand ceased its movement. She held his gaze for several moments. Her eyes had the shine and color of aged bourbon, liquid and rich and unblurred by the marijuana.

"Would you do a job for me? Take a risk, a big risk?"

Bobby drew a deep breath.

"What kind of risk?"

"Does it matter?"

"Sure, it matters."

It was over. Both of them knew it. Over and done. A line crossed.

He was wilting in her grasp. She released him and drew her hand from his shorts, out from under the sheets. She wiped her hand on her bare thigh.

"I don't think you're going to be my hero after all," she said. "I think you're a Boy Scout, Bobby. Sweet and simple-minded and boring. I think the two of us could make love until you couldn't breathe and your spine would remain a steel rod. You'd still salute the flag, sing the national anthem word for word."

"What job is it that I'm not up to?"

She rose and bent to her pile of clothes, plucked out her panties and stepped into them and tugged them into place. In his chest an enormous weight was sinking, the missed chance, the risk not taken, an ungodly pleasure forever lost.

Savannah held his eyes as she pulled on her jeans and buttoned her blouse.

"What job?" he said.

"Sorry, Bobby. That's something you'll never know."

But she was wrong. The task she had in mind for him soon became apparent.

Sometime late on the following night the *Flying Dragon* vanished. No replacement rudder had ever arrived. Clearly, it had never been needed. The lost rudder was simply a ruse.

The next morning Colonel Snyder summoned Bobby to his office and with downturned eyes, he asked if Bobby knew why Savannah and her friend had left so abruptly. Bobby said he had no idea. The Colonel lifted his gaze and stared at Bobby with suspicion.

"Were you intimate with my girl?"

Bobby's throat clenched.

He said, "I barely knew her, sir."

"And the other men? Did any of them?"

"I can't say, sir."

"Can't?"

"No, sir. Not that I know of. I can try to find out if you want."

Colonel Snyder turned his head and looked out his office window at the airstrip where a Micronesia Air flight had just touched down.

"You should get to work, Captain. There's a plane to unload."

Three days later during a routine inventory in the Red Hat area, munitions were discovered missing. Two dozen M23 landmines. Steel disks thirteen inches in diameter weighing twenty-three pounds a piece. Each mine was filled with an additional ten pounds of VX nerve agent—the deadliest gas in the U.S. arsenal.

It might have taken an hour or two, humping those twenty-four armaments from the Quonset hut to the docks, but it would have been an easy enough job for the muscle boy, Judson. And that eight hundred extra pounds wouldn't slow down the *Flying Dragon* to any great degree.

Snyder put the island on lockdown. Everyone confined to quarters except for personnel performing essential services. Snyder notified D.C. of the theft, and the Navy immediately launched two P-3 Orion turboprops and the Air Force sent out four C-130's, also turboprops designed for flying low level search missions. The Navy sailed all available vessels toward Johnston Island, carriers and other helo bearing ships.

The Defense Department dispatched a DOJ lawyer and two FBI agents to investigate the situation and interrogate all base personnel, military and civilian. But before the interviews could begin, Corporal J.T. Munson, a member of the Red Hat team came forward to admit that he was the damn fool they were looking for.

Munson was a strapping farm boy from Minnesota. What hadn't worked on Bobby had succeeded flawlessly with Munson. Enticing him with dope and sex, Savannah took a single evening to work her twisted magic on the boy. Hours after Corporal Munson opened the gate into the Red Hat area to give Savannah the forbidden tour, he was helping Judson lug the landmines to the sailboat. He had no idea why they wanted the landmines, or where they were headed. Munson confessed to having only foggy memories of that night.

After two weeks of fruitless effort, the search for the sailboat was suspended. All ships were recalled to their home ports, and the Air Force abandoned further reconnaissance efforts. The *Flying Dragon* had officially disappeared.

For Bobby Tennyson every detail of the night Savannah entered his room, the shape and texture of her body, the exact words spoken, the fateful choices made would haunt him the rest of his days.

As the years passed, his initial relief that he had not succumbed to Savannah's seduction metastasized into a deeply rooted ache of guilt that he had not done more to thwart her plans.

Whatever the hell her plans were.

Four

When Bobby finished his tale, the silence in the room stretched for half a minute. Outside the front window on the branch of a gumbo limbo a mourning dove cooed several times, lamenting its fate and the fate of every living thing.

Finally Sugar, cleared his throat and said, "And that's only the first chapter."

"It sounds like a love story," Sofia said. "The way you tell it, how your voice changed when you got to the Savannah part."

Bobby looked down at his lap and was silent.

"It was obvious," she said. "Don't know if the guys heard it, but I sure did."

Bobby nodded.

"It's like it happened yesterday," he said. "I remember every second of that night she appeared in my room, and yeah, I think what I should have done, I should have said, yeah, sure, I'll go along with her, pretend to help her do whatever it was she wanted me to do. And once I found out her plan, I could've taken action, kept it from happening.

"But I didn't. I got self-righteous, went cold, pushed her away. But if I'd been thinking, I'd have realized I was on an island full of horny guys. Take your pick, lady."

"So she found another sucker and escaped with two dozen weapons of war."

Thorn asked who else knew about the theft.

"Only a small group on Johnston got the exact details. Munson, Snyder and me, and the inspecting Red Hat officer who discovered the missing armaments.

"A few of the airmen and soldiers might have had an idea what was going on, there was gossip, but mostly the affair got buried. Snyder was busted down to Captain, shipped to Da Nang.

"And the brass put a turd in my file that kept me from further promotions. Which was fine. I left the Air Force when my time was up, flew for Pan Am, then Eastern, then United."

"It's a fascinating story, Bobby. But why tell us?"

"Show them, Bobby," Sugar said.

Bobby dug his cell phone from his pocket, tapped it a few times and handed it to Thorn.

The message on the screen was brief and cryptic:

M23's stolen. Bad things are coming.

Thorn handed the phone to Sofia.

"It's a text message," Bobby said. "Just showed up on my phone. M23's are the landmines with VX."

Thorn asked who sent the text.

"The number was blocked. I don't know for sure."

Sugar said, "With blocked numbers the service provider would need a warrant from the court to reveal the caller."

"Naturally, I think it's from Savannah," Bobby said. "She's the last person to have them. I mean, yeah, she could have passed them on, they could have changed hands a bunch of times, but if it's some stranger, why contact me? How would they even know who I was?

"So maybe Savannah has been safeguarding them all these years, couldn't dispose of them, couldn't hand them over to the authorities or she'd wind up in jail. So they've just been sitting somewhere, then boom, they're stolen. And she has reason to believe the thief means to use them."

Sugarman said, "Bobby called FBI headquarters in DC. Couldn't get anyone interested. Called Miami field office, same thing. And he contacted the State Troopers out in Texas, Border Patrol, Texas Rangers."

"They blew me off, every one, treated me like a crackpot," Bobby said. "Maybe I am."

"How about Frank Sheffield?" Thorn said.

Sugarman explained to Bobby that Sheffield was the Special Agent in Charge of the Miami field office. A friend to Sugar and Thorn. They'd worked together a couple of times in informal arrangements.

"Yeah, I spoke to Sheffield," Bobby said. "He's the one that blew me off. Laughed in my face."

"You told him that whole Johnston Atoll story?"

"I couldn't do that. I just said something vague, like I had reason to believe there were some landmines filled with VX nerve gas about to be used by someone."

"That's vague all right," Thorn said. "No wonder he blew you off."

"So I just dropped it," Bobby said.

"Except he didn't drop it," Sugar said. "The book, Bobby, show them."

Bobby picked up the leather-bound album from the side table and brought it over, handed it to Thorn.

"The last page," Bobby said. "Happened two days ago along the Mexican border between Van Horn and El Paso."

Pressed flat beneath a plastic sheet, the article was from the *El Paso Times*, a single column long, headlined: **Five Migrants Die In Mysterious Blast**

Sofia leaned in and read it along with Thorn and when she finished, she said, "You think this was one of the stolen landmines?"

"It has the earmarks," Bobby said. "Asphyxiation, an explosion from beneath the vehicle."

Thorn paged through the album, scanning other headlines about explosions and death.

"What is this?" Thorn said. "This book."

"Bobby collects news stories," Sugar said. "His computer is set up to search for keywords that sound suspicious, anything that hints of landmines or nerve gas."

"Ever since Johnston Atoll, I was afraid this was going to happen."

"This El Paso thing, it <u>is</u> suspicious," Sofia said. "You've got to admit."

"Nobody listens to me." Bobby cast a forlorn look around the room, studying each of their faces. "You guys don't believe me either."

"What exactly do you want from us?" Thorn said.

"I know you two have helped other people in the past, I mean, you know, with their confidential problems."

Thorn glanced at Sugar, giving him a 'you take it' flick of the eyes.

Sugar said, "It's my business, yes. I investigate things privately."

"I'll pay the freight. Whatever it is."

"Let me get this straight, Bobby. After all these years you want us to track down these landmines?"

Bobby nodded, sheepish but resolute.

"Before something really bad happens."

Sugarman lifted his gaze to the ceiling as if consulting the rafters. Not an outright refusal, but close.

"And you, Thorn?" Bobby said. "I'll pay your way too."

"I'm no gun for hire. Do you even have a plan in mind?"

"I have an airplane at my disposal," Bobby said. "We can fly out to El Paso, sniff around, see if we can pick up the trail."

Thorn shot Sugar a searching look which Sugar answered with a non-committal shrug. After an uneasy stretch of silence, Sugar came to his feet, clapped Bobby on the back, steered him to the door, then suggested they all sleep on the idea and meet up tomorrow to decide what they'd do.

"Come to the Lorelei," Sofia said. "My shift starts at three. I'll stand you all a round. But just one."

"The second's on me," Bobby said. "And the third."

On that cheery note, the gathering adjourned.

"Arizona, Mama. See the sunrise. Are you happy? We are in America."

The girl gestured through the narrow rip in the side of the metal truck, their only view and meager source of fresh air for the last week days. There were several larger openings in the truck's opposite side, but other travelers had claimed those, pushing the girl and her mother aside.

"Arizona," her mother repeated. "Pretty America. Very happy."

The girl's name was Dulce. She was fifteen and was trying to teach her mother English, but it was not going well. Maybe her mother was too old for new languages. Or maybe in her grief she could no longer learn anything at all. Sister Kathleen had told Dulce that she must be patient with her mother in her time of sorrow. She had lost her husband, Dulce's father, when he was shot down by the *Maras* gang on his way home from the sugar cane fields—his weekly wages stolen.

The floor of the truck bed was covered in straw. All the others sat with their backs again the metal sides of the truck, some with their eyes down, others sleeping. There were three teenage boys in one group, traveling without an adult. There were twin girls with their father. The twins were five or six and wore matching pink frilly dresses that were probably their best frocks. The dresses started out fine but now were soiled and rumpled. Their father slept a lot and when he woke he spent most of his time coughing. There were also two young men in their twenties who wore ragged street clothes and had tattoos on their arms. They carried no suitcases or knapsacks. Those two worried Dulce for she had seen the flash of metal under the shirt of one of them, a knife or gun. That one kept eyeing her in a hungry way.

At the outset of their journey, the driver handed out five plastic jugs of water. The men with tattoos grabbed two of them. The others did not protest but shared what was left, small sips only. The food Dulce's mother had brought in her shopping bag was nearly gone. Only a darkened banana and two corn tortillas.

The days had been hot and dusty and the air was thick with the stink of piss and shit. In the back corner of the truck was a single bucket full to the brim.

Before they left San Pedro Sula in Honduras, the driver told them they would be locked in the truck and not allowed to exit until they crossed into America. It would take six nights and seven days of driving with only stops for petrol.

"We will be free soon," Dulce told her mother. To console her. To give her hope. Her mother had barely spoken the entire journey.

Dulce learned her English from Sister Kathleen who came to San Pedro Sula from the town of Phoenix. Phoenix was where Dulce and her mother were headed.

They paid for their passage with money her father saved from working the cane fields outside of Planeta. For years he saved so the three could leave Honduras and go north to Mexico and maybe one day cross into America. It was his dream and when he died it became Dulce's.

Sister Kathleen brought magazines to the school and showed pictures of America, the streets, big new cars, women in their white kitchens. Dulce collected some of the photographs and taped them into a scrapbook that she carried in her pink knapsack, along with some coins and a change of clothes.

The man who took the money for the trip to America was honorable. Dulce knew him from church. A religious man who smoked cigars and had four sons who were very polite, except for one who looked at Dulce and hissed dirty words. But the father was a good man, someone to be trusted. Not like the devils she'd heard of who took the money and left their travelers locked inside the trucks to die in the heat without water or food.

The driver of Dulce's truck was the boss man's brother. He was also from San Pedro Sula and lived alone in a cabin behind his brother's house. He was a good driver, and had taken others from Dulce's neighborhood to Arizona and some of them had written letters back to their people in Honduras to praise the man and his skill at driving. After they made the long journey, some of them were happy in their new home but some wanted to return to Honduras.

Dulce believed such *nostalgia* was a weakness of spirit.

"We are on a good road now, Mama. It is more smooth."

"A road," her mother repeated. She tried to say "smooth" but could not manage it and mashed her lips together and shook her head in frustration.

The blast was louder than any thunder Dulce had ever heard. It shook the truck, throwing it from side to side and tearing open a large hole in the floor. The vehicle came to a violent stop.

During the explosion the two men in ragged clothes were thrown upward and smashed into the roof of the truck, their faces and arms were slashed by metal fragments. Their mouths were wide but she heard no screams, no wails. She heard nothing. The truck was full of wild movement, but everything was silent as if Dulce was only dreaming.

Perhaps the truck's engine had exploded. Dulce knew nothing of motors or trucks, so she had no idea what had gone wrong. The truck was old. It had made many journeys like this, long, hot, difficult trips. Maybe gasoline was leaking and blew up.

Fragile daylight shone through both sides from ruptures in the metal. The straw was on fire. Dulce's mother had frozen, eyes looking upward.

Dulce saw the shiny piece of metal shaped like the blade of a knife sunk into her mother's throat. Blood trickled from the wound.

Dulce tried to scream but had no voice. The flames from the straw moved to the twins' dresses and lit them ablaze. Their father slapped at the burning cloth but the fire spread quickly, the girls continued to scream without sound.

Through the ragged opening in the floor a fine mist rose. For a few seconds it looked like steam from a broken pipe, then the spray disappeared. The teenage boys began to cough, the young girls in the burning dresses were gasping.

Dulce's mother fell sideways, landing on Dulce. She was a heavy woman and her weight trapped Dulce facedown on the floor. Dulce's lips jammed against a rip in the metal flooring. She could barely breathe. The air tasted of acid and gasoline.

Mashed flat by her mother's weight, Dulce was too weak and shocked to shift her away. She was beginning to hear again—the cries of pain, the coughs, the gasps and gagging.

Then came thumps and bangs as if someone was trying to break into the truck. Dulce could see nothing but the sandy ground below the truck. She budged her head beneath her mother's weight and caught sight of the twin girls lying on the floor. White foam flowed from their mouths like soap lather.

Dulce's mother shook and trembled then was gone. Dulce could feel the terrible weight of death bearing down against her own body, crushing Dulce into the straw. Again, her lips were pinned to the open gash in the floor. The air outside the truck was hot and now an odor like nail polish remover was burning her nostrils.

She heard voices far away. A man and woman speaking. Someone coming to rescue them.

Dulce turned her head beneath her mother's wide belly and

looked for the people. If they had come to save the travelers, they were too late. Dulce had seen the others in the truck. None were moving, bloody wounds and white foam on their lips. It seemed that only she had survived the explosion.

Or perhaps she had already perished and her mind had not yet left her body.

The man's voice was closer. Dulce shifted her head and saw her scrapbook lying on the floor a foot in front of her. The knapsack was torn apart and the book had fallen open to a page that showed a beautiful kitchen. White tile, blue curtains on the windows, daisies in a glass jar, a tomato sliced open. Its sweet red juice glistening. The fire in the straw was close to the scrapbook. A flame slithered like a bright snake through the straw, until the fire began to eat the pages, turning them black, melting the plastic cover.

Someone opened the rear doors on the truck and light flooded in.

She could see the shadow of someone moving on the straw in front of her. The stab of fear made her squirm, but she caught it and hardened herself. Stiff, unmoving.

Dulce watched his feet pass by her face. His boots were black rubber.

The man stopped next to Dulce and squatted down as if he'd seen her move. He was wearing a mask with goggles, and a rubber suit like ocean divers she had seen in magazines. He was holding up his phone and moving it around slowly like a movie camera.

She shut her eyes before the man saw her face.

This man had not come to rescue anyone.

The man rolled Dulce's mother part way off of her and poked a finger into the side of Dulce's throat. Dulce didn't move. She made no sound. He pinched her cheek hard and twisted. Dulce stayed still, enduring the pain.

Play dead. This was her father's instruction if the gangs came with guns. If there was shooting. Play dead. They will not waste bullets on a dead child. Bullets cost money. Dulce had asked him if this worked, if this was all it took to save yourself when the gangs came. He looked her in the eyes and told her, yes, some of the time it worked.

It wasn't much, but it was her last hope.

Play dead.

When the man released Dulce's mother's body, it settled atop her again, then he moved on and checked the other passengers. When the man passed by Dulce a second time, he halted. Dulce stayed very still and through eyes almost shut she saw the man squat down and place something small and shiny in the straw not far from Dulce. Then he bent over the shiny object, held his phone in front of it then lifted the phone and swept it across the dead bodies. Making a movie. Dulce had seen others do the same with their phones, that same movement.

When the man finally left the truck, Dulce continued to lie still, flattened beneath her mother's bulk, struggling to breathe the hot dry air that rose from beneath the truck. Maybe an hour went by.

Dulce whispered, "Mama?" Got no reply, whispered it again a while later and again there was only silence.

Dulce stayed still. She breathed carefully. Her throat was sore. She looked toward her scrapbook and stared at the shiny object on the floor next to the book.

Dulce squinted to see the object more clearly. It was the same size as the American coin Sister Kathleen had given her. A silver dollar. Perhaps it was something she might use later to exchange for food or water.

Dulce listened carefully, no longer hearing any voices. She reached out for the coin, stretching as far as she could manage and snatched the object and tucked it into her pocket.

Then she closed her eyes and kept her lips pressed to the gash in the floor. The hot dry air was making her sleepy. She closed her eyes. She would rest for a while and when she felt stronger, she would push her mother away and try to stand. Stand and leave the truck, find help. But first she would rest. Rest and maybe sleep.

FIVE

Category five hangover. Inside Marco's skull a jackhammer was chipping bone, trying to open a crater in his forehead. An excruciating beam of sunlight ricocheted from the front window of the hotel room off the mirror across from the bed and blinded Marco even with his eyes closed.

And oh, Lord, Marco needed to piss.

His bladder was about to erupt. But he couldn't sit up, couldn't lift his thumping head off the pillow, and forget about trying to stand. He rolled onto his left side, opened his eyes and struggled to remember where he was, the day of the week, how he'd arrived in this room, trying to reconstruct the night before, any detail, a place, a face, a song on the jukebox.

But all he found inside his head was swirling haze and pounding.

On the side table a foot away was an empty bottle of Patron tequila. His favorite, the gold one, expensive, a splurge.

A clue. They'd been whooping it up.

Yeah, yeah. A big day. Of course. They blew up the truck of illegals.

Afterwards they'd celebrated with Patron, sparing no expense. Staying in a four star Tucson hotel so they could use the super-fast Wi-Fi to upload the video. Yes, the plan was finally kicking in.

Marco tried to focus on the tequila bottle but it kept dancing on the tabletop. He blinked, rubbed his eyes, worked to keep the room stationary, lower the volume in his cranium.

He heard Ingrid speaking. Trying to get Marco's attention.

Marco struggled to lift his head again, but failed.

A few throbbing seconds later, Ingrid was hissing in his ear.

"Wake up. Wake up, goddamn it."

Ingrid was standing beside the bed in her pink panties and matching bra.

"You fucked up. Fucked up big time."

Ingrid had the TV remote in one hand, using it to raise the volume.

"What's going on?" Marco may have said the words aloud or maybe not.

"Watch this. Open your eyes and watch."

With a stagey flourish a voice said, "And now for KOLD News At Noon."

Marco managed to haul his head upright. On the screen a man and a woman sat behind a sleek desk. Both of them unbearably perky. He shut his eyes and listened to their report.

When the story was over, Marco tried to say something but his mouth was too caked to open.

"One of the little darlings got away," Ingrid said. "Now we have to find the bitch. You hear me, Marco? You hear what I'm saying? We have to get up and go finish this off."

Marco hadn't pissed the bed since he was seven years old. Back then when his old lady discovered what he'd done, she made Marco lie in the wet sheets until supper. All day lying atop his soaking mattress, cold on a winter day.

Some folks would call that child abuse. But hell, as punishments went, Marco considered it a fair trade-off.

Because, by god, when the piss finally flowed, back then and again now, it felt so fine, at least for the first little while, a warm, secret relief, it was worth any price he might have to pay later on.

☣☣☣

"Arizona," Bobby Tennyson said. "A few miles south of Nogales. This is it. This is definitive."

Bobby slid the printout across the bar. Thorn scanned it and slid it back to Bobby. Bobby passed it to Sugar who was sitting on his other side.

The article was from the Arizona Daily Star.

Eleven Border Crossers Found Dead In Truck Explosion

No photos and only a few specific details like the name of the rancher who found the gutted truck and the eleven dead Hondurans on her property. A couple of ID's showed the immigrants were from a town in Honduras. Initial analysis by the local coroner indicated that several of the victims died of wounds sustained in the initial blast while several others were the victims of asphyxiation. The coroner suspected they succumbed to carbon monoxide poisoning or smoke inhalation.

Thorn pushed the bottle of Red Stripe away. His thirst was gone. After delivering their drinks, Sofia had stepped down the bar to tend to a group of tourists in gaudy shirts and sunburns.

"This happened yesterday?" Thorn said.

"Yeah," Bobby said. "On the border. South of Tucson, same exact pattern."

Sofia returned and dabbed her towel at a damp spot in front of Bobby. Thorn slid the article to her and Sofia read it.

Sugar leaned forward and said, "Very convenient."

"What's convenient?" Bobby said.

"Blast occurred in a rural area, a long way from a city."

"Meaning what?" Thorn said.

"Means you've got ordinary, untrained folks taking care of the bodies. Nationwide we've got a haphazard system for dealing with the dead. In most rural locations a local justice of the peace will decide if an autopsy is needed to confirm the cause of death. Most times deaths like these migrants will land on the local coroner. The coroner might be elected or he might be appointed. Could be the director of a funeral home, or the local sheriff. Doesn't need medical training, doesn't need to be a pathologist. In Arizona there's only a dozen or so medical examiner offices for all the counties in the state. So do the math.

"Way I see it, if you want to kill people using an exotic poison or nerve agent and have a high probability no one would put two and two together, backwoods Arizona is a pretty good place to pull it off."

"That's impressive info," Sofia said.

Sugar had spent years as a deputy with the Monroe County Sheriff's Department before quitting that job and going into business for himself as a private investigator. Given Sugarman's modest and unassuming manner, it was easy to forget what a hardcore professional he was. And how well-informed.

"Wouldn't first responders be contaminated?" Thorn said. "I mean, if this stuff is so potent, it would infect anyone coming in contact with it, no?"

"Protective gear, rubber gloves, breathing masks," Sugar said. "These days even for backwoods law enforcement that's standard protocol. Worried about AIDS, blood borne infectious diseases. Same with the medical team."

Bobby said, "A speck no bigger than the dot over an *i* will kill you. But VX is heavy. It doesn't stay suspended in the air. It'll remain in the soil for a while, on clothes and such. But gloves and protective gear would keep the EMT guys safe."

"Okay," Thorn said. "Then what's the motive?"

"Isn't it's obvious?" Bobby said. "They despise illegal immigrants. There's a lot of that out there, always has been. Back in the day, I was stationed at Laughlin Air Force Base for two years, right on the Mexican border. Guys I knew cruised the desert at night, playing freelance border patrol, vigilantes, that's how they thought of themselves, out in their Jeeps with spotlights and pistols keeping America safe."

"Killing people?" Sofia said.

"Never heard of any killing," Bobby said. "But scaring the ever-loving bejesus out of them. Forcing them back across the border. It was sport. I never went along on those outings, but I heard about it happening. I knew guys. They weren't evil or political, or anything. To them it was like herding jack rabbits, see how fast they could make them run back to their burrow."

"That's awful," Sofia said. "Those people are only trying to survive. Americans should know that. Americans are supposed to appreciate that."

"A lot do," Thorn said.

Eyes misting, Sofia turned away.

Despite dealing with a steady onslaught of drunks and pushy tourists for eight hours a day, Sofia remained a gentle soul. Oh, sure she kept a judge's gavel behind the bar and Thorn had seen her whack a few guys who got too grabby at closing time. A sharp, measured tap on the skull, or crack on the knuckles always cooled them down.

From the use of that gavel and her quick, biting comebacks to raunchy remarks, she'd acquired a hard-ass reputation with the locals and fishing guides who frequented the joint.

But beneath the tough exterior Thorn had found Sofia was an unapologetic flower child. An idealist and dreamer who often made her point by quoting lyrics from the Beatles in a earnest voice as if they were sacred lines from the Gospel.

"I'm flying out there," Bobby said. "Leaving tomorrow. Who's in?"

"Flying where?" Thorn said.

"Tucson," Bobby said and tapped the printed out page. "The Cessna 441 cruises at 300 knots. Leave at dawn, with the time change, puts us there by noon. Rent a car, from Tucson it's a short hop to the border where this last one happened. Get there while the trail's still warm. I already called the sheriff out there, little town called Frontera, told him I had information he might find useful."

"Bobby, Bobby," Sugarman said. "You're getting way ahead of yourself."

"Sheriff's name is Castillo. He's eager to hear what I have to say."

Sugar sighed and looked at Bobby for a long moment, then sighed again, and explained that his twin girls had birthdays next week. No way he could miss that.

Bobby nodded that he understood. He was quiet, watching a flats boat edge up to the adjacent dock. Resignation had hardened his features, making him look ten years older.

Thorn had a backlog of bonefish fly orders to fill. Days of work. Work he loved, work that gave his days a quiet meaning. Bobby's concerns didn't involve Thorn in any personal way. No one he knew was at risk and Bobby's evidence was flimsy. An anonymous text, a news article.

But as the silence ticked by, it was Thorn's turn to bail or sign on. Bobby didn't turn his way. He didn't say the words. Didn't need to. Thorn owed him. Owed him his damn life.

"I appreciate you guys hearing me out," Bobby said, staring down into his drink. "I understand you got your own lives to attend to. Don't need to waste your time on some silly expedition that more than likely won't come to anything."

"I'll go, Bobby," Sofia said. "This is important. I got sick days stacked up."

She patted Bobby's hand then peered at Thorn, the harsh Florida sun blazing in her brown eyes. For a dizzy half-second Thorn saw this moment from Sofia's viewpoint. They'd been given a rare chance to nudge the universe a half degree back on course. A watershed occasion for her, as well as a painful recognition that Thorn, her lover of late, could dismiss this opportunity with such casual disregard.

A week ago, he wouldn't have understood that look. But during the boisterous seven days in Key West mingling with the Mendoza clan, Thorn had gotten a privileged glimpse into the complicated heart of a migrant family. Though he'd known countless Cubans since he was a kid, and had many Cuban friends over the years, that week with the Mendozas had been a revelation.

The family was thriving in a foreign land and doing it with such relish it was easy to miss the undertone of grief in each wistful story about their past and their homeland. Some of those rambling tales were cut short with a sharp intake of breath, or a sudden shudder and shake of the head as if the memory had cut too deep. At other times their stories simply trailed away into a shared silence, a communion of loss.

Last week as Sofia and Thorn were cruising back to Key Largo, Thorn had switched off the engine and they'd drifted for a while, watching the sunset off the bay side of Marathon, sharing a bottle of red. Thorn wondered aloud whether Sofia felt more American or Cuban.

She laughed at him, then quoted the Beatles line, "'Imagine there's no countries. It isn't hard to do. Nothing to kill or die for. And no religion too.'"

"Okay," he said. "Which means what?"

"Borders are the problem. We're all in this together, everybody, all of humanity. Doesn't matter which side of which border you're on."

"But borders are real. We can't just wish them away."

"I can wish for whatever I want."

Hard to argue with that.

"And you, Thorn? Do you think of yourself as American or a Keys guy?"

"Those my only choices?"

"You're terrible, you know that? We're having a serious talk and you make smartass jokes."

"Touché," he said and considered the question for a moment. "Okay, I don't consider myself a member of any group. I'm a guy who loves the place he lives, has a few buddies and a beautiful, intellectually stimulating lady friend. A great thing about America is that it leaves me alone to experience all that."

Sofia raised her glass and they clinked, turned back to the rest of the flamboyant sunset, and no more was said about nationalities or borders.

But the conversation kept nagging at him.

'Imagine there's no countries. It isn't hard to do. Nothing to kill or die for.'

Despite mulling over the sentiment for the last few days, he couldn't decide if it was naïve or profound.

Navigating a flimsy raft, the Mendozas had risked their lives to cross the Florida Straits, and settled in Key West, so close to the land they'd loved and lost they could almost smell the exhaust fumes of those ancient Chevys and Fords cruising the Malecón in Havana. As risky as their journey was, no one had tried to blow them up or poison them, mainly because the vagaries of American politics favored their nation's refugees over migrants from other territories. They'd gotten a pass while Haitians in similar rafts or Mexicans plodding across the border hadn't. Still, despite their favored status and despite escaping the tyranny of a despot, the Mendozas lived as outcasts, never fully at home in their adopted country. Once abandoning his or her original country, maybe no refugee was ever fully at home again.

"Hell, yes, Bobby," Thorn said. "Count me in."

Sugarman smiled. He knew the story of Thorn's near drowning. Must have known from the moment he brought Bobby over to his house that Thorn would have no choice but to enlist in this adventure.

Bobby turned to Thorn and in a solemn voice asked if he was sure.

"When do we leave?" Thorn said.

"The Cessna can seat all of us, no sweat. Long as everyone travels light."

Sugar said, "You ever try to track down Savannah or her dad?"

Bobby sighed.

"I tried every way I could think of. But no, they both disappeared."

Sugar nodded, flattened his lips, mulling something.

Thorn said, "Your buddy know you intend to fly his airplane to Arizona?"

"Hector doesn't care. He's at Raiford, finishing up a ten year hitch. Used to fill that Cessna with bales of grass, now it's just sitting at Tamiami Airport, sprouting rust. They're like boats, worst thing you can do to an airplane is let it sit, that's Hector's philosophy."

"Sticking your nose into this," Sugarman said. "I mean, okay, it's a worthy goal, but come on, honestly, what do you think you can accomplish?"

Bobby said, "Find the rest of those landmines, that's what. Return them to the U.S. government for disposal. Rid the world of one more danger."

"Would VX still be good after all that time?"

"Shelf life for VX could easily be fifty years. It's thick and heavy like motor oil, doesn't degrade over time like Sarin or some of the other nerve agents."

"Bobby knows his stuff," Sofia said.

"Those things disappeared decades ago," Sugar said. "Tracking them down now would be next to impossible."

"There's nothing you can do that can't be done," Sofia said.

A bright Beatles twinkle in her grin.

Thorn smiled across the bar at her.

"Lady's got a point," said Thorn. "And you, Sugar, you're sure you're going to pass on this?"

He sighed and shook his head.

"You go on if that's what you want. I'll do what I can from this end. I've had some success running down missing persons. That'll have to be my contribution."

"I don't believe it," Bobby said, his own eyes growing muddy. "You guys are actually going to help me make this right."

"Whoever's doing this, Bobby," Thorn said, "they're not going to take kindly to someone sniffing their trail."

"I know," he said. "But we can handle them. The bunch of us."

"We can try," Thorn said.

"No way in hell one of them survived that gas."

"Marco, you were in too much of a hurry, like always. You should've noticed the girl was moving."

"I'm inside that suit, goggles fogged up, I'm squinting at the image on the phone camera, I can barely see a thing."

"Stop making excuses. Bottom line, if that girl saw what you were doing, the whole deal could fall apart."

Marco swung them around two more whipsaw turns, then blew out a breath as he settled into a long empty straightaway. He hated this top-heavy yellow van. Even their ancient Suburban hugged the road better than the van

"Okay, I did see one girl squirm. I poked her in the neck, she didn't squeak."

"Well, you didn't poke hard enough."

"Look, we could let this go. That girl was too scared to open her eyes, see what I was doing."

"You'd risk that? Put this whole thing in jeopardy. If the feds know there's a video, what with all the high tech shit they got, they'll start combing the dark web until they find the damn thing, and we're fucked."

"Aw, Christ."

"Say it, Marco. What do we have to do to fix your fuckup?"

He was silent, focused on the road ahead.

"The words, Marco. What do we have to do?"

He felt like bawling. Almost forty years old, could break Ingrid in half with his bare hands and she still had that power over him, could turn him into a ten year old whenever she used her drill sergeant voice. Been happening since they were teenagers, even after Marco made all those trips down to Detroit to see a shrink.

The doc listened, asked about Marco's childhood, his missing father and fucked-up mother, typical shrink shit, then after four sessions Marco told the guy, okay, time to stop with the questions and give Marco some answers, how to break free of his girlfriend's dominance.

"Sorry, buddy, doesn't work that way."

Marco saw a patronizing smirk flicker across the guy's lips.

"Anything else you want to address today? We have five more minutes."

"My face," Marco said.

"What about your face?"

"Never mind."

"No, help me here. You're not a movie star, okay, I'll grant you that."

"My mouth, my chin. They don't fit with the rest of my face. I look in the mirror, I don't like what's there."

"Sure, sure. I can understand that. But hell boy, I'm no plastic surgeon. There's one down the hall if you want to make an appointment. Just a joke, Marco, just a little humor. So next session we'll talk about your self-consciousness. How's that sound?"

Marco got out of his chair, marched out of the office, climbed into his Mustang, drove a block down the street and parked, waiting for hours till the doc called it a day and headed off in his sleek red Lexus.

Marco tailed him home, hung near the guy's fancy house in Bloomfield Hills till dark, waited a few more hours till all the lights in the house went out. From what Marco could tell from peeping, the shrink had a teenage daughter, a young son, and a wife with blond hair. Guy was enjoying a perfect life on the backs of fucked up individuals like himself.

An hour after the house went dark, Marco rang the doorbell. A few minutes later the shrink stuck his head out the door and Marco clocked him in the nose, grabbed him by the pajamas and dragged him onto the porch, kneed his groin, and when he was down and squirming, Marco stomped his head, kept stomping with his work boots until the shrink was limp and drew his last raspy breath.

Marco squatted down beside the dead man and said, "Hey, thanks, doc. I think I'm cured."

Of course that wasn't true. Didn't matter how many people Marco wasted, Ingrid could still turn him into a whimpering ten year old.

After doing the shrink, Marco was officially a killer. Not that it changed him. Nothing life-altering. His stomach was a little iffy for an hour after, but that passed. He plumbed his conscience, tried to feel around for a trace of guilt, or maybe even a hint of pleasure. Nothing.

Did that make him a psychopath, a stone-cold killer? Maybe it did. Spending years on the Whitman's farm where killing was a daily chore, Marco wasn't squeamish about it because it was a necessary duty. Chickens, pigs, humans, not a lot of difference when you got down to the blood and guts of it. So if he was a psychopath then most farmers were too.

"Go on, say it, Marco. What do we have to do now?"

He heard the words coming from his lips, but they sounded small and far off.

"We find the little girl and take her out."

By the time they made it to Frontera, it was dark, all the shops closed up on the shabby main street, nobody walking around, not even a stray dog. Kind of street you'd expect a big tumbleweed blowing down the middle of it.

The sheriff's office was dark.

Ingrid told him to stop a half block down and she jumped out of the van and walked back down to the office and tried the door. Locked.

"I say we get on back to the ranch," Marco said when Ingrid climbed back in. "Regroup. Start prepping."

"No, we'll find a motel up the road," she said. "Return here in the morning, get up close and personal with Castillo, find out what he did with the girl."

Marco was out of comebacks. His headache was down to a Category 2, meaning he'd survive. Actually about now he could use some hair of the dog. Just a glass or two of something. Beer, bourbon. Anything but tequila. Yeah, Christ, anything but that.

SIX

"We're going to miss our flight," Thorn said.

He spooned Sofia tight, kissed the back of her neck then started to draw away, but she clung to his arms, locking him in place.

Through the eastern window, he watched a rosy plume of clouds rising from the horizon. Dawn filled the room with light so delicate and pervasive it seemed to dust Sofia's flesh in rouge.

"Bobby will wait for us," she said.

"Listen to the temptress."

He kissed her shoulders, held her for a while, felt himself firming against her backside. When his hand strayed to her breasts and he began to caress, she gripped his wrist, halting him, then turned her head to see his eyes.

"You're right," she said. "We should go."

He exhaled.

"Sorry," she said. "I got you all worked up."

"Duty calls," he said.

"It's true," she said. "I'm a bad influence."

"Hell with that. You're the best influence I've had in a long time."

"How long exactly?"

"So long I can't remember."

"Sure, Thorn. Sure. I guess some girls buy that."

She rolled over to face him.

"You're positive about this, Sofia? Flying off with Bobby, no plan, nothing."

"A few days in Tucson. Might be nice. You ever been?"

"Haven't had the pleasure. Hot, a lot of desert, that's how I picture it."

"I hitched through there once," Sofia said. "It's a pretty place."

"Except for the truckload of dead refugees."

"Yeah," she said. "Except for that."

Thorn sat up, swiveled away and slipped his legs over the side of the bed. Sofia reached out and touched the knobs of his spine, slick with sweat. Counted them slowly from T1 to L5. He felt goose bumps tickling his arms. A quick shiver.

"You want the first shower?" he said.

"Why bother with two?"

"Because otherwise we'll never get out of here."

He was rising from the bed when she said, "Who are you, Thorn?"

"What do you mean?"

"I'm about to fly off with you, I'd like to know who you are."

He settled back onto the mattress beside her.

"You don't know already?"

"I don't mean how you are in bed, which by the way is great, and I don't mean the witty guy, quick with the quip, or Henry David Thoreau sitting on his dock, watching the light change and the birds ride the breeze, all meditational and sensitive. Yeah, I know that Thorn. But there's another one, isn't there?"

"Where's this coming from, Sofia?"

"I've heard things, stories about your past. Bad shit you were into. I want to know how much of it is true."

"I don't know what you heard, but okay, probably some of it is true."

Thorn was silent, looking into those eyes, the glimmer, the shadowy depths.

"I've had adventures, maybe more than my share."

She motioned with her hand. "Let's hear all of it."

"The point is, Sofia, I don't go looking for trouble. But a few times in the past, when friends or loved ones were in danger, some who even lost their lives, I've done what I could to make sure they got the justice they deserved."

"Like a vigilante?"

"No," he said. "I'm just a guy who likes things to turn out fair."

"But if you had your choice, you'd rather the world left you alone?"

"I'm fond of solitude, yeah. But I'll make the rare exception."

"Like for Bobby."

"Yes," he said. "And for you."

Sofia smiled and leaned forward, cupped the back of his head, tugged him to her and kissed him with such fervor that the room around them and the birdsongs beyond the windows and the coral island and the turquoise waters, all of it dissolved like a flimsy daydream until Sofia was finished with him and drew away.

"Okay," she said. "I guess I'll take that first shower."

☣☣☣

Ten till nine Mountain Time, Ingrid and Marco parked half a block down from the Frontera sheriff's office and waited. Marco was pissed, feeling the pressure mounting in his chest, his headache threatening to resurface.

For the last hour he and Ingrid had argued. Marco making the case for kidnapping the secretary or sheriff, whoever showed up first, take them into the desert and employ some serious stress on their various joints until they revealed where they'd stashed the kid.

Ingrid called him crude and idiotic. She wanted to extract the girl's location without alerting anybody to their presence. Move so stealthily they wouldn't even ruffle the air. It was the way she talked sometimes, poetic.

She said she had a plan but wouldn't share it with Marco. He was supposed to stay put, not say a word and let her work her magic.

"And when that fails," Marco said, "I'll start cracking bones."

Ingrid unbuckled her seatbelt, squeezed between the seats and duck-walked into the back of the van. In the rear view mirror Marco watched her dig through one of her duffels.

"Keep your eyes on the sheriff's office," she said.

She rustled around for another few minutes, then squeezed back between the seats and settled into hers.

"Jesus," he said.

Ingrid had on a wig, blonde and frizzy, a pair of aviators. She cocked her sun visor down and checked herself out in the little mirror, applied a large helping of slut-red lipstick, then swirled a tiny dab of lipstick from her fingertips against her cheeks.

"You look like a foxy badass."

"Yeah," she said. "Exactly what I was going for."

She leaned forward and opened her purse and drew out a manila folder, dug through it and after half a minute plucked out a laminated ID card.

"Which of those you going to use?"

"I'm the brains, remember. You're the brawn. Don't get confused."

Marco shut up and they sat in silence until five after nine when a heavy-set Mexican-looking woman with black hair swirled up in a beehive showed up at the office in a tiny white car, got out and unlocked the office door and walked inside. She was wearing a yellow dress with big blue flowers on it. Marco guessed she was fifty, maybe a little older.

"I shouldn't be but a minute."

Ingrid got out and walked across the street and went in the office.

Marco knew he shouldn't, but he jogged over, waited till Ingrid was inside then opened the door a crack so he could see her work.

The secretary was futzing with the radio on a shelf behind her desk, her back to the door. Ingrid stepped forward and waited while the secretary tuned in a country music station. When the woman turned around and saw Ingrid, she gasped and snatched at the throat of her blouse.

"Sorry," Ingrid said. "Didn't mean to frighten you."

Ingrid smiled, came forward and held out the laminated ID. The secretary picked up a pair of reading glasses from her desk, leaned forward, read the ID, looked up at Ingrid's face and said, "Has there been a terror attack?"

"No, not yet."

"Then what in the world is the Department of Homeland Security doing way out here in the middle of nowhere?"

SEVEN

Just after ten local time, Bobby touched down in Tucson. Thorn, not a seasoned flyer, had grown queasy in the rocky stretches of the flight. Slamming through eight-foot swells in his Chris Craft was one thing, but the Cessna's sudden dips and jolts at 35,000 feet rattled his composure and unsettled his breakfast.

"You're not getting sick, are you?" Sofia asked him somewhere over Texas.

Thorn managed a smile.

"Piece of cake."

"Don't worry," she said. "Bobby seems to know what he's doing."

Thorn nodded. But his gut floundered for most of the trip and only calmed after an hour on the straight, flat Arizona highway.

Bobby rented a big black SUV and they made it to Nogales by noon and kept heading southwest toward the border on a two-lane blacktop that was nearly deserted. By three they pulled into the gravel lot of the Frontera Sheriff's Office, a building resembling a repurposed 7-Eleven.

The secretary, a cheerful, robust woman in her fifties with an intricate concoction of black hair, said the sheriff was running late from a county commission luncheon, but was on his way, and the three of them were welcome to wait in the outer office with her.

Sofia and Bobby sat together on a wooden bench and Thorn wandered the room, humming along with Johnny Cash's "Ring of Fire" on the radio. He paused by the front door and read a framed news story from the Nogales paper that featured Raoul Castillo, the sheriff of Frontera, receiving an award from a county commissioner that honored the sheriff's bravery for apprehending a trio of bank robbers who'd been terrorizing southern Arizona for months. Dressed in a suit and tie, his face glossy with sweat, Castillo seemed to be strangling from embarrassment and his tight white collar as he received the plaque.

As Thorn turned from the framed article, the door opened, and the sheriff strode into the room, halted, then took his time examining his three visitors.

"I'm Bobby Tennyson, I talked to you on the phone," Bobby said. "About the explosion, the migrants."

Castillo was a short, husky man about fifty with a froth of curly white hair, a resolute jaw and the dark vigilant eyes of an underfed raptor.

"And these folks?" Castillo said.

"Like I told you, friends from Key Largo. This is Thorn and this is Sofia Mendoza."

"Are there any more stashed somewhere?"

"No," Bobby said. "Just us three."

"Sheriff," the secretary said. "I need a word."

"Let me deal with this first, okay, Tensia?"

With an aggravated sigh, he waved for them to follow him into his office.

Castillo instructed Thorn to shut the door then took a seat in his high-backed leather chair and eyed each of them in turn, settling his probing eyes on Bobby.

"All the way from the Florida Keys," he said.

"That's right," Bobby said. "Been there?"

"Got as far as Miami once," he said. "Just for business. Too many people, everyone in a rush, a lot of pushing."

Thorn was scanning the office, taking in the framed commendations, photos of Castillo with civilian leaders, politicians, civic groups. Handshakes, big smiles. Nearly everyone on the walls seemed to be of Mexican descent. The office décor was scrupulously official, objects one would expect in any bureaucratic workplace. But the fragrances in the room revealed a distinctive personality, lime-scented aftershave, well-worn leather, the clinging hint of wood smoke, and the pungent whisper of strong whiskey. It was the masculine musk of a man who spent a lot of his waking hours laboring in the outdoors, marinating in the aromas of this desolate, parched land.

Beyond Castillo's office door, his secretary had turned up the country station, more oldie-goldies. Dolly, Willie and Tammy.

"So this young lady would be Sofia Mendoza, bartender at a tavern in the Keys, Cuban American, daughter of hotel owners in Key West."

Sofia nodded and said, yes that was all correct.

"You told him all that, Bobby?"

"No, just your name. He must've dug up the rest himself."

"Then there's Thorn," Castillo said. "Thorn being his family name, or so Bobby says. Thorn is a man who as far as I can ascertain never entered a database of any kind. No birth certificate, no driver's license, social security card, no passport, voter registration. Do I have that right, son?"

Thorn nodded.

"Managing to accomplish that in this day and age is a minor miracle. The authorities down in Key Largo let you get by with that, do they?"

"So far."

Castillo gritted his teeth in a pained smile. He lay his large hands flat on the desk and stared down at them.

"Somebody better start explaining your presence here. I got

about a minute of patience left."

"Like I said on the phone, we've got some time-sensitive information concerning these migrants killed in the truck explosion."

"If it was so time-sensitive, you could've just told me on the phone. You didn't need to come all this way."

"Look, Sheriff," Thorn said. "We don't want to lock antlers with you. We'd just like to assist if we can."

Castillo considered Thorn while nodding sagely like a man whose best conversations were those he had with himself.

"You're down to thirty seconds."

"All right, the quickie version," Thorn said. "Bobby was an Air Force officer stationed in the Pacific when two dozen landmines were stolen from his base. We think they may have resurfaced here."

"Landmines?"

Thorn said, "Yes, only these mines weren't conventional ordnance, these were packed with VX nerve gas."

The sheriff rocked back in his chair, giving Thorn a wary squint.

"And what exactly is your interest in this, Mr. Thorn?"

"Bobby feels responsible for the landmines that went missing. He's our friend, so we're trying to help him track down the miscreants who stole them."

"Miscreants?" Castillo said.

"Bad guys," said Thorn.

"I know what the goddamn word means," he said. "Just never heard anyone feel the need to speak it out loud before."

Castillo rubbed his thumb slowly across his chin as if feeling for stubble his morning shave missed. His face had relaxed and Thorn watched his chest fill and empty again, a measured cadence like a brand of yoga he employed to reclaim his composure.

"Illegal border crossings," said Castillo at last. "Central Americans fleeing violence, poverty, seeking asylum in the U.S. or just plain sneaking in. How in hell's name could this be connected with nerve gas?"

"We're not sure," Thorn said. "That's why we're here."

"These devices are anti-tank mines," Bobby said. "Four pair of ridges along the top surface. Each has two fuse wells on top of the primary, so it can be set for anti-vehicle or anti-personnel. When it's activated by sufficient pressure, the bursting charge breaks open a thin steel casing, heating and spraying the nerve agent so it forms an aerosol. A droplet no bigger than the head of a pin will kill a full-grown man. If one of those landmines went off in a crowded indoor space, it could kill hundreds."

Castillo nodded and continued to nod, his face so slack Thorn couldn't tell if he was absorbing Bobby's information or ticking off the last few seconds before he ordered them from his office.

Bobby continued his riff.

"How VX works, it prevents the proper function of an enzyme that shuts off glands and muscles. When that switch doesn't work, the glands and muscles will start racing flat-out. Like a seizure times ten. Breathing stops, lungs fail. You sweat, you twitch, you die."

More nodding from Castillo, eyes half-closed as if he might be drifting off.

"Other thing you should know. VX isn't volatile. It's slow to evaporate from liquid to vapor. So in average weather, it can last for days on objects, clothes or the skin of victims. A long-term hazard. Any object it contacts can be contaminated and be a threat for weeks.

"Am I being a bore?" Bobby looked at Thorn then Sofia.

Sofia said, "This is all interesting, Bobby. And relevant. You're an expert."

"All right, all right," Castillo said. "You made your point, now what do you want from me?"

"What can you tell us about the explosion?" Thorn said, trying to keep the edge out of his voice though the sheriff's scorn was starting to irritate him.

"It destroyed a truck and caused the death of eleven migrants riding inside."

"Have any forensics been done at the scene?" Thorn said.

"Not yet."

"When did the explosion occur?"

"Near as I can tell it was Tuesday, early morning, just after sun-up. Wasn't till Wednesday mid-day I learned of it."

"How could that be?" Thorn said. "A day and a half before you find out."

"Desert is a big place. The event occurred in a remote region."

"And how did it come to your attention?"

"The owner of the ranch contacted me."

"Are there suspects?" Sofia said.

"Can't be suspects without a crime. Like I said, it looks like there wasn't anything unlawful about the deaths except the undocumented folks being inside the country."

"Newspaper story said the medical examiner believes some of the deaths were caused by smoke inhalation or carbon monoxide poisoning."

"That was his initial impression, yes."

"Has he finished the autopsies?" Thorn said.

"Haven't been any."

"Isn't it required with a violent death or one that's suspicious or unnatural?"

"You a lawyer?" he asked Thorn.

"I know some law."

"The law is one thing," Castillo said, "politics is another."

"What's political about this?"

"Pima County ME says it may be another week before he gets to it. Not his fault. His department is overworked and underfunded. They don't have the budget. These eleven go to the end of the line."

"Because they were migrants?" Sofia said.

"Illegals is the word most folks use around here. To those folks, migrants are a threat to their way of life. Don't ask me how they reach that conclusion. But for them, shoot them, blow them up, whatever it takes to slow down the flow."

"Is that your suspicion, this truck was targeted? Attacked?"

"I've not ruled out any possibility."

"You know people who would do that, blow up a truck full of migrants?"

"About half the citizens I'm sworn to protect fit that description."

Thorn said, "The owner of the ranch where this happened, does he fall into this category? Hateful toward undocumented."

"It's a woman owns the ranch," Castillo said. "She's eighty-seven. And she leaves water and food out for them, lets them rest up on her property if they want. I think we can rule out Marjory Banfield."

"The road where this happened, do border crossers use it regularly?"

"You just keep pushing, don't you, son?"

"Normally he's pretty laid back," Bobby said. "But we think this is important."

Castillo sniffed, rubbed a rough hand over his face like he was scrubbing away a bad dream.

"Okay, yes, there's a steady flow of border crossers on Banfield's property."

"So if someone wanted to ambush a truckload of migrants?"

"It would be easy to accomplish," Castillo said. "That area of the border is not heavily patrolled and there's a clear dirt trail smugglers follow."

"Well, we'd like to see the site," said Thorn. "Can you spare somebody to show us the way? Or give us the GPS coordinates and we'll do it."

"And any photos or physical evidence you've gathered so far," said Bobby. "If you could share that, we'd be grateful."

"Don't be ridiculous," Castillo said. "Your story's intriguing, I'll give you that, but where's the link between those landmines and these migrants? I've been patient with you, but look, you can't walk in here, complete goddamn strangers, and start demanding to see evidence."

Bobby said, "Before we get any farther along, there's something else I need to tell everybody. Kind of a confession, I guess."

Bobby was about to continue when Castillo's secretary tapped on his door and peeked around the edge.

"I really need a word, Sheriff. This may be important."

The sheriff asked her what it was.

"Your sister called just now. A van pulled up in front of her house. She doesn't recognize it. She was worried someone's come for the girl. In the middle of our conversation she hung up. I tried calling back but there was no answer."

The sheriff's jaw hardened and he shook his head.

"How'd anyone find out about the girl?" Castillo said.

"It was on TV. That Rappaport fellow at KOLD reported it. Probably one of the EMT boys who moved the bodies fed him the story."

"But you and I were the only ones knew where she's staying."

"I guess I messed up," the secretary said. "A woman came in first thing this morning. She had ID from Homeland Security, and wanted to know where the girl was located. I should have waited for you to get out of your meeting to clear it."

"Why would Homeland Security be involved in this?"

"I asked her that but she said she wasn't authorized to discuss it."

"All right, Tensia. I'll take it from here."

With a weary wave, he motioned her out of his office.

"Something wrong?" Thorn said.

Castillo stood up and took his hat from the rack behind his desk.

"There's a girl," he said absently.

"What?"

"A survivor from the truck explosion. Fourteen or fifteen. Won't talk. Hasn't said a word. Scared, traumatized. Probably lost her mother, maybe her father too and brother or sisters. It is hard to say how those people were related to one another. They didn't have many papers, and what they had some of it burned up."

"Were you planning on telling us about this girl?" Sofia said.

"I'm telling you now."

Sofia said they'd like to meet her.

"I need to get out to my sister's place, see what the hell's going on."

"Mind if we tag along?" Thorn said.

Castillo didn't answer, just brushed past Thorn and headed for the door.

"I'm taking that as a yes," Thorn said.

On the way out, Castillo told his secretary to call his sister, let her know he was on the way. Keep her door locked, don't let anyone inside no matter who they claimed to be.

As Castillo started his truck, Thorn hauled open the passenger door and climbed aboard.

"Get out," Castillo said.

"When we get to your sister's I'll get out."

"You're an idiot."

"You're not the first to notice."

"I don't know who the hell you are, son. Or what you're doing here."

"I'm beginning to wonder myself."

Castillo slammed the pickup into gear and roared away.

The truck had to be at least thirty years old, dented side panels, a blue flasher fixed to the dash. The muffler was either missing or its bowels were rusted out. The racket rattled the windows and made further conversation impossible.

In the side mirror Thorn saw Bobby following in the rental.

The road shot straight across the valley. The surrounding mountains were a dozen shades of dusty brown, treeless and wind-scarred, stark ridges rimmed with rows of broken incisors. The plain stretched into the endless distance, a desert floor dotted with cactus plants and a lone palm here and there rising from gray scrub.

The sheriff left the main highway and drove fast out a series of dusty, back roads past boarded up farm houses and road signs riddled with bullet holes. He tried three times to make a cell call but couldn't get through and slapped his phone into the cup holder.

He sped up, bouncing hard over the rutted one lane until they reached a narrow track that led into a grove of mesquites and willows, the first shade in miles. Thorn recognized an acacia and a stunted oak, then saw through the branches a white mobile home with a green compact car parked nearby.

The sheriff cut the engine and coasted to a silent stop about fifty yards away. In the rear-view Thorn watched Bobby and Sofia park a few yards behind them.

He leaned forward and squinted through the low limbs. A yellow panel van was parked in near a cluster of trees a few yards away from the double-wide.

Castillo reached in front of Thorn and punched open the glove compartment and drew out two holstered handguns.

"I shouldn't do this," he said. "But I don't know what kind of business this is."

"You can trust me."

"Can I?"

Thorn looked him straight on and nodded.

"Can you handle one of these?"

"Sadly, I can."

"And your friend, Tennyson?"

"He was military, so yes, pretty sure."

"Only to protect yourself, don't fire unless fired upon. You got it? My sister and the girl are in that trailer."

"Self defense only," Thorn said.

They got out, left their doors ajar. Castillo hustled back to the truck bed, opened the storage box and took out an AR-15, snapped in a mag, thirty rounds, maybe more, then he slipped two more magazines into his trouser pockets.

Bobby and Sofia joined them. Bobby hesitated for a half-second when Thorn held out the pistol. He took it finally, racked the slide, chambering a round.

"What's the trouble?" Bobby said.

Keeping his voice low, the sheriff said, "Whoever drove that van, they're inside the house. I don't recognize the vehicle. It's got out-of-state plates. My sister's not answering the phone. Someone flashing government ID to get her whereabouts. Worrisome set of facts."

"I don't like this," Sofia said. "These weapons, why do you need them?"

"I hope we don't," Castillo said. "Young lady, you stay here and stay low. And you two men keep your damn heads down."

Castillo trotted off toward the far side of the trailer. Thirty yards away, he swung around and motioned Thorn and Bobby into the woods east of the trailer. Castillo cut through dense shrubbery to the west.

Thorn stole forward, Bobby hanging a half step back. Sofia brought up the rear, a stiff, unnatural frown on her lips.

Still wearing their travel clothes, Bobby in blue jeans, red short-sleeve shirt. Thorn in neon yellow Snappers T-shirt, jeans. Sofia wearing a white blouse and dark jeans. Bad camouflage for tramping through this gray and brown landscape.

Thorn lost sight of Castillo, then three heartbeats later saw him emerge from behind a tangle of cactus and willow branches. The sheriff held up a fist. The three of them halted.

"What is it?" Bobby said.

"Don't know," said Thorn. "He must see something."

The single rifle shot was a flat pop, sounding small and so far away Thorn had no sense of its direction. A second after the crack, Thorn felt a hard pluck at his left sleeve and a sting in his upper arm.

"Well, damn."

The rip in his shirt sleeve darkened with blood, and his upper arm was numb.

Shots strafed the leaves and branches above them, a flurry, then another. Sounded like a long rifle on full-auto accompanied by a handgun. Behind them Bobby Tennyson made a strangled *whoof* and staggered backwards into a hedge.

"I'm okay," he called out in a husky voice. "Just tripped."

"Stay put, Thorn," Sofia said. "Let the sheriff handle it."

Thorn shook his head and got down on hands and knees and angled to his right toward the dusty apron surrounding the trailer, a thirty foot fully-exposed dash to the front door. Sofia crabbed up beside him and scowled at his defiance.

"Their legs," she whispered. "Under the van, one in front, one in the rear."

His arm was beginning to throb, blood tickling down his triceps. He craned to the right to better see the legs of the two shooters under the van. Jeans and shiny black boots.

"Where'd the sheriff go?"

"That idiot," Thorn said, as Castillo broke from behind a flowering shrub and jogged across open ground toward the side of the trailer. Fast for his size and age.

A burst of automatic fire spurted the dust near his feet. At least one round caught him mid-body and spun him sideways to the ground. He was sprawled on his back as a series of convulsions twisted him left and right.

Thorn rose and unloaded on the van, blew out the back window, put two more slugs in the door. The auto fire ceased.

He peered through the thicket, saw the shooters' legs were gone, caught a glimpse of a man hustling around the back of the van and ducking into the driver's seat. Hindered by a stand of saplings, Thorn couldn't get off a decent shot, but could tell the man was wide-shouldered, burly with close-cropped dark hair.

"They're running."

Thorn stepped out of the cover as the van rumbled to life and lurched forward, slewed to the right, missing a gear, engine revving high, the clutch caught and the van burst forward across the yard.

Fully exposed in the clearing, Thorn fired again, taking out the back windows.

He sighted on the right rear tire, the one most exposed and shot twice, then a third time, blowing out the a tail light and missing with the rest of the clip before the van disappeared down the narrow entrance drive. Out of ammo, badly out of practice.

EIGHT

Thorn hauled Castillo to his feet. The sheriff's Kevlar vest had blunted the impact of the two slugs, one in the chest, the other in the stomach. He was alert, but waxen and sweaty, and his breath was hoarse and labored as if the trauma had damaged a rib or two.

Thorn led the way up the wooden steps to the front door of the trailer. With his foot he nudged the door open, keeping the Glock extended as he stepped inside. He panned the pistol across the living room, then lowered it when he saw the woman bound to a chair with what looked like an entire roll of Saran Wrap.

"Did you kill the bastards?" the woman said. "Tell me you did."

Castillo's sister had a mass of sable hair tumbling to her shoulders and eyes that glittered like black marble. She was younger than her brother by several years, a gaunt figure with a long skinny neck, cheekbones so sharp they could've severed twine.

"They got away," Castillo said. "You all right, Jenny?"

Thorn found a steak knife in a kitchen drawer and began to cut her free.

"Almost sweated to death, but I'm still here. Hurry up with that knife."

While Thorn sawed through the plastic wrap, Jenny gave a description of the two assailants: both in their late thirties, the man just over six feet, clean-shaven, bulky body, brown hair worn in a short crew-cut, blue eyes, the woman was tall, close to six feet, skinny with short spiky hair, blood red, looked like a bad dye job. Pretty copper-colored eyes, no make-up, with a wide mouth and thin lips. No jewelry, no tats, or visible scars. Both wearing blue jeans, denim shirts and black combat boots with a high polish.

"Dressed so much alike, they might be in uniforms."

The sheriff used the landline to alert the state police, giving them a quick summary of the shooting, then a description of the man and woman and the yellow panel van they were driving. When he clicked off, Jenny said, "Who are these people in my house, Raoul?"

"Long story," Castillo said. "They're harmless."

The sheriff slumped into a lounge chair, wincing at an intake of breath. Sofia went to the sink, ran some water and filled a glass which she brought to Castillo. His face had grown paler and had a clammy sheen. He drank a few sips and handed the glass back to Sofia with a nod of thanks.

"They were after the girl," Jenny said. "I told them I didn't know nothing about any girl, but they didn't buy it, so they wrapped me up and were about to start carving on my face when they heard your truck. Thank the lord you haven't fixed that damn muffler. What's wrong with you, *hermano,* you been shot?"

"Vest saved me," he said. "Where'd you hide the girl?"

"You been bad-mouthing that vest for twenty years, how hot it is. You owe it an apology."

"Where is she, Jenny?"

Thorn cut away the last of the plastic and Jenny tried to stand. As she wobbled and almost went down, Thorn grabbed her elbow and steadied her. She looked down at his hand, then smiled up at him, her dark eyes alight.

"Is this fellow a cop too?"

"The girl, Jenny," Castillo said.

"When I saw them drive up in that van, I quick put her down below," Jenny said. "After she heard all this shooting that thing isn't ever going to speak again."

"Where's 'down below'?" Thorn said.

"This way." Jenny motioned toward the hallway that led off the living area.

In the middle of a bedroom floor, she pushed aside a Mexican serape runner, and motioned to the hatch cut into the floor.

"Storage locker," Jenny said. "She barely fit."

Thorn squatted down, tugged the recessed handle and drew open the hatch.

The girl was tucked in a fetal position, chin pressed to her chest.

"English or Spanish?" Sofia said.

"From the looks of her, Spanish," Jenny said. "But who knows? She hasn't answered to either."

"I'm going to lift you out," Thorn said. "It's safe. The bad men have gone."

Sofia repeated it in Spanish: *"Voy a sacarte. Es seguro. Los malos hombres se han ido."*

"Not bad," Jenny said. "What're you, Puerto Rican?"

"Help me get her out."

Sofia positioned herself on one side of the trapdoor, Thorn on the other, and together they pried the child out of the compartment, lifted her upright and settled her on the edge of the bed.

The girl was short and thick-bodied with the mature facial features of an older teenager. Her black hair was knotted in a braid that hung to her waist. She wore a soiled white peasant blouse and torn jeans and her bare feet were filthy. She kept her eyes shut as Sofia tipped her face up to the light. She had a round face, high cheekbones and wide set eyes. Her skin was the color of polished mahogany.

"Still wearing the clothes she came in?" said Thorn.

"Do I look like the Salvation Army?" Jenny said.

"And she hasn't bathed?"

"I fed her, gave her a place to sleep. It's more than most people would do. I'm not running a Ritz-Carlton."

Thorn took hold of the girl's right hand and cradled it lightly in his. He felt her hand twitch as if she meant to yank it away, but after a moment or two her hand quieted and some of the tension seemed to drain away as though she had been starved for a soothing touch.

Jenny said, "To me she looks Mayan. Maybe she doesn't even speak Spanish."

The girl opened her eyes and looked down at her hand, then up at Thorn.

"My father Maya," she said. "My mother from Chiapas. I speak English."

"And you do it very well."

"Sister Kathleen teaches me. My mother and I go to Phoenix to be with her."

"My name is Thorn and this is Sofia. You already know Jenny."

The girl flicked a stinging glance to Jenny then came back to Sofia.

"What's your name?" Sofia said.

The girl's eyes strayed to the far wall, and she drew a deep breath as if weighing the danger of entrusting these strangers with her identity. Again she looked down at her hand still clasped in Thorn's.

"Dulce," she said in a whisper. Then after a pause: "Mérida."

"Hello, Dulce."

"I tried everything to get her talking," Jenny said. "Don't know what the hell you did."

"Where's my mother?" Dulce murmured.

Thorn said they didn't know.

Dulce's brown eyes were flecked with gold and though she was only inches away she seemed to be peering at Thorn from a far off place where her childhood ended long before she was ready. Whether it was from some freakish accident or her own ingenuity or strength of will, this girl alone had survived what her fellow travelers had not, and Thorn sensed in the girl's halting demeanor an uncertainty that she deserved her good fortune.

"My mother is on truck. She die with the others. Where she now?"

"I don't know," Thorn said. "But we'll find out."

"*Ella debería ser enterrada en América.*" She should be buried in America.

"Of course," Sofia said. "We will do everything we can to make that happen."

"You have blood." Dulce reached out and pointed at Thorn's wound.

"Yes. But I'm okay."

"Did you kill them, the bad ones?"

"We tried," Thorn said. "But they got away."

The girl bowed her head and shook it in silent resignation.

"It's okay, Dulce. You're safe. Nothing is going to happen to you now."

"This one said the same." Dulce swiped her hand at Jenny as if with that bitter gesture she meant to banish all the fairytales she'd ever been told.

"Hey, look, kid," Jenny said. "It's not my fault some crazies showed up."

"Thorn." Castillo stood in the doorway. His color was returning but his face was still sheened with sweat.

"What's wrong, what happened?"

"I radioed for an ambulance," he said.

"I'm okay. Just a graze."

"Not you," the sheriff said. "Your friend, Tennyson."

"What happened?"

"Used my kit to stop the bleeding. He took one in the upper leg, another in the gut. The gut shot looks bad."

Bobby was conscious. Castillo had stretched him out on a bed of leaves in the shade of an acacia. His shirt was open and pants pulled to his knees, exposing his bandaged right thigh and a square of blood-soaked gauze taped to his belly inches from his navel.

The EMT's arrived within half an hour. During the wait, Bobby worked to appear jovial as if to reassure Thorn and Sofia that all was well. Sofia held Bobby's hand and wiped the sweat from his forehead and played along with his act.

But eventually his wisecracking faded and Bobby began to chatter about his tenure on that island in the Pacific back during the Vietnam War.

Rehashing the story he'd told two days before, this time in rambling detail: plutonium, Agent Orange, Sarin gas, VX, the Chinese junk, the beautiful young lady who was the base commander's daughter, gorgeous coral reefs, spectacular sunsets, a caged rabbit inside a storage facility, a broken rudder, a novel he'd been reading about Travis McGee the night Savannah appeared in his room. The fragments of his babble linked by the flimsiest narrative thread with lots of doubling-back and broken sentences and non-sequiturs.

"I'm not the man I pretend to be," he said.

Thorn gripped his soft cool hand.

"What're you saying, Bobby?"

"Not that man," he said, then fell silent as the paramedics loaded him onto a stretcher and slid him into the ambulance and headed off to a trauma center in Tucson. As the sheriff stepped away to talk with his sister, Sofia motioned for Thorn to join her in the shadows of a willow tree. Her face was flushed, her eyes bleak and determined.

"Are you in pain?" she asked.

"It's manageable."

"I don't like guns," she said.

"I'm not fond of them either."

"But you accepted the one from Castillo, and you did it so casually like it was something you do all the time. Without hesitation, without a second thought."

Nothing he could say.

"And don't claim you were defending yourself or me. It wasn't like that. It wasn't do or die. You were shooting at those people, at the van, it was only to stop them, to kill or injure them. You didn't have to fire. You didn't. You shot at them because you were angry. You lost control."

"I wasn't angry."

"Don't lie, Thorn. You were angry."

"Okay," he said. "Maybe a little, mainly I was scared."

She shifted her eyes, looking past him as if she could no longer bear his face.

"Can you promise me you'll never use a gun again?"

"I wish I could."

"But you can't. You won't."

Silence was all the answer he could muster.

"I know it's not your fault, Thorn, not really," she said, bringing her gaze back to him. "I should've listened to my girlfriends, guys too, everyone telling me to keep my distance, don't get serious, how dangerous you were, sooner or later you were going to attract something terrible, people would be hurt just being around you, there would be violence. But I didn't listen. I didn't believe them. It sounded crazy, like some stupid jinx. I like you. I like you a lot. And I thought they were exaggerating. You'd just been unlucky a few times, that's what I thought. I believed that. Until today."

Thorn didn't argue. Didn't try to defend himself. Sofia was right. A shit magnet, that's what he'd become. Karmic toxin circulating in his veins.

"I can't accept this," she said. "Bobby getting hurt, and the sheriff and you wounded, all those bullets flying around. This isn't what I was expecting. This kind of madness. I'm sorry, Thorn."

Her words rang with finality. Thorn understood. He didn't blame her. It was bound to happen. He'd hoped their time together might last a few more months, maybe longer, maybe a lot longer.

"You have anything to say?" Sofia searched his eyes.

He didn't speak aloud the measly words humming in his throat.

All you need is love.

It sounded true but wasn't. You needed a hell of a lot more than that. You needed tolerance and self-control, and you needed empathy and strength and discipline and flexibility. You needed serenity and good luck.

"You should go home, Sofia. I need to finish this, follow it where it leads."

"Why?"

"For Bobby."

"Oh, come on, not just for Bobby. This is what you do, Thorn. This is what you live for, your reason for being."

"And for that little girl," he said. "For Dulce."

At Frontera's storefront urgent care office, Dr. Diego Martinez stitched up Thorn's arm with swift efficiency. He was in his early forties, a few inches taller than Thorn, and lean as a whippet, with gleaming, swept-back hair and the long lashes and astonishing white teeth of a matinee idol. Back home Thorn might have mistaken him for a South Beach Lothario.

The doc assured Thorn the wound was a clean through-and-through, whisking a quarter-inch below the surface. Lucky, very very lucky.

"Don't see many flesh wounds like this," the doc said. "Around here people are better shots."

"Good thing I ran into an out-of-towner."

The doc smiled indulgently.

Back in the waiting room Thorn sat beside Sofia while she spoke on her cell to the Northwest Medical Center in Tucson where Bobby had been taken. Put on hold for several minutes, then passed between departments until finally someone told her that Bobby was still in surgery. No updates on his condition, so she left her number and pleaded that someone call her when Mr. Tennyson was out of the OR.

A half hour later, at four that afternoon, Sofia and Thorn were seated in silence while the doctor X-rayed Castillo's ribs. Dulce Mérida was in a second treatment room with the nurse, a graceful Hispanic woman who'd introduced herself as the doctor's wife.

Sofia's hands were folded in her lap. She'd been staring at the blank wall across from the room for the last half hour. All the rosiness had drained from her face. She looked exhausted. Thorn's throat was packed with sawdust. Nothing to say, no way to say it.

All the easy banter and intimacy that for these last few weeks had come so naturally was gone. He was beginning to feel the new distance separating them was unbridgeable, truly no way back across that span.

Castillo exited the exam room and took the vacant seat between them.

"Dulce is going home with the doc and his wife."

"Is that a good idea?" Sofia said. "Will she be safe?"

"Dr. Martinez is ex-Marine, two tours in Iraq, and Maria, his wife, was a State Trooper for ten years. They met on the interstate. Diego was breaking the sound barrier in his Porsche. Maria wrote him a ticket, and took down his phone number. They've been married two years. I can't think of anyone I'd trust more than those two to keep the girl safe. During the day she can stay here at the clinic, work on her English, go home with them at night."

"What about Border Patrol or ICE?" Thorn said. "Or whoever it is that'll want to scoop her up and send her back?"

Castillo knew the regional staff of both departments quite well. If necessary, he'd claim Dulce was an essential eyewitness in a murder case and should be held in protective custody until her testimony could be established. That should keep them at bay.

"But just in case," Castillo said, "it's best we keep the girl under wraps, as far from the feds as possible."

Across the lobby, Dulce stepped out of one of the exam rooms flanked by Maria Martinez. Maria came over while Dulce hung back at the exam room door.

"She's dehydrated," Maria announced. "Her electrolytes were dangerously low, but we'll monitor her for the next few days, make sure she gets plenty of fluids and rest and she should be back to full energy very soon."

"Good to hear," Thorn said.

Maria said, "Dulce would like a word with you in private."

"Me?" Thorn said.

"You can use the exam room."

Inside the room Dulce motioned for Thorn to shut the door.

When he turned back to her, Dulce was staring down at the

floor.

"Are you a good man?" Her hooded eyes were still down.

"I try to be."

She lifted her head and met his gaze, considered his answer and studied his face for a long uncomfortable moment then nodded her acceptance.

The girl dug a hand in her jeans pocket, drew something out, hiding the prize in her fist.

She extended her hand to Thorn and uncurled her fingers. On her palm lay a disk the size of a silver dollar. Etched on its face was an image of two interlocking triangles intersected by a lightning bolt. He turned the medallion over and found the same image on the other side. It had the weight and feel of a pewter stamping blank, used for crafts and cheap jewelry.

"What is this?" Thorn said.

"A man left it in the...I do not know the word...*paja*."

"Straw, I think."

Dulce repeated the English word.

"Which man dropped this?" Thorn was keeping his voice quiet, reassuring.

"The man in ocean diver mask with suit of rubber."

"This man was in the truck after the explosion?" Thorn said.

"He dropped this in... straw. I thought it had *valor*."

"Value, yes," Thorn said. "It might. You were smart to pick it up."

"I give it to you alone."

"Not the sheriff?"

"No confio en el." Dulce didn't trust him.

"He seems a good man," Thorn said.

"Confío en ti." He wasn't sure why, but Dulce trusted Thorn.

"I'll find out what it is and what it means, and I'll make sure you find out."

"Tell no one else, please."

Though he wasn't sure it was a promise he could keep, he said he would.

Back in the waiting room, Sofia asked him what Dulce wanted.

"I'm not sure."

"Well, what did the girl say?" Castillo was giving Thorn a wary look.

"There was a language problem. I think she just wanted to thank me for helping rescue her."

The sheriff grunted and stepped close. His hazel eyes, slitted with distrust, were fixed to Thorn's.

"Boy, you better be leveling with me."

Thorn assured him he was speaking the truth. Working to keep his face slack, and his eyes defying as best they could the sheriff's prying glare.

"Sheriff Castillo, excuse me, but I'd like to go see Bobby now."

Sofia's words broke the spell. Castillo drew a breath and released Thorn from the face-off.

He turned to Sofia and said fine, he'd have Tensia drive her to the hospital where they'd taken Mr. Tennyson.

Outside in the dusky lavender light, Sofia followed Thorn onto the sidewalk. She drifted up to him, brushing her arm against his, then turned, arched up, shoulders back, and for a moment Thorn thought all might be forgiven. They could find their way back to the warm sheets and happy evening conversations, the long lazy, limber afternoons on the deck of the *Heart Pounder*, gliding directionless across easy seas.

Sofia leaned close, brought her mouth up and at the last moment tipped her head to one side and pecked Thorn on the cheek.

Though it was soft and quick, her lips left a stinging imprint, an unmistakable finality to the gesture, the latest in a long history of parting kisses.

When she drew away, her strained smile sealed it, and the luster in her eyes was gone, now only a desolate, lightless shade of brown.

"Good-bye, Thorn. Be careful, please, unless you've forgotten how."

With an aggrieved thrust of her chin, Sofia left him and joined Castillo at the clinic door.

While the sheriff walked Sofia away, Thorn stayed put, looking off at a stretch of gray and brown desert that commenced just across the blacktop and seemed to expand into the infinite distance. The sky was changing to a pale mauve, the shade of a fading bruise.

For a long while his eyes roved across those empty miles and he considered the fragile web of causalities that brought him to such a place, so far removed from home, at such an impossible distance from all he loved and all that mattered to him and how, in such a short span of hours, the first shoots of tenderness and commitment between Sofia and him had been trampled by circumstance.

He ran it through, moment by moment, and ran it through again, considering each step along the way, but could find nothing in these last hours he would or could have done differently even had he known that he was risking his bond with Sofia.

When Castillo returned, he stepped close, squinted up at Thorn and cocked his head as if to appraise the level of his misery.

"Is it that obvious?" Thorn said.

“Women are a different race of beings,” he said. “Superior in every way.”

Thorn nodded in agreement, and said, “Is there enough daylight left to take a look at the crime scene?”

NINE

Marco Snyder was mechanically gifted. That's the phrase Judson used to describe Marco to his biker buddies when Marco was ten. Far as Marco could remember that was the only praise the old man ever gave him.

At sixteen living with the Whitmans, Marco dropped out of tenth grade and apprenticed for a local locksmith, Billy Joe Martinson.

Marco sponged up every trick he could: traditional locks and keys with driver pins, key pins, cylindrical pin-tumbler lock with a push-button locking mechanism, then the modern stuff like biometric data locks, fingerprints, facial recognition, security tokens and RFID tags where blasts of infrared light or sequences of ones and zeroes opened doors.

But what got his heart racing was mastering the ins and outs of car security systems, including how to break into a vehicle and steal it. From Billy Joe he learned how to assemble the necessary equipment using junkyard parts and a soldering iron. Billy Joe believed a locksmith needed to know how to defeat any system he was working on.

Once Marco had acquired the necessary skills, he spent most of his free time down at the Detroit Metro Airport perfecting his new sideline.

Cruising through the airport parking garage with the simple code grabber turned on, Marco could pop open any vehicle a few seconds after the owner chirped them locked, and rolled his suitcase toward the terminal.

Once inside the car, by-passing the ECU, the car's computer brain, was a little more complex. He had to unscrew the ECU from its nest of wires, which was usually inside the glove box, then unplug the wires one-by-one and replug them in the universal ECU that Marco carried with him. ECUs were about the size of a cigar box, easy to conceal as he prowled the parking lots. Soon as the security system was circumvented, the car was his.

Sure, it was more challenging than stealing cars in the old days when all you had to do was break open the steering column and touch wires together, but once he'd done the ECU exchange a few times, Marco got the process down to three minutes max.

Cars he couldn't unload to chop shops around Detroit, he drove to Chicago and sold them to a Chinese fellow who had them on a boat to Asia two days later.

Right up until he left Bad Axe, Marco continued boosting cars and never got caught. Not a single close call. Even worked up the nerve once to use a Range Rover's GPS system to guide him to the owner's home and activate the garage door opener to get inside. He never did that again, too creepy walking around inside a stranger' house, not sure if he was the star on a home security video. Just did it that once, made off with some diamond jewelry, a vial of Xanax, a bottle of first-rate bourbon, two handguns, and bam, he was out of there.

Now because they had to dump the van, Marco drove into the Tucson airport, found a parking spot and organized their weapons, luggage and the duffel bags, locked them in the van, and for the next twenty minutes Ingrid followed him up and down the parking garage aisles, Marco with his grabber activated, waiting for a chirp.

Turned out the first one came from a Lincoln SUV, two years old, not his favorite vehicle, but what the hell.

Marco drove back to the van, got their parking ticket, tossed their equipment into the back of the Lincoln and left.

At an exit off I-19 south of Tucson, he pulled behind a McDonald's and tossed the duffel with the contaminated suit into a dumpster then leaned over the side and pulled some other garbage on top of it.

"Should toss the guns too," Marco said when he got back in the car. "If that sheriff dies, those guns could put us away for good."

"When that little girl is no longer a problem, we'll find a nice deep river for the guns. Right now, job number one is what?"

"The girl," Marco said. "The girl, the girl, the girl."

They drove through the late afternoon and arrived in Nogales at close to sunset. They'd decided to stay a safe distance from Frontera in case there was a BOLO on them. Marco tooled around the scruffy town looking for a place to stay, and finally pulled into the gravel lot of the Arroyo Motel and turned off the engine.

"Ratty enough for you?" Marco said.

There was duct tape crisscrossing the office window and a single rusty pickup parked in front of one of the six rooms.

"Dump like this, I should be able to add to my scorpion collection," she said.

Marco rang the counter bell and the manager, a hefty Mexican woman wearing a pink T-shirt, looked him over and kept staring at him as Marco counted out the thirty dollars for the room, a single with two twins.

"No funny business," the woman said.

"I look like I'm into funny business?" Marco said.

"Hell, yes," the woman said. "Or else I wouldn't have said it."

Back in the Lincoln, Marco peered into the rear view mirror but could see no trace of anything that might have tipped the woman off.

Inside the room, Ingrid locked the door, shut the blinds. Marco drew out his phone, brought up his encrypted app, checked new messages.

"Jesus," he said. "The video is bringing them in."

"How many hits?"

"Too many to count. Fifty maybe."

"We'll need to up the price. Supply and demand."

"Where do we start tomorrow?" Marco said. "What's the plan?"

"Start at Castillo's office. Grab him or that secretary."

"What about those other two that were shooting at us?"

"Probably a couple of locals Castillo deputized."

"I'd rather we took the secretary."

"Yeah, maybe she'll be a fun-time girl."

"That would be a bonus."

"Maybe you'll want to kiss her, fondle her. Maybe we both will."

Ingrid talked this way when she wanted to warm things up. A technique she'd learned from her fucked-up mother. Flora Whitman was a specialist in lewd talk, ways to stimulate a man. Inflaming his cheeks, revving the hum in his gut, sending the blood sprouting down into his tingling taproot.

Ingrid tugged her blouse over her head, let it rustle to the floor. Stood there giving Marco a chance to absorb her fine breasts. Even after all these years, they were still holding their perfect shape. He'd been mesmerized by them since she first showed them to him at twelve.

"Did you enjoy shooting your weapon?"

"Yes," he said.

"Did you enjoy being shot at?"

"It was all right."

"Just 'all right' or was it stimulating?"

"It was a little stimulating."

"Are you still stimulated?"

"Yeah, I guess I am. I'm still fairly stimulated."

She unzipped her jeans, kicked off her boots, peeled the jeans down to her ankles and stepped out of them.

She edged close, lifting her chin, offering her throat.

Her coppery eyes were hard and gleamed like polished pennies. In a well-practiced move, he seized her neck and dug in with his thumbs.

Ingrid knew to get a quick breath down before he cut everything off. He gripped harder until her lips worked as if she was pleading for him to stop.

But she knew there was little risk he'd seriously hurt her. The two of them had practiced this for years and knew exactly how much pressure to apply to bring the other to the ecstatic edge of consciousness. A technique he'd learned from his mother who once in a fit of rage wrapped her hands around Marco's throat and clenched, her eyes glazing as she brought her face close to his and whispered that she loved him, loved him, loved him.

Savannah's knowledge of strangulation started in March 1970, Honolulu.

She was studying nursing at the local junior college when Marty returned from Vietnam. Eight years older, her dashing brother had followed in their dad's illustrious footsteps, Colonel Joshua Snyder. Marty enlisted, became a Screaming Eagle in the 101st Airborne, shipped off to the rice paddies early in the conflict.

After two rotations and the Battle of Hamburger Hill, he returned a wraith, so frail she could count his ribs, eyes dimmed, face gaunt, so haunted by the horrors he'd partaken in, he'd turned to heroin, hash, uppers, downers, anything he could steal or bargain for.

With their father stationed at Johnston Atoll, and their mother bedding a string of officers at Hickam Air Force Base, it fell to Savannah to attend Marty.

She dropped out of school, spent her days with him, steering him from his suicidal fantasies, hour after hour, devoting herself to his grim, hopeless rehab, urging him to clean up, searching out his latest stash and flushing it, dealing with his lies, his false promises, dragging him out of alleyways and drug houses, fighting dealers and junkies for possession of his soul.

Didn't work. None of it. Nothing could purge his demons, bring him back from the steamy jungle, the trip-wired vines, the machine-guns rattling day and night, choppers blown from the sky, buddies shredded around him, nothing could salvage Marty from his desolation.

It would be crazy not to be crazy after living through all he'd seen and done.

He screamed through the nights, howled in the afternoons, bayed in between. His terrors filled the house with sweaty raving. He'd tramped away into the wilderness in his mind and was lost there. Savannah could not save him, though god knew she tried.

Even performing that one forbidden service. The greatest sin. Even that did not calm Marty, or quiet his gibbering. Later she agonized that it might have been their intimate hours together that pushed Marty past the breaking point.

One full moon night her beautiful brother climbed a mast on the *Flying Dragon*, Colonel Joshua Snyder's restoration project that sat in a cradle in the side yard waiting for the old man to return. Marty worked his way out a yardarm, looped a line around his neck and jumped.

Minutes later Savannah found him alive, twisting, bucking on the deck. The spar had snapped under his weight. When Marty revived, he pleaded with her, begged Savannah to help him die.

Strangle him. A mercy killing, that's all he wanted. His wish beyond all wishes. If she loved him she would end his misery. No one would be able to tell the difference between his hanging and what he was asking her to do. Tighten her hands around his throat and tighten them more until the light was gone from his eyes, his pain ended.

Strangle her glorious brother.

TEN

Castillo drove south along dirt roads with neither speed signs, markers nor fences. The roadways were straight and untended and had washboard patches that must have been carved by the wind or rare flash flooding. The desert that spread around them was empty and endless. There were no power poles, no phone lines, no sign that this part of America was in any way connected to the distant bustle of cities or ceaseless agitation of world events.

After twenty minutes of silence, Castillo came to a stop at a closed metal gate. He got out, unlooped the chain, swung the gate aside, drove through, stopped and shut the gate. It was the first of five similar gates.

Thorn volunteered to open and shut the others, something to do, something to distract from the throb in his wounded arm.

"A lot of gates," Thorn said. "But no cattle."

"The gates are for people," said Castillo. "Marjorie's a bit of a recluse."

Thorn asked if Ms. Banfield knew they were coming.

"No way to let her know," the sheriff said. "No phone, no power, nothing. She has a primitive life out here, even by local standards. Marjorie's an uncommon lady but she can be as hardheaded as a burro."

The sheriff left the main road and headed southwest over the trackless desert which was neither simply sand nor dust nor scrub, but some gritty mixture of all three. They drove for another ten minutes over the rough terrain.

When Castillo came to a stop, the upper rim of the sun was slipping past the horizon. He shut off the engine and leaned forward to peer out the windshield and said, "Well, goddamn it all to hell."

"What?" Thorn saw only a large darkened patch in the scrub.

"Somebody hauled it away, the truck. It's gone."

"How'd that happen?"

"I'm damn well going to find out." Castillo rocked back against the seat and sat there for a moment sighing with exasperation. He cranked up the truck and headed south through the thickening desert gloom.

After twenty or thirty minutes it was fully dark, the headlights barely penetrated the shadows. Thorn yelled over the muffler's racket to ask if they were taking the same route back and Castillo shook his head no, but didn't elaborate.

A short while later Thorn saw a golden glow just beyond a sandy knoll. They mounted the rise and coasted down the other side and Castillo downshifted and drifted up to the outskirts of a bonfire where a couple of dozen people were squatting in the flickering light. Overhead streaming embers scribbled bright messages against a black, star-splashed sky.

As the group took notice of the truck's arrival, several of the men scrambled to their feet and stood tensely until a woman's voice called out, *"Tranquilo, hombres. No te preocupes. Él es mi amigo."* Don't worry, he's my friend.

"Marjory," Castillo said.

Marjory Banfield emerged from the shadows. A woman of average height, her hair loose across her shoulders was glowing like burnished pewter in the firelight. She wore a leather skirt that clipped her knees, and cowboy boots tooled with elaborate designs. The cape over her shoulders hid her body but she moved with the sure-footed grace of an athlete forty years her junior.

Castillo climbed from the truck and met her just outside the circle of firelight. Marjory opened her arms for an embrace, but the sheriff shied away and turned his back on her, extending a hand toward

Thorn.

"Who have we here?"

Castillo made introductions, then said, "I've come about the truck."

"Yes, yes," she said. "I'm sure I committed a terrible offense having it hauled away. But I couldn't leave that hulking crematory out in the pathway where more poor souls would see it and be frightened off."

"You had it towed?"

"Yesterday," she said. "Emmitt Peterson at Last Chance Salvage took it. By now it's the size of a bread box, riding on the deck of a ship bound for Malaysia, or wherever they're paying the most for scrap metal these days."

"That truck could have contained evidence of a crime."

"Sorry, Raoul, it's gone. Are you going to arrest me for removing junk off my own land? Or will you come have a cup of Sangria like the good man you are?"

"You shouldn't have done it."

"We'll add it to the list of things I should not have done."

"Has there been any more trouble?" Castillo asked.

"The Whitmans, you mean?"

The sheriff nodded.

"When the wind is right, I can hear their shooting range, but otherwise they've stayed on their side of the fence. You don't suspect those lazy hooligans. I thought it was an accident."

It probably was. As for the Whitmans, even they aren't so stupid to try something like that in their own backyard."

"That explosion rattled my china. Sounded like a bomb going off."

Castillo said he was looking into it, the investigation was on-going.

"And the little girl I found, she spoken yet?"

"She's fine," he said. "She's opened up, needed fluids and a little time."

Marjory turned to face the assembly, stepped forward into the light, and introduced Castillo and Thorn. Though she said they'd only appeared this morning, Marjory knew each of their names and country of origin and a detail or two about every one. Jorge from Guatemala, who ran an auto repair shop out of his garage. Catalina who left her abusive husband in Costa Rica and a profitable sewing business of her own. Each of them stood and shook hands with the visitors and some spoke a timid English greeting, while a couple of the men ducked their faces when the sheriff looked their way.

Thorn accepted a paper cup of Sangria and squatted on the ground near the fire. The night had turned chilly and the sky was dense with stars. No lights shown in the vicinity. If Marjory's house was nearby, it remained invisible in the darkness.

In his half-assed Spanish, Thorn spoke with a young woman who was sitting next to him, nursing a baby wrapped in a striped beach towel. No more than sixteen, the girl said her name was Audrey and she'd come from Honduras. She'd connected with the others on the southern edge of the Sonoran Desert and relied on these strangers to steer her and her child to welcoming waypoints along the trek. The whereabouts of these safe havens were passed on from previous travelers.

Cheered that Thorn responded in her tongue, Audrey chattered on about her homeland, its dangers, its poverty, its daily torments, but even as she described the privations of the place, her voice was wistful as if despite all its hardships, the land she'd abandoned still governed her heart. An echo of Sofia's family.

She pointed out other members of the group who had helped her in some critical way, offering food, carrying her son for miles to relieve her of the burden, offering salve for her blistered feet at the end of the day.

"Mi hijo y yo no habríamos llegado tan lejos sin su ayuda." She and her son would not have made it this far without their help.

The moon had climbed a quarter of the way into the sky by the time Castillo rose and announced that he had to return to Frontera. Thorn stood and bid Audrey good-bye and wished her a safe journey and told the others the same.

Marjory walked arm in arm with Castillo back to the truck and kissed him on the cheek.

Castillo steered them back into the night, the racket of the muffler again making speech impossible.

They'd been driving for less than a minute when Thorn heard the sound.

He reached over and switched off the ignition key, silencing the muffler.

"What the hell, boy?"

"Listen," Thorn said.

To be sure, he lowered his window, tipped his head into the chilly air.

Another rapid burst came from behind them, back towards Marjory's. Distant but clear, one barrage overlapping another—either a string of firecrackers or an automatic weapon.

Castillo cursed, restarted the truck, slammed it into gear, fishtailed through a U-turn and roared back the way they'd come.

The bonfire was still burning when the truck topped the knoll and slewed down the other side. But the migrants who'd been ringing the flames were gone.

Castillo switched on the spotlight mounted on the windshield post. With the interior handle he panned the light across the grounds, holding briefly on a knapsack and the jug of Sangria they'd been drinking. As he rotated the light, Thorn saw the ground littered with cups and blankets and bedrolls.

Castillo raised the beam and illuminated the terrain beyond the bonfire, lighting up a flat-roofed adobe house, and an ancient Army Jeep parked nearby.

Castillo had one leg out his door when in the darkness an engine roared to life. He grabbed the spotlight handle, jerked the beam upward, swung it right then left until it caught the chrome roll bars and the churning wheels of what looked like a dune buggy or a high-powered ATV with two long-haired men in the front seats. The vehicle crashed through the shrubs and hedges and spun away across the open plain.

Castillo settled back in the seat.

"Why aren't we chasing them?" Thorn said. "They're getting away."

"No need," said Castillo. "I know where the assholes live."

He worked the spotlight back across the open yard and the beam lit up a pair of cowboy boots. He moved the light up to the hem of Marjory's leather skirt, and worked it midway up her body but didn't shine it in her face.

"I'm okay, Raoul," she called out.

Castillo switched off the spotlight and Marjory walked over to the truck and leaned close to the sheriff's window.

"The Whitman boys," he said.

"Of course. They were pitching firecrackers like drunk teenagers."

"Anybody hurt?"

"I don't think so," she said, "but we'll need to check."

"Why?" Thorn said. "To scare off your guests?"

"Yep," Marjory said. "Welcome to America."

Armed with flashlights and lanterns, they combed Marjory's property for the next hour. Castillo called in Spanish that the travelers could return to the campfire, there was nothing to fear. The sheriff would protect them. And Marjory sang out their names over and over.

But if any of the migrants could hear their reassurances, they were not persuaded. No one answered back. None reappeared.

"Word will spread," Marjory said, when they'd assembled back at Castillo's truck. "First the truck explosion, now with this there'll be no one passing this way any time soon."

The sheriff volunteered to camp out for the rest of the night to make sure the Whitmans didn't return.

"They won't be back," she said. "Too chickenshit."

He asked if she wanted to press charges. Castillo would be happy to round up the whole lot and lock them up for as long as any judge would allow.

Leave them be," she said. "Their karma will be punishment enough."

"How many are there?" Thorn asked.

"Two brothers," Marjory said. "They're the troublemakers. There's a sister and her boyfriend. Haven't seen them lately. I'm not even sure they live over there anymore."

"How far away is their place?"

"What're you after, Thorn?" Castillo said. "You plan on going over there and starting something?"

"Maybe somebody should."

Marjory said, "The mobile home where they live is maybe four or five miles from here. The place used to be owned by Charlie Whitman. An uncle or something. A decent man, kept to himself. Raised horses. He died a long while back, left the place to those kids. Nobody works as far as I can tell, probably living on an inheritance."

"Do they show up in town, Sheriff?"

"The brothers have a couple of times. Just to start trouble. Never met the sister or her boyfriend, heard about them but never laid eyes on them. But trust me, going over there, Thorn, trying to straighten them out, talk sense into them, it's useless. Those two are fully-committed assholes."

Castillo drove in silence back across the desolate landscape. Thorn closed his eyes and tried to will away the gloom that had settled on him hours earlier and had deepened on this long Arizona day.

At last Castillo pulled into his office parking lot, switched off the engine.

"Who have we here?" the sheriff said.

Stepping into the faint halo of a single overhead bulb, Sofia Mendoza raised a hand in solemn salute. As downhearted as Thorn had been these last few hours, seeing Sofia emerge from the shadows revived him. At least until he saw her stony look and her trudging step as she came forward.

Thorn jumped down from the truck, hustled over.

"What is it? What happened?"

"We should never have come. We should have stayed in Key Largo and none of this would have happened."

"What? Is it Bobby?"

"I was with him, holding his hand. He was fading in and out, mumbling. I leaned close and he made a terrible hacking noise like he was drowning, like his lungs had failed. Gasping and wheezing. I ran into the hallway and screamed for the nurses, the doctors, anyone. The hallway was empty, no one at the nurse's station. I ran back to his bed, took his hand again and he opened his eyes. That was the first time he'd opened them in the hours I'd been beside his bed."

Castillo joined them, listening in, his face a bland mask.

"Tell me, Sofia. Go on, say it."

"He wanted you to have this."

She pressed Bobby's cell phone into Thorn's hand.

"Talk to me, Sofia."

"When Bobby finally spoke, his voice was clear and vibrant. What he said was, 'Let it be. Just let it be.'"

Thorn looked away down the dark, empty road.

"I was still holding his hand and I could feel everything seep away. Saw his head slump into the pillow. Thorn, listen to me. Bobby wanted us to stop, just stop this madness and go home. Those were his last words, his dying wish. Let it be.

"Can you do that, Thorn? Can you do what Bobby on his deathbed asked of us, just step back, let go of this? We'll return to Key Largo, sort things out between us. Can you do that for me?"

PART TWO

ELEVEN

Thursday morning, after Bobby, Thorn and Sofia Mendoza flew off to Arizona, Sugarman began a computer search for the Snyders, father and daughter, Joshua and Savannah. At least those were the names Bobby Tennyson knew them by.

Over the years in running dozens of background checks for local businesses throughout the Keys, Sugarman found you didn't need to be an FBI most-wanted killer to feel the need for a fabricated identity. Husbands fleeing child support, tax dodgers, women hiding from abusive boyfriends or stalkers, foreign dictators fleeing their plundered nations, and all the other permutations of people wanting desperately to disappear. Naturally, starting fresh usually meant assuming an alias and all the ID's that went with it.

Then there was the chance that Savannah Snyder might have married and taken her husband's name—another variable that made the job of locating her even more problematic.

Still, he needed to start somewhere, and maybe Savannah Snyder was one of those lawbreakers so foolhardy and cocksure that she'd kept her maiden name. If so, he thought the name was uncommon enough the search could strike pay dirt in hours. But after logging into all three databases he subscribed to and scanning the lists, he discovered there were lots of women named Savannah Snyder scattered over the U.S. Three hundred and ten all told.

Two of the sites he used also listed family members associated with the search name, so he scrolled through the entire list of Savannah Snyders looking for a relative named Joshua.

None appeared.

He footed the extra cost for a more in-depth search that took an additional three hours and netted him nothing more. He spent that entire morning and most of the afternoon scanning the search sites, scrolling through financial data, criminal records, foreclosures, mortgages, vehicle registrations, county, state and federal tax information and all the social networks known to man, including a few he'd never heard of with names so raunchy there was little doubt about the clients they catered to. He was looking for any reference to sailboats or Air Force service or anything that might associate with Johnston Atoll.

Nada.

Next he turned his attention to Joshua Snyder, a veteran of the United States Air Force. First he went to the National Archives and spent a morning in the Combat Air Activities Files, searching for the records of any Joshua Snyder who'd died in military action or while still in the service. There were sixty-seven thousand names listed in the file but none with that name.

He broadened his search to any Joshua Snyder in the entire archival database. There he found three. One died in Iraq and two others were killed in accidents. All three were too young to fit the profile of a commander of the base at Johnston Island during the Vietnam war.

Widening the search even farther, Sugarman found eleven Joshua Snyders who'd served in some branch of the military, one born as early as 1918. But none of the death records for these men showed a birth date which would have made them eligible to serve as an Air Force colonel in 1971. Most of the dead Joshuas were decades too young.

So after all that work, Sugarman had learned only one simple fact. He could now assume that Colonel Snyder who was busted to major after the Johnston Atoll incident had probably survived at least until retirement age.

To have had an adult daughter in 1971, today Snyder would have to be in his late eighties or mid-nineties. So as a last resort Sugarman used Google to search for Joshua Snyder coupled with the words Air Force and Johnston Atoll.

After an hour of scrolling down and down and down through the results, he came across a site dedicated to the memory of service personnel who'd served on Johnston over the years. A two page history of the island, lots of washed-out amateur photos of the landing strip and dock, and even some of the officers who'd staffed the island in decades past. But no sign of Joshua Snyder.

A creeping sense of doubt was building in Sugarman as again and again he came up empty. True, he'd confirmed that the island had been a storage site for banned chemical weapons, and much of the rest of Bobby's story checked out. But the missing commander was worrisome. Could Bobby have been embellishing some incident from his years on the island? Had he misremembered the names?

After a grouper sandwich at Snappers, Sugarman was back at work. He started out with Google, but the searches were tedious and slow, made even more time-consuming by Sugarman's poor Internet service. After only an hour of work his brain was already getting fuzzy when he looked up from his computer screen and peered through the two-way mirror that looked into the Hairport, Key Largo's premier beauty salon which occupied the space next door.

The shadowy mirror ran the length of the wall he shared with the salon. It had been installed by a previous owner of the salon who believed her employees were stealing from her and wanted to catch them in the act.

Sugarman always felt vaguely guilty about snooping on the salon even after the shop's new owner, Molly Bright, gave him permission, in fact encouraged him to keep tabs on things next door in case a jealous husband or boyfriend showed up and caused a disturbance. Such disorderly conduct had occurred twice in the handful of years Sugarman had rented this office space. And he'd successfully defused both situations.

Now as he observed the bustling salon full of Key Largo ladies getting permed and manicured for the weekend, his eyes came to rest on one of the framed movie prints he'd seen so many times that it had virtually disappeared into the background. It was a promotional poster for a Bruce Lee film of yesteryear, and featured an elaborate Japanese image of a fire breathing dragon. It took him a few seconds to realize why the poster had snagged his attention.

The image was a version of the figure Bobby described emblazoned on the prow of the sailboat Savannah Snyder had been sailing on. A Chinese junk christened the *Flying Dragon*.

That was an investigative avenue Sugarman hadn't considered and one with tantalizing possibilities because in the last few years, motorboats and sailing vessels had become one of Sugarman's sub-specialties.

Stolen boats, sunken boats, vandalized boats, he'd handled all of them. And in a couple of divorce cases Sugarman had been hired to track down the community property one spouse was trying to hide from the other. Both of those divorces involved the disputed ownership of boats, and in both cases, the husbands were trying to hide the vessel in question in a marina or private boatyard where the wife's attorney could not locate it for an appraisal.

It was during those cases that Sugar came to depend on the United States Coast Guard National Vessel Documentation Center database. Type in the name of a boat and up pops a list of vessels with that name along with the year built, length, type of service, such as passenger or recreational, and the home port. The database also provided the registration number affixed to the bow of the boat, an identifier that most marinas and boatyards used to log in their vessels and keep track of their location.

As he typed in Flying Dragon, Sugarman drew a full breath, expecting the list to be so long it might prove daunting or even useless. He clicked Enter and after a long interval the list of registered boats with that name materialized.

Only six of them.

Even better, he saw that only one had been built in a year prior to 1971. That *Flying Dragon* was constructed in 1947 and was forty-two feet long and its home base was Port Austin, Michigan which Sugarman soon discovered was on the tip of the thumb of Michigan, which put it on the southern shores of Lake Huron.

He clicked on that boat's italicized name and was sent to a page listing the complete details of the *Flying Dragon*'s Coast Guard registration. Call sign, official number, gross ton, net ton, length, breadth, depth, hailing port city, hailing port state, and the owner's name and address. And there she was, Bobby's seductive dream girl.

S. Snyder, 85 Taggart Road, Bad Axe, Michigan.

Bingo, double bingo.

After only a single day's work and without leaving his office, he'd found her. That is, if she was still alive and still living in Bad Axe. And then, of course, there was the possibility, even the likelihood that she'd parted with the stolen landmines decades ago and would have no way of knowing where they were located today.

The more he considered how easily he'd tracked her down, the less it felt like a breakthrough. He had a specific location with a clear linkage to Bobby Tennyson's missing munitions, a juicy clue that seemed a little too juicy.

If someone was using nerve gas stolen from a military arsenal to murder migrants, then surely that person would take more care to conceal themselves from the inevitable investigation.

Unless, of course, they wanted to be found.

Sugarman set his reservations aside and plowed on. Now that he had a fix on Savannah Snyder's location, the problem of collecting more information about her was simplified. Her address opened up a myriad of new avenues. Tax records, mortgage info, social media, even photos of her residence could show up online on real estate sites, all the breadcrumbs a person in the modern world left behind whether they meant to or not.

He hardly slept that Thursday night, wondering what he'd missed in his search, or what he might have got wrong. Something seemed off. Savannah Snyder had made no apparent attempt to hide. Could that mean she simply didn't have anything worth hiding? Had he found the wrong Savannah Snyder? No. She was the owner of the *Flying Dragon.*

He got back to work early Friday morning, locating the Huron County tax rolls, and he was digging through their clunky database for any more signs of Savannah Snyder's presence when his cell phone buzzed—Bobby Tennyson calling.

"We're never gonna use them," Judson would say. "We need to unload those fuckers before the feds track them down, send us to prison forever. Dig a hole, throw them in and be done with them."

For years the munitions remained in their sealed crates. A row of six stacked four high in the padlocked shed behind their white frame house on Taggart Road. A few feet away from the crates was a domed bird cage where she kept Big Blue, her hyacinth macaw. An old girl, still feisty, and after all that time the bird hadn't yet detected a leak.

Feeding Big Blue was Savannah's daily reminder of what was yet undone—the bird's reproachful braying, its guttural rebukes. "When will it be?" "When, when, when?" "Why wait?" "Just do it."

Judson trained the bird to squawk those phrases, and the kids schooled it in senseless curses. "Fuck you in the ear." "Limber dick, limber dick." "Shit on your cereal." "Fart, fart, fart."

Every morning Savannah opened the padlock, stood back a safe distance in case there was an overnight discharge, and when she saw the bird was still upright, she swung the door open. And every morning for all those years, Big Blue said, "Time to eat. What took so long? Limber dick, limber dick."

Almonds, dried fruit, whatever flowers were in season. Big Blue watched Savannah approach with her food, then turned her head away as Savannah grew near as if that damn old bird sensed her own disposable function and was bitterly unforgiving.

Judson was right. Savannah was never going to do it. Her rage over Marty's death still burned, although not as hot as it once had. Time had cooled all her passions. She had dutifully raised Vegas, worked part-time as an LPN in a VA hospital down in Saginaw, where a dozen times on every shift Savannah confronted versions of Marty's unreachable eyes, his broken spirit, his empty shell.

But mostly day in and day out Savannah simply survived. Enduring all those Michigan winters with their icy winds, and endless snows with drifts so deep a woman could wade into one and vanish forever.

TWELVE

After Sofia left, chauffeured by Castillo's secretary, Thorn climbed into the rented SUV and drove off. He searched out the main highway that headed north to Tucson and by just after midnight he checked into the Sagebrush Inn off I-19. He had no plan. He wanted nothing beyond a night's rest. He would call Sugarman tomorrow and they could discuss the options, decide if there were any.

At two that morning he came fully awake and lay looking at the clock's red digital glow and after a while he realized what he must be feeling was jet lag. A first for him. Not much of a traveler. First time venturing out of his time zone.

He climbed out of bed, showered, put on fresh underwear, a clean T-shirt, the same jeans, same boat shoes.

He brushed his teeth and brushed them a second time to clear away the gunk of traveling and the disastrous day. He peered at himself in the mirror. He seemed to have aged in the last twenty-four hours—same sun-scorched hair, same hard cheekbones, but a new set of pouches beneath his blue eyes and an unbecoming puffiness in his cheeks, and wrinkles at the corners of his mouth where there had been none before.

His wound was aching and his belly rumbled. He tracked back through the hours and realized he hadn't eaten since yesterday, mid-way through the long flight out from Florida—a turkey sandwich that Sofia packed.

At least his hunger was one problem he could solve.

Through the warm, airless dark, he drove the empty streets until he found a Waffle House. He ordered eggs and bacon and a short stack of pancakes and ate at the counter alongside two chatty off-duty hookers and a doughy man in a trucker's hat, and a gang of teenagers in flashy duds who looked they'd been recently evicted from a two-bit dance club. After breakfast and three cups of coffee, he drove around some more and at sun-up he finally returned to his motel room.

He was unlocking the door to his room when Bobby Tennyson's cell phone buzzed like a trapped hornet in the front pocket of his jeans. He dug the damn thing out, saw the caller was 'Unknown,' and he tapped the green button on the screen and a voice said, "Where the hell are you, Thorn?"

"Who is this?"

"Castillo. Now where are you?"

"In a motel south of Tucson. Why? Did something happen?"

"Name of the motel."

Thorn told him.

"Room number?"

"What's going on?"

"What's your damn room number?"

Thorn gave him the number.

"Stay put, don't go anywhere till you hear from me again."

Thorn clicked off and went inside the room and shut the door.

He'd never liked phones of any kind, but in the last few years he'd acquired a particular distaste for cell phones, mainly for the way they'd invaded every private space, and monopolized way too much of even his sensible friends' precious time.

Thumb-typing texts, scrolling through emails, cell phone talkers who lost all regard for their surroundings, blundering through restaurants and bars and public spaces while bragging about business conquests or dating calamities.

God knows, Thorn had no interest in snooping on strangers, but with cell phones so prevalent, you had no choice but to eavesdrop on one side of the most intimate exchanges, and in some cases because the speaker was apparently deaf, you were forced to hear both sides of insufferably mindless chats.

It seemed to him that nearly every person he encountered recently had been taken hostage by the damned things, using them to shoot photos of their fish dinner or their king-sized margarita, or to ask the genie who lived inside them to solve problems so trivial the answers were rarely worth recalling afterwards.

The phone in his hand was probably no different in appearance or function than any other, but because it had been Bobby's, its heft seemed inexplicably to far outweigh its size and shape. That it was Bobby's dying bequest to Thorn made the damn thing impossible to discard. And maybe somehow it would prove useful. Even though he knew little about the operation of such devices, he assumed the phone contained the names and numbers of relatives and friends who should be alerted to Bobby's passing.

Thorn perched on the edge of the bed and made his first-ever cell phone call, punching in Sugarman's office number.

It took several minutes to bring Sugar up to date, ending with the bitter news of Bobby's final moments and his last words. After he'd finished the account, such a length of silence followed Thorn had to ask if Sugarman was still there.

Sugar said yeah, he was there, then: "I'm sorry, Thorn, but frankly that doesn't sound like Bobby, something he would say. 'Let it be.'"

"I know. But it does sound a lot like Sofia."

"Would she do that? Lie about Bobby's deathbed words?"

"I don't know. I hope not."

"Just doesn't sound like Bobby. He was passionate about this thing."

"Obsessed," Thorn said.

"Anyway it's not like you have to follow Bobby's last wishes," Sugar said.

"Maybe I should just let it go."

"But you aren't going to do that, are you?"

"Are you?"

Sugarman paused. Thorn could hear his breath, slow and steady.

"Tell me more about that coin the girl gave you."

"Two triangles with their bases overlapping and a lightning bolt intersecting their juncture. Etched or stamped, it's hard to say."

Over all those empty miles, Thorn heard Sugar typing on his laptop. While he waited, Thorn gazed across the room at a mass-produced painting on the far wall—a couple of buzzards circling high over a stretch of barren sand. A jolly image.

"What're you doing, Sugar?"

"Running an image search," he said. "That coin sounds familiar. Something I've seen before or heard about. Give me a minute, okay, hang on."

Thorn listened to Sugarman clicking his computer keys, cruising the Web. It still struck Thorn as unfathomable that so much information could be floating around out there, archives of facts and trivia and songs and treatises on subjects from Archimedes to birdcalls, nearly anything you could wonder about, someone had deposited it in cyberspace and provided access to anyone who knew the tricks of searching.

As a kid Thorn had learned to navigate the local library and had spent hours tracking down details about the habits of bonefish and tarpon and sharks. He'd learned about tides and celestial navigation and he'd read novels of nautical heroics, great sea battles that unfolded in parts of the globe whose names still resonated with enchantment and whose authors and their protagonists had activated Thorn's youthful imagination and shaped the trajectory of his adult life.

Melville, Conrad, Patrick O'Brian, the yarns of swashbuckling Captain Blood, and the Horatio Hornblower series that followed the seafaring adventures of its hero as he climbed the maritime ladder from midshipman to Lord. Jack London's Sea Wolf and Nordhoff's doomed mutineers on Captain Bligh's Bounty.

Books and more books. But Thorn had never made the leap to computers and the universe of the Internet. He'd been duly impressed by what Sugar had shown him, the wonders of the online world. But Thorn never felt comfortable with electronic wizardry of any kind, even the ones his boating buddies swore by.

Maybe those marine toys pulsed with such supernatural abilities they could outperform their human rivals, but Thorn was stubborn and would rather trust his own eyes to read the flickering shades of the shallows to safely navigate around sandbars, shoals and coral heads than follow the guidance of a satellite beaming down coordinates to a gadget on his console. He'd rather rely on his long acquaintance with the shadows and outlines of the underwater landscape that could be spied from above to guide him back to productive fishing spots than to mark them on an electronic screen.

He could still hear Sugarman clicking the keys to his laptop when someone knocked lightly on his motel room door. A tap so faint it was almost imperceptible as if the intruder was painfully shy.

"Hold on, Sugar, somebody's here."

Thorn placed Bobby Tennyson's cell phone on the foot of the bed and went to the door. He leaned forward and squinted through the peephole and saw a short woman with curly blond hair. She was gazing to her left as if she knew she was being inspected and wanted to present her better side.

Thorn drew the door open.

She was an elfin figure, barely five feet tall. She wore dark slacks and a beige top. Her eyes were large and a piercing blue, and her nose slightly uptilted. In the harsh radiance of the motel's exterior lights, she looked lost and vulnerable. As he would quickly discover, neither was remotely true.

"Can I help you?"

"Are you Thorn?" Her quiet voice was only a decibel above a whisper.

"I'm Thorn, yes."

"Then we're in the right place."

"We?"

Thorn registered her move a half second late, though in truth even if he had been on full alert, his reflexes would not have been quick enough to block the sweeping kick that hooked his right knee, crumpling him sideways.

He caught hold of the doorframe and was regaining his balance when a man pushed past her. A big man, huskier than Thorn, as wide as a beer truck.

Thorn registered that much in the chaotic blur, and he remembered protesting to the woman, a few words from his mouth before the black bag fit over his head and a hard sting, something cold and ugly, jabbed into the side of his neck.

Time staggered about in a disjointed series of images. Bumpy, weightless, lying flat on his back, immobile. Maybe he talked, maybe not. It was a gray twilight that ended with him sitting up in a hard chair.

Waking slowly, but too groggy to speak. His hands were numb, wrists locked behind him, his biceps digging into the edges of a straight-backed chair. Fingers prickling with needles of numbness. Darkness. The cloth against his mouth was soggy from his breath. The hood smelled of dry cleaning solvent, or maybe the aftertaste of the drug in his bloodstream.

The room was cold. Meat locker cold. His lungs were singed with frost. He was shivering and feverish. A Florida boy stranded in arctic detention. His mind was bathed in mud. He opened his mouth, tried to find a word, any word. Failed.

He shut it, drew a long breath through his nose. Tried to think.

Failed at that. Let his mind rest. Tried to picture some recent event. Today, yesterday, last week. Anything that might explain why he was here.

Desert light. Soft lavender sky. Mountains as jagged as broken teeth.

Tried to remember the last thing.

Arizona. A motel room. Knock on the door. Light knock.

Why the hell was he in Arizona?

Sofia Mendoza kissed him on the cheek. See you later or maybe never. Sofia, her Cuban parents. The whole tribe naked in downtown Key West, everyone out of sight behind the high stucco walls.

It was cold. Icy air, a freezer.

"Who are you, why are you here?"

A woman's voice asking quietly, sympathetic, as if attempting to bond. Woman at the motel door. Petite, quick as a snake. She'd taken him down then her pal stormed in, a needle in the neck. Oh, yes. Arizona. Bobby Tennyson. An island in the Pacific. Thorn had been on that island. Or imagined it. Not sure.

"What's your name, what's your mission? Think."

Someone pinched his right nipple and twisted. His bare nipple. He was naked. Naked in an icehouse. His bullet wound throbbed, his nipple stung, the Waffle House breakfast sloshed in his gut.

"Take the goddamn hood off." It was Thorn's voice, but someone else speaking on his behalf. Someone with clarity of purpose, someone with definite ideas. Maybe the old Thorn was still alert inside this scrambled, vulnerable Thorn. A ventriloquist pulling the strings, Thorn, the dummy, given voice by Thorn the tough hombre.

The hood came off.

Blinding white sparkles and flashbulbs popping, the glare of searchlights."Leave him," a man said. Behind him.

"Let it wear off. He's no good for now."

A murky figure moved past him. Thorn blinked again and again but couldn't clear the blur.

He swallowed the gurgle in his throat, an acid belch of eggs, bacon and coffee.

He breathed. He was alive. That was a good thing he supposed. Alive.

The room went dark. Freezing cold and dark.

THIRTEEN

"Why should I tell you anything if you're going to kill me anyway?"

"Now why'd we do something extreme like that? We just want to know where the girl is. You tell us that, you go on your merry way."

"Oh, come on. Don't bullshit an old lady. I've seen your faces up close and can identify you later in a line-up when you're apprehended, which you will be."

"You already saw my face yesterday when I was in your office," Ingrid said.

"You were disguised. If yesterday was all I had to go on, I'd never be able to pick you out. But now it's different. I can describe you down to the last detail, like that earlobe scar where somebody must've torn out one of your pierced earrings. That's some hard living you've been doing. Some mean-as-a-rattlesnake boyfriend probably did that. So see, you're going to kill me anyway, why should I cooperate?"

"She has a point," Marco said. "Maybe torture her, test her pain threshold."

Marco dug the pocketknife from his jeans, flicked it open. Stroked his thumb across the blade. Plenty sharp. He held the point close to the secretary's nose.

"Cut on me all you want," she said. "I'll scream and howl but I won't tell you where the girl is. Go on, if that boils your eggs, give it a try."

They'd parked the Lincoln at the dead end of a dirt road about five miles beyond Frontera. No houses, not a tree, nothing.

The secretary had her back against the passenger door, Marco on her right side, Ingrid on her left, blocking her escape. Though this woman was no runner. From the looks of her, she probably hadn't run more than ten feet in her entire life.

"Her name is Dulce," the secretary said. "I'll tell you that much. The little girl is Dulce, which means sweet. She's from Honduras. You know how far away that is, how many miles that girl had to hike to get here? It's sixteen hundred. And those are hard, terrible miles, full of dangers."

"So?" Marco lowered the blade.

"You the ones blew up her truck?"

"I don't know what you're talking about," Marco said. "What truck?"

"Truck Dulce was riding in. Truck you blew up. I see it in your face. You can't be all bad if it bothers you enough I can read it in your eyes. If that's why you want her, because you think maybe she could identify you, well, that's the least of your worries."

"She's just trying to confuse you. Just shut up, don't talk to her anymore."

Marco said, "Who were those other people shooting at us?"

"One of them is dead," the woman said. "You killed him. The other two are friends of his from Florida. Key Largo, I think."

"Key Largo? What the fuck are they doing out here?"

"Tracking you," the woman said. "They know all about you, the bombings you've done."

Ingrid cursed and Marco said, "What're their names, these Florida people?"

"One of them is called Thorn, and his girlfriend, I don't know her name."

"What kind of fucking name is Thorn?"

"What I'm telling you is, forget those people and forget Dulce. They're not what you got to worry about. The sheriff's sister, Jenny, she lives out in that trailer where you were. Jenny gave Sheriff Castillo detailed descriptions of you both. He's already had sketches drawn up, which now that I'm looking right at you, I can say those sketches are damn close. That artist nailed it."

"Christ on a stick," Ingrid said. "We should've killed that scrawny bitch the minute we saw her."

"So go ahead," the secretary said, patting her puffed up hair, tucking a few escaped hairs back in place. "Murder me if you want, chop me up, sprinkle my parts all over the desert, won't do you any good. Law's closing in on you as we speak."

"She could be lying about the drawings," Marco said to Ingrid. "Those sketch artists never get it right."

"Yeah, and why lie, how's that benefit her? Unless she's got a death wish."

"If I might suggest an option," the woman said. "Leave me out here, just drive away. Take a good look at me, do I look like I'm fast on my feet? It'll take hours to plod back to town. By then you two would be long gone. Naturally I'll tell the sheriff everything that happened, but I'm not going to be able to add much to the description of you two, not more than what they got already."

"You've seen our car."

"Yes, well, there's that. But I don't know one car from another, unless it's a Maserati. That one I know because of a TV show I watch, star drives one."

"I know it's weird," Marco said. "But I'm starting to like this old broad."

"Jesus, Jesus, Jesus." Ingrid turned and stalked back to the rear of the SUV.

Marco told the secretary to stay put and he joined Ingrid. She'd opened the rear hatch and was digging through one of the duffels.

Marco asked her what she was doing.

"Getting a gun."

"Knife is better."

The secretary yelled back to them.

"One other thing I should tell you. They got the lab results from the dead bodies and they know you used poison gas to kill all those poor people. Because of that, the FBI is stepping in. FBI and some other federal agency too, and the sheriff's moving aside so they can take over. I'm thinking if you two ever want to sleep in your own beds again, you better get on down the road, as far from here as you can as fast as you know how. That's my advice."

Ingrid selected a Glock 43 and walked over to the secretary.

"It wasn't my boyfriend tore that jewelry out of my earlobe."

"Your husband," the secretary said. She was staring at the pistol.

"Not my husband either," Ingrid said.

"You want me to guess?"

"Are you a mother?" Ingrid said.

"Two boys, both in the service. One Navy, the other Marines. Good boys."

"And were you a good mother?"

"Did the best I could. My husband died when the boys were in grade school."

"You ever strike your children?"

"Never, not once. Though there were plenty of times I wanted to."

"It was my mother ripped it out of my earlobe. Tore out the earring because I disobeyed her. I can't even remember what I did wrong, it was so trifling. That's the house I grew up in."

"That's terrible. I'm sorry."

"So, see, I'm not real fond of mothers."

Ingrid raised the Glock, inches away from the woman's chest.

"Last chance," Ingrid said. "Tell me where the girl is, you can go."

"All right, I'll tell you only because I know you'll be walking into a buzz saw."

Ingrid held her aim.

"The people protecting her, they'll chew you up, spit you out."

"You got two more seconds then you're a dead lady."

The secretary gave Ingrid an address.

Ingrid lowered the pistol and fired into the woman's thigh.

The woman lurched back, slid down the side of the car, her butt thumping on the bare ground. She groaned and whimpered and said, "Don't, please don't."

Marco turned away and walked back to the rear of the Lincoln and stood looking out at the vacant landscape while Ingrid finished with the woman.

"If you're lying to me, bitch, we're coming back and my man is going to start in on you with his blade."

"I'm not lying. I don't lie."

Marco watched the woman bleed for a few seconds, then said to Ingrid, "What do you think she meant 'walking into a buzz saw'?"

FOURTEEN

"Thorn?" A whisper from deep within his delirium. "Thorn, is that you?"

A woman's voice, a woman he knew. A trick. Had to be a trick.

"Who is it?" Thorn's voice was croaky, unused for hours, his throat parched.

"It's me. It's Sofia. Is that you, Thorn?"

A hoax, a ruse. His captors' trickery.

"I'm tied to a chair, Thorn. Is that you? Did they kidnap you too?"

"Sofia?"

"It's me."

It did sound like her, but considering Thorn's current daze, he was leery.

"Can you prove it?"

She was silent for several heartbeats, then, "You always order Red Stripe. On special occasions it's margaritas, but only top shelf, Patron, Grand Marnier."

She sounded close, ten feet away, maybe closer.

"Did I pass?" she said.

"Sorry," said Thorn. "Did they hurt you? Are you okay?"

"Injection in the neck that hurt like hell. But yeah, I'll survive.

Groggy, a headache, like a terrible hangover and I'm freezing."

"They could be listening to us," he said.

"Let them listen. What's there to hide?"

"Did they say anything to you, interrogate you?"

"They just asked my name, then the needle. I heard them ask you what the next target is."

"Yeah," Thorn said. "It's mistaken identity. Has to be that."

"Please let it be that."

"Unless they're not cops," he said. "They sure as hell didn't act like the law."

"My hood is still on, is yours?"

"No, but it might as well be. I can't see a damn thing."

"They stripped me," she said. "I'm getting frost bite."

"Same here."

"That's no police procedure I ever heard of."

"No," Thorn said. "It's not."

"You have any idea where we are?"

"Feels like a meat locker, weird smells, chemicals I don't recognize."

"We should never have come out here. Bobby dead, now this."

"I'm sorry, Sofia."

"No, it's all my fault. I bullied you into it. You wanted to stay home."

"We'll be okay. We'll set them straight and they'll let us go."

"You're sure of that?"

No, he wasn't sure, not even close. But Sofia's voice was frail, a quaver he'd never heard from her before, so he faked it.

"If they're law enforcement, they have rules. Have to read us our rights, allow us a phone call, legal counsel. All that."

She was silent. Thorn had always been a lousy liar. Even as he'd spoken the words, they'd tasted unconvincing on his tongue.

"How'd you wind up here, Sofia?"

"Hortensia, you know, Castillo's secretary, she dropped me at an airport motel. I was going to fly back to Florida tomorrow. I'm in my room half an hour, knock at the door, I open it, then, I don't know, it happened so fast, some kind of injection knocked me out, and here I am."

He thought he heard her sniffling.

Thorn fetched for a Beatles line, something to break the dismal spell. But he couldn't recall anything, not even a single phrase echoing down the long corridors of memory.

"About that shootout," he said. "You were right. I was angry and lost control. I didn't need to fire at the van. That was wrong."

"It's more than that, Thorn, and you know it. I don't want to change who you are. We've been really good together. I'm grateful for that. My parents liked you, even my brother, Rodrigo, and he never likes any of my boyfriends. But this situation, sitting here in the freezing place with a hood over my head, and the shooting, and Bobby killed. That's too much. I know you think I'm silly, just a bartender in a local pub. The girl who quotes The Beatles all the time.

"Don't deny it. I know what you think. But there's a reason for that, something I never told you." She paused for a moment as if gathering herself, then continued in a resolute voice: "Growing up in *Cienfuegos*, Rodrigo would play his Abbey Road album and the white one, over and over on his little turntable. We would lie in bed at night, falling asleep listening to them sing. It's how we learned English. How we glimpsed the world beyond the island. So, yeah, I know it's sappy always quoting them like they were some great gurus on a mountaintop. But when I do it, it gives me solace. Reminds me of that magic place where I grew up and was forced to abandon.

"Do you understand?"

Thorn said, yes, he understood.

She was starting to say something more when across the room a heavy door squealed open and the dazzling overhead lights flared on.

When his stunned eyes adjusted, he counted ten stainless steel gurneys with naked bodies lying atop them, each with a red toe tag and in the far corner were two empty carts. From his angle, he couldn't make out the faces of the dead, but their sizes ranged from those of young children to heavyset adults, male and female. All of them were brown-skinned and dark-haired.

Sofia and Thorn were imprisoned in the refrigerated locker of a morgue.

"All right, Mr. Thorn," the woman said. "Are we ready to talk?"

She settled into a folding metal chair, leaned forward, elbows on her knees.

"Who are you?" he said.

"Name is Perkins. This is agent Doyle."

"What kind of agent?"

Perkins was silent for a moment, eyes half-closed, weighing her answer, then said, "The kind you don't want showing up at your door."

"Your worst fucking nightmare," Doyle said, "times ten."

Perkins had the sinewy body of a marathoner. Lanky arms with a rash of freckles running from wrist to upper arm. Her face was also gaunt and the corners of her mouth were downturned as if her gloomy disposition left its bitter imprint there.

"Now tell us what you know about Odin." With a spidery finger she tucked a coil of hair back behind her ear.

"Who?"

"Come on, dick wash," Doyle said. "Odin. O-d-i-n."

He was a burly man with grizzled stubble on his cheeks and a gleaming, shaved head. Doyle was eyeing Thorn with smug contempt, an invitation to try something. If Thorn hadn't been bound to a chair he was pissed enough to accept the challenge.

The heavy metal door squealed open and Sheriff Raoul Castillo stepped into the room. He was dressed in civvies, faded jeans, a pearl-button checked shirt and hard-worn cowboy boots with square toes. His off-duty duds.

He glanced around the morgue and winced at the display, then locked eyes with Thorn and shook his head in disgust—either for the grotesque setting or Thorn in particular.

"Can somebody please take off my damn hood," Sofia said.

Perkins nodded to Doyle, and he walked over to Sofia and yanked it away.

Blinking against the lights, Sofia settled her eyes on Perkins and said, "Odin, the Norse god, is that what you're talking about?"

"Okay, that gets us started," Perkins said. "So, young lady, walk us through the details, who you are, what you're doing here? What's your scheme?"

"Scheme? I don't know what you mean."

"Start with these people, why don't you?"

Perkins swept her hand at the gathering of corpses.

"The victims of the truck bombing," Thorn said.

"Exactly," said Perkins.

Until that moment, Sofia must not have noticed the gurneys. She stiffened, closed her eyes and rocked her head back and groaned in anguish.

"Does it give you a buzz," Doyle said, "seeing your victims like this?"

Thorn said, "You've made a mistake. We're not involved in this. Sheriff Castillo can tell you our story."

"Oh, he did," said Perkins. "Castillo was kind enough to give us a very thorough account. But he couldn't explain this."

She slipped her hand in her trousers pocket and drew out a silver disk. She held it out, flat in her palm, presenting it to Sofia, then stepped over and showed it to Thorn.

"What is it?" Sofia said.

"Ask your friend. We found it in his pants pocket."

"Thorn?"

"Let her get dressed," he said. "There's no reason for this."

"Oh, there's a reason," said Perkins. "A good reason."

"Sheriff, who are these assholes?"

The sheriff dodged Thorn's eyes, his gaze ticking from the shelves on the far wall to the wheels of the gurneys. Ashamed or furious, Thorn couldn't tell.

Then he said, "They're Defense Department. Counter terrorism hotshots."

"That's right," Doyle said. "We track down creeps like you and root you out."

"Well, sorry to say," Thorn said, "you've captured the wrong creeps."

"Guy wants to play dumb," Doyle said. "Let me see if I can smarten him up."

Perkins shook her head at Doyle, smiled vacantly at Thorn and said, "Tell us then, how'd you happen to have the disk?"

"Dulce gave it to me."

"And who is Dulce?"

"You don't know? Castillo didn't tell you?"

"Who is she?"

"The sole survivor of the truck blast."

"And the sole survivor gave you this?"

"Yeah, we were at the medical clinic in Frontera."

"And the girl just handed you the coin?"

"That's right."

"Were there witnesses to this transaction?"

Doyle had begun to circle Thorn's chair.

Since he'd wakened, Thorn had been tugging at the nylon zip ties gripping his wrists. From decades of fly-tying his fingers were strong and nimble, practiced in the art of knotting and unknotting. So far, he'd only managed to loosen the binding enough for the feeling to return to his hands.

The straight-back chair he was strapped to was creaky with age. From what he could tell it was vintage oak like the ones used decades ago in schools and government buildings. To test the chair's sturdiness, Thorn had been making cautious rocking motions, pressuring his spine against the back until he heard the crackle of brittle wood, then letting off the tension. He'd begun to sense a give in the screws that held the chair together. Rocking and loosening, rocking and loosening.

Thorn said, "Dulce and I were in an examining room when she handed me the medallion or coin, or whatever it is."

"Yes, right. Whatever it is."

Doyle was behind Thorn, out of sight. His breath against Thorn's neck was as foul as rotting shrimp.

Perkins said, "Why did she give you this?"

"She told me the killer, the man you're looking for, left it lying in the straw inside the truck. Dulce thought it might be important or valuable, so she grabbed it."

"And she gave it to you, this important, valuable thing."

"She did."

"You sure it wasn't you left it in the straw?"

Thorn shook his head, still dizzy from the drugs or perhaps it was these outlandish claims.

Doyle came around the chair, hunched down to peer into Thorn's eyes. He licked his lips, shook his head, chuckling with scorn then blew a gust of his rancid breath in Thorn's face.

"Knock it off, Doyle," Perkins said. "Step away."

Though the odds of taking on these three hand-to-hand were in the minus column, prudence had never been Thorn's guiding light.

As Doyle moved away, Thorn flattened his bare feet against the floor, stiffened his torso, thrust backwards, felt the splintering of wood at the juncture of seat and back. And thrust again until the chair broke apart.

Wobbling to his feet, he saw Doyle coming for him. Thorn ducked and plowed his right shoulder into Doyle's gut, ramming the big man backwards.

Keeping him off-balance, Thorn pumped his legs while Doyle windmilled. Thorn drove him against a stainless steel tray, tumbling it sideways, spilling the corpse of an elderly man onto the floor. Doyle tripped over the body and fell, his skull clipping the edge of another steel tray. He roared and went down hard.

Perkins clapped a hand on Thorn's shoulder, sharp nails digging in, spun him around and rammed the barrel of a pistol into the side of his jaw.

"Okay, cowboy. Twitch and you're done."

"Oh, Jesus, Thorn. Can't you ever just stop?" Sofia wriggled against her restraints, her face crimson and gleaming with sweat.

Castillo dragged over another chair and shoved Thorn down. Perkins slipped the pistol barrel lower, jamming it into the side of Thorn's throat.

"You see those empty gurneys?" Perkins motioned to the two carts in the far corner. "Try anything else, smart guy, that's how you're leaving this room."

FIFTEEN

When Castillo finished securing Thorn's wrists with a new set of zip ties, Doyle settled the corpse back in place on the cart.

"Now, where were we?" Perkins' tone was off-hand, as if Thorn's eruption wasn't worth comment. "Oh, yes, discussing how you came by this coin."

She reached out and snapped her fingers so close to Thorn's face he felt the pulse of air.

"Wake up, Thorn. You've been caught. Your plan is thwarted."

"I have no idea what you're talking about."

"Why'd the girl give you the coin? Did she know you? Did she trust you? Did she simply want to bestow a gift on you because you're a rugged, fine-looking fellow or because you remind her of daddy? You're asking us to believe a bullshit absurdity. You should've worked harder on your story, Thorn. This isn't cutting it."

Her blue eyes held on Thorn's for a few scathing seconds.

Perkins pinched the coin's edge, held it up for Thorn to see.

"You put this inside the truck after the explosion. You've done that before on previous terrorist acts. Rapes, church fires, bombings."

"Jesus," Thorn said. "And why the hell would I do that?"

She examined him with eyes as hard and depthless as blue enamel.

"To grab headlines, get your name out there, build up your brand."

"You've lost me."

"Enough of this good-cop shit," Doyle said. "I'll get my tools."

"Not yet," said Perkins.

"You're not feds, are you?"

"We are exactly who we say we are. The question, Thorn, is who are you? Castillo tells us you live off the grid, way off. In my experience there's a reason people are off the grid. Usually it's not a good one."

"Screw the grid," Thorn said.

"Wouldn't that be nice," Perkins said. "We all go live in huts by the sea."

"It's your choice," said Thorn.

With a half smile, she shook her head.

"Here's how I see your situation, Thorn. With your bombing in Frontera, you got careless, maybe in a hurry, or lazy or you panicked, who the hell knows, but you forgot to leave the medallion. That's why you returned, buddied up with Castillo, looking for a chance to slip this calling card inside the truck. Otherwise, all your efforts are for naught because nobody would know it was your outfit that killed all these people. A phone call taking credit wouldn't cut it. You needed the medallion to be found amid the bodies, physical proof. But alas, Ms. Banfield had the vehicle hauled away."

"Come on," Sofia said. "Do Thorn and I look like terrorists to you?"

"You people come in all shapes and sizes," Perkins said. "And listen up, don't trot out that fairy tale you gave the sheriff. We know all about Johnston Atoll, and the events of '71. And we also know about Marco."

"Marco?"

"Ray's son," Perkins said. "You can stop the cute act."

"Who is Ray?" Sofia said. "We don't know a Ray."

"Raymond Murphy," said Perkins. "Guy you've been calling Bobby Tennyson."

"Oh, man," Thorn said. "This is nuts."

"Go on," Doyle said. "He thinks we don't have the goods. Lay it out, rub his fucking face in it."

"Yeah, okay," she said. "We know that in 1971 your buddy Ray Murphy helped steal two dozen landmines filled with VX nerve gas from the Johnston air base, and just recently you and Ray and your pretty friend carried out an attack using one of those stolen munitions. The lab finished the blood work on these eleven corpses a few hours ago, and there's absolute confirmation. These people were killed with VX and you and Mr. Murphy are the ringleaders."

"No way," Sofia said. "Bobby was trying to track down the explosives because he felt responsible. He felt guilty."

"Oh, he was guilty, all right." Perkins drew a folded square of paper from her back pocket, opened it and held it up for Thorn to see.

Two side-by-side mug shots in black and white. A much younger Bobby Tennyson, one photo had him facing front, the other was a side view, with **U. S. Department of Justice** printed in bold across the top.

"Read it," Perkins said. "It's your friend's inmate file from Leavenworth. Charged under the Uniform Code of Military Justice, found guilty of larceny of military property. Served a fifteen year sentence. That's your buddy."

"And the other photo," Doyle said.

Perkins' hand went back to her pocket and she withdrew a glossy color shot and thrust it inches from Thorn's face.

Bobby's naked body was laid out on a stainless steel morgue tray.

"His shoulder," Perkins said. "Look closely."

Thorn had to squint, but yes, he finally saw it.

Just above Bobby's left biceps a crude tattoo was inked into his flesh. The same interlocking pyramids with a jagged lightning bolt at their juncture.

"That's why you're naked," Perkins said. "So we could locate your matching tattoos."

"But you didn't," Thorn said.

"Well," Perkins said. "Nobody bats a thousand."

Doyle marched over to Sofia, used both hands to gather her dark mane and lifted it to expose the white flesh at the nape of her neck.

"But 500 isn't bad," Perkins said.

Doyle jerked Sofia's head to the side so Thorn had a clear view.

It was no larger than a thumb print at the base of her skull—the same image as the one on the coin was tattooed to her skin. Thorn's fingertips had roamed that area dozens of times but he'd never examined the flesh.

"I can explain," Sofia said. "It's not what it looks like."

"Oh, this should be good," Doyle said.

"What is that image?" Thorn said. "What does it mean, Sofia?"

"Tell him, girlie," Doyle said. "Go on, you know what it means."

"It's a Valknot," Sofia said, her voice small and faraway. "Also known as a 'knot of the slain.' That's the interlocking triangles part. Bobby told me about it. I wouldn't know otherwise."

"Valknot," Thorn said, trying to muffle his anger. "And what is that?"

"Norse symbol for the afterlife," she said. "Also an emblem for the Norse god Odin. Certain groups adopted the image as a sign they're willing to give their life for Odin. You know, like willing to die in battle."

"And the lightning bolt?"

"That's a sub-group," said Sofia. "They call themselves Abyss. They don't have an ideology, morality, religion, it's all bullshit to them."

"And killing immigrants? Where does that fit?"

"I only know what Bobby told me," said Sofia. "For members of Abyss, everything and everybody is fair game. There's no taboos. Destroy, destroy. Incite mayhem, turn Americans against each other. A civil war, blood in the streets, that's their goal, anarchy, chaos. Overthrow all forms of authority."

"Oh, it goes on," Perkins said. "Tell him about the initiation rites."

Sofia claimed she didn't know what Perkins was talking about.

"Okay, I'll do it," said Perkins. "Abyss kidnaps migrants, cages them, feeds them dog food, just enough water to keep them going. When they have a new recruit wants to join up, Abyss pulls a teenage kid or old lady out of their cage and uses them as a loyalty test. Have the recruit shoot them, cut on them, whatever he's ordered to do."

"Oh, Christ." Sofia sank back into her chair.

"That about sums it up, little lady," said Doyle. "Now tell us, Sofia Mendoza, the thing we all want to know. Why are you wearing the tat?"

As Sofia opened her mouth to answer, someone hammered on the door. Perkins and Doyle exchanged a glance. After another round of knocking, Castillo who stood closest, swung it open.

A smiling Sugarman filled the doorway. He peered into the refrigerated room, his grin melting away. He shook his head gloomily the way he often did when confronted with another of Thorn's catastrophes.

"Who the hell're you?" Doyle puffed himself up, inching close to Sugar.

"Name is Sugarman. I'm here to emancipate my colleagues."

SIXTEEN

Perkins gave Doyle a cool-it pat on the shoulder, and edged in front of him.

"Emancipate your colleagues?" she said. "How do you plan on doing that?"

Sugar craned his head to the side to check out Sofia and Thorn.

"You two okay?"

"Fine and dandy," Thorn said.

"Who are you?" Perkins said, "and what the hell are you doing here?"

"Your supervisor in D.C. was kind enough to steer me to this location." Sugar held up his phone and panned its face around the room. "You getting all this, Frank?"

A familiar voice came from the phone in Sugar's hand:

"Good afternoon, folks. I'm Frank Sheffield, Special Agent in Charge of the Miami Field Office of the FBI."

Perkins squinted at the phone and said, "What kind of bullshit is this?"

"You would be Agent Margie Perkins, I assume. If you want to verify what I'm about to say, I suggest you place an immediate call to your boss, Martin Bessemer. I have the number to his cell if you've misplaced it."

Perkins swung to Doyle and ordered him to call the home office.

Coming back to the phone in Sugarman's hand, she said, "What the hell?"

Frank explained that Thorn and Sugarman and Sheffield had joined forces on several cases in recent years. That much was true. Twice before Thorn had blundered into Frank Sheffield's investigative territory when a couple of Thorn's vigilante crusades went seriously astray. If Frank had been an uptight, straight-shooting *federale*, Thorn would probably be serving a stretch at Raiford at this moment, but happily Sheffield and Thorn had hit it off.

After a rocky start, they discovered they were equally unimpressed with bureaucratic authority and both shared a dry, irreverent view of the follies of mankind, not to mention a passion for the sea and all that it sustained.

But today, after a sentence of truth, Frank veered into make-believe.

"Thorn and Ms. Mendoza are assisting the Bureau in a covert capacity."

Doyle finished his mumbled phone call and leaned close to Perkins, hissing at her ear.

She swung around, glared at Thorn then said, "Jesus, Mary and Joseph."

Sheffield said, "Seems your investigative activities have been following a parallel course to ours until recently when your work and our work, well, they intersected, resulting in this awkward situation.

"I have an extraction team on its way from Tucson. They're about two minutes out. But I hope we can resolve this peacefully without their intervention.

"So," Sheffield said, his voice as coolly understated as always. "If you would kindly release my people and let them get back to work, we will continue down our fact-finding pathway and you can continue down yours and maybe if we all do our jobs in a professional and courteous manner we'll meet again at the finish line and raise the trophy together."

Sugarman was holding the phone up so Perkins and Frank were eye to eye.

Thorn called out from across the room, words he'd thought would never cross his lips. He wanted his damn cell phone back.

"I'll stay on the line," Sheffield said, "until I see my people are released from their bonds, fully dressed and out the door. And before they leave, would you please return Mr. Thorn's phone."

☣☣☣

Sugarman tossed Thorn's duffel and Sofia's overnight into the back of a white Chevy Tahoe and pulled out of the parking lot of the county morgue.

While he drove, Sugar explained how he'd arrived on the scene. First, he'd overheard the whole takedown in Thorn's motel room on the open phone line because Bobby's cell was lying on the bed while Thorn answered the knock on the door.

After what sounded like a scuffle, Sugar heard nothing more from Thorn, but did catch a conversation between a man and woman. He wasn't sure if they were FBI or what, but they had a brisk, no-bullshit exchange about questioning Thorn, using language that Sugar registered as federal jargon.

When they discovered the cell phone lying on the bed, a female voice came on the line and asked who she was speaking with. Sugarman was silent but figured that since they now had his phone number, it wouldn't be long before one of their kind showed up at this door in Key Largo.

He clicked off and called Frank Sheffield, filled him in on Thorn's latest debacle, then asked if Frank would consider using his contacts to find out what kind of law enforcement operation was underway in the Tucson area. After cursing out Thorn for a colorful half-minute, Frank agreed to look into it, told Sugar he'd call him back as soon as he had something.

Not sure if Sheffield would follow through, Sugar packed, drove up to Miami, made it by eleven, got super lucky and nabbed a seat on a flight to Tucson that was currently boarding, and as he was sprinting down the concourse to the gate, Frank called back.

Some kind of task force run out of the Department of Defense was tracking a hate group that appeared to have acquired landmines containing VX nerve gas, part of the cache stolen from a base in the Pacific decades back.

"I know about the nerve gas stuff," Sugar said.

Frank wanted to know how the hell he had that kind of info.

So Sugar gave him a quick rundown of Bobby Tennyson's version of events and Frank agreed to poke around, see what else he could find.

Early afternoon when Sugar landed in Tucson, he checked in with Sheffield. By then Frank had an address where Thorn was being held. He'd bullshitted the head of the DOD task force in D.C., convincing him the Miami field office was running an operation targeting the same hate group, and the overlap had resulted in a fucked up case of mistaken identity with Thorn and Sofia wrongly taken into custody.

Frank coaxed an informal agreement with the DOD guy, promising to share all the FBI's latest investigative notes—handwritten, video, audio, phone intercepts, everything they'd collected, as soon as his undercover operatives, Thorn and Sofia, were released from custody.

"Conning a federal official," Thorn said.

"Guess it worked."

"Generous of Frank," said Thorn. "Anything in return?"

"He'd like you to put him on a school of tarpon sometime soon, mentioned fishing the flats off Flamingo."

"I believe I can manage that."

"But that's it for Sheffield's help. He wants me to bring you back to Miami, stop by his office so he could debrief us. He's looking at retirement in a year or two and wants to play this by the book. I'm assuming this is one last favor for old-time's-sake. He didn't put it that way, but in so many words."

Through mid-afternoon traffic they drove a few miles in silence, Sofia riding shotgun, Thorn in the seat behind her. For a while he watched the desert scenery flash past, desolate, dry, a land of sun-bleached scrub dotting the endless stretches of sand and in the northern distance was a treeless mountain range rimming the city.

His gut was clenched, a growl of blood in his ears. He drew shallow breaths and stared at the back of Sofia's head. Her hair hung over the seat and a lustrous skein brushed his knees.

He flipped back through the last weeks, all their bright, vivid hours together. Their laughter, their talk, her smartass take on things, her goofy-ass Beatles fixation, her warm, nurturing family.

The hours of nestled ease, basking in the sunlit sheets, or the moon's silver radiance, the taste of her lips, the writhing elasticity of her arms, her legs, the raw, wildcat power in her hips as she arched to meet him, opened herself, her breathless groans that seemed to arise from deep in her viscera. The lightshow that left its fiery imprint on the inside of Thorn's eyelids: comets with their trails of sizzling dust, the eerie, melting glow of northern lights. Stoned on sex. Gorged on oblivion. Hours of flesh and flesh and flesh.

Thorn had thought they were a flawless physical fit. Every contour matched, a congruency that rivaled any Thorn had known, and Sofia claimed the same. Their timing was perfectly in synch, the rising scale of their voices and heartbeats as they worked toward a mutual final thrust and embrace and long series of shivers fulfilled her needs at the exact moment it satisfied his, and when that ultimate moment fell away into astonished laughter or a drowsy hour with their bodies entangled, Thorn had been repeating silently to himself the word he found so difficult to say aloud, trying it out in his mind, coming closer and closer to giving it breath.

Now he wondered what fraction of their time together had been genuine and what part scam. It seemed he'd put too much trust in sensual evidence. Idiot Thorn. Once again mistaking lust for something more.

At the wheel Sugarman had begun to fill the tense silence by recounting his recent efforts of tracking down Savannah Snyder. A computer search for the *Flying Dragon*, the sailboat in Bobby's story that was towed into Johnston Atoll. Sugar's online search led him to a small town in the thumb of Michigan. A street address, tax records for Savannah.

"Bad Axe?" Sofia said. "Weird name."

"After the Civil War, a military surveyor mapping the region came across a rusty axe left at an abandoned campground where two major trails intersected. He wrote the name on an early chart and it stuck. The town's on Lake Huron, three or four thousand people."

"Pull over," Thorn said. "We need to talk."

Sugar heard the bite in Thorn's voice because he glanced back at him with a look of alarm. Thorn's face felt like cold stone.

Sugar found a Wal-Mart parking lot and chose a space on the outer edge.

When the car stopped, Sofia swiveled around to face him.

"I'm ready," she said. "Go on."

"The tattoo on your neck," he said. "You and Bobby were scamming us. This whole thing was a setup. You're part of this Abyss group."

"No, no. That's not true."

"What the hell's going on?" Sugar said.

Thorn gave him a quick recap of the last couple of hours. Bobby Tennyson's real name. His fifteen-year hitch at Leavenworth for stealing munitions from the Johnston stash. The Valknot tattoo on his arm. An identical one on Sofia's neck.

"Bobby was going to explain everything to both of you," Sofia said. "He needed your help and he didn't think you'd go along if you knew it all upfront. He needed someone strong, willing to take a risk. He didn't think that he and I could do it by ourselves. He wouldn't let me tell you anything because he was afraid you'd bolt. He was about to reveal the whole plan when he was shot."

Sugarman looked back at Thorn and with a shrug, said, "Hear her out."

"What do you want to know?" Sofia said. "I'll tell you everything."

"Why the tattoo?"

"All Abyss members wear one. It was going to be our admission ticket, to prove we were one of them. We were going to try to talk you into getting one too."

Unsure he'd fully trust anything Sofia said again, he asked, "Who is Marco?"

Marco was Savannah's first born. Ray Murphy's boy. Conceived during their three-day dalliance.

Savannah's old man, Colonel Joshua Snyder, commanding officer at Johnston, was attending a two-week briefing at Edward's Air Force Base in California to review plans for the giant incinerator to be built on the island. An incinerator that was meant to destroy the complete U.S. stockpile of nerve gas.

For those fourteen days with the Colonel gone, Ray would be in control of Johnston. Just enough time for Savannah to execute the plot she'd been fantasizing about since her brother Marty's death the year earlier.

Savannah had met Ray Murphy twice on his leaves to Honolulu, and after a little exploratory flirting, she determined that Ray was susceptible to her charms.

And she'd been right. It took nine days to sail to Johnston but only three days of moonlit fucking in the fertile heart of the Pacific with the silver sea flickering in every direction and the sky packed tight with stars, to soften Ray's resistance until he was ready to help her rip off the landmines.

At his court martial Ray never ratted her out. Just called her an anonymous girl on a sailboat with a hippie friend sailing off with twenty-four deadly weapons. He testified that he didn't know why she wanted the armaments. She'd mesmerized him, he admitted that, and one night, under the woozy spell of Savannah's charms and some powerful weed, he'd help her load the weapons on her boat. Yes, he was a sex-dazed sap. Guilty, guilty, guilty.

All that was true. Ray had no idea Savannah intended to use the explosives against the war-mongers, the Pentagon establishment, the military industrial complex, the evil fucks who recruited naïve, vulnerable boys and shipped them off to battle then abandoned them when they returned, didn't give a shit those warriors were tortured by nightmarish memories, and wound up withering in despair and shame and self-hatred.

She stole the weapons to help kick start the revolution everyone knew was coming. Yeah, that was an article of faith in 1971. War in Nam becoming more vile every week with thousands of sweet young boys chewed up, and bloody chaos in the American streets, student protestors shot down, sit-ins shutting down universities, calls to topple the government, bombs set off in recruitment offices and government buildings, even a bomb in a bathroom at the Pentagon.

But none of her radical contacts would touch the landmines. Took one look at the goodies in the back of her van and backed away. Every one of those phony anti-war militants. A month of turndowns in midnight parking lots and nameless streets.

"I told you," Judson said. "All the risk we took, we can't even give the shit away."

She and Judson drove them back to the Michigan farm where Judson's mom was in her final days of cancer. Stowed all those beautiful weapons in the shed out back, and there they sat. And sat.

SEVENTEEN

"All I know," Sofia said. "Marco is Bobby's grown son. He grew up somewhere in Michigan, Bobby didn't say where, then left home as a teenager. I've never seen him, not even his picture. I know he's the leader of Abyss. Bobby was in contact with him, starting a month ago, right after he got that text from Savannah. I don't know how Bobby and Marco stayed in touch, maybe an encrypted app or burner phone, but they communicated, I know that.

"He found out where Marco and his group were based, but he wouldn't tell me. He wanted to infiltrate the cell, pretend he sympathized with Abyss and find a time when we could kidnap Marco, or at least sabotage what he was doing, keep him out of jail."

Sugar looked back at Thorn and shot him a prying look to see how he was taking this. Not well.

Which must have been obvious because Sugar said, "Why recruit us?"

"Strength in numbers," she said. "Bobby knew about some of your past exploits and thought you might be helpful, thought you could handle the stress, and the physical stuff that Bobby and I couldn't manage."

"Like what?" Thorn said.

"I don't know all he had in mind. Maybe carting off what landmines remained. Bobby has a bad back and me, I'm strong but probably not strong enough for that."

"So we were going to be your beasts of burden."

"Most of what Bobby told you was true."

"You knew about Leavenworth? His real name? The other

version of his story?"

"No," she said. "But that doesn't change anything. It was still a worthy mission. Get Marco to stop the killing, and rescue him."

Thorn held back for a few moments, the anger constricting his throat.

Finally he managed to ask about her tattoo.

"When did you have it done?"

"I went up to Miami, found a guy in a strip mall."

"When?"

She shook her head and with pained reluctance said, "Early September."

"A month ago," Thorn said. "So this was in the works before you and me."

"Yes."

"You seduced me."

"It wasn't hard."

"And this, you and me together, it's all been a con."

"Not all of it, no. Maybe it started out that way."

"Oh, come on."

"You come on, Thorn. What isn't a con? Haven't you heard? Men con women, women con men. Happens every day."

"No, somehow I missed that message."

"We all live in a yellow submarine. Everything's some kind of lie, everything's absurd."

"Everything's a lie," Thorn said, echoing her flat tone.

"Yellow Submarine," Sugar said. "I thought that was a children's song. Or about LSD or something."

Thorn leaned back in the seat and looked out at the Wal-Mart lot where people were wheeling their shopping carts brimming with goods back to their cars. Groceries, clothes, toys, sundries, all of it a little cheaper than the same items in the mom and pop stores on Main Street. Consumers consuming. All the shoddy, plastic-wrapped, disposable necessities of modern life. Things, things and more things overflowing everyone's baskets.

Maybe Sofia was right, everything was absurd, nothing more than an endless shopping spree at cut-rate stores selling trashy goods, and people working for low wages at jobs they despised to buy the gewgaws and toilet paper, cheap jeans and fake jewels, the Christmas gifts and the wrapping paper. A never-ending cycle of earning, spending, consuming, sending the leftovers to the dump. A spiritless sequence that provided spurts of pleasure in each new acquisition before the item lost its luster, wore out or broke. A mass addiction. Everywhere you looked consumption passed for consequential because every message on every billboard or TV ad said as much. An enormous con, a nation built on that lie. Belief in the advertising fantasy everyone had been programmed to believe.

Hell, everyone craved a fairytale. A story to explain their past, their dashed hopes, their postponed dreams, their boring present. Everyone chose the memories that fit their chosen narrative, abandoning those that didn't. Stories, stories, stories. A way to give the chaos shape as we do with the random spatter of stars, grouping them into coherent constellations, assigning names and dramatic histories—all to make us feel snug in a universe of wild confusion.

Even the elegantly told tales of Thorn's youth, those treasured seafaring yarns in leather-bound volumes that he'd latched onto as a child, the ones that propelled him, defined him, guided his steps for the rest of his years, those too were no more than fabrications, elaborate lies contrived to make an imaginary world seem real.

Everyone was riding in a yellow submarine, and their friends were all aboard, a thousand feet deep in an ocean of deceits.

As tempting as it was, Thorn didn't completely buy that easy cynicism. Stories might be lies, they might be man-made inventions, but the purposes they served were absolutely necessary. They gave respite and order in the face of chaos. They were temporary strongholds pitched in the wilderness where we hunkered down, lit our fires, cooked our food, and breathed easy as the night beasts howled incessantly beyond the make-believe walls.

"Where do you want to go now, Sofia?" Thorn asked.

"I'll call an Uber, go to the airport, fly home. I've had enough, way more than enough. This was all a terrible mistake."

"I can take you to the airport," Sugarman said.

"No, I need to be on my own right now. Are you okay with that, Thorn?"

"Do what you want."

It sounded cold and dismissive, but in his chest Thorn felt something like heavy fabric ripped apart by brute force.

She climbed out, went to the rear of the SUV, retrieved her bag and came back to the passenger door and leaned inside to meet Thorn's eyes.

"I'm sorry. I'm very sorry to have deceived you."

Before he could fashion a reply, she shut the door and walked away.

Sugarman let a few seconds pass then said, "So what now, buddy? Wash our hands of this craziness, go home, get back to our lives? Bobby's dead, you and I don't have anything invested in this."

Thorn watched a family of Hispanics, four small children, their mother and grandmother stuffing their purchases into the bed of a rusty pick-up.

"I want to see the girl," he said.

Sugarman asked what girl.

"Her name is Dulce. Castillo will know where she is."

"Okay," Sugar said. "You going to tell me why you want to see her?"

"If there is a point to all this, it's Dulce. That girl knows something that made her a target."

"You want to pursue this? Way out here in the desert, finish Bobby's quest. Because he saved you from drowning a long time ago."

Thorn said nothing.

Sugarman sighed, resigned, not fighting it. He headed south, located I-19, and they were back in Frontera by seven that evening with a dusky blue twilight hovering just above the horizon and a gathering darkness that seeped in from the desert like wood smoke.

Even though it was after closing time, the sheriff's office was lit up. Sugar parked in front and followed Thorn into the office.

At his desk, Castillo's elbows were planted on his ink blotter, head slumped into his hands.

"Sheriff?"

He looked up, eyes damp and inflamed.

"What in god's name do you want now?"

"What's happened?"

He shook his head as though answering was more than he could bear. He shoved himself to his feet and came around the desk and closed in on Thorn, mouth gritted.

"You..." Castillo looked up at the ceiling but found no obscenity sufficient to label Thorn. "I don't know who the hell you are or why you're here, but what I know is that you have single-handedly brought more mayhem and tragedy with you than this town has ever known."

The sheriff balled his hands into fists, but his arms hung limp at his sides.

"Tell us," Thorn said. "What happened?"

The air seemed to leak from him. His head sagged, eyes half-closed.

"They killed her. Murdered her like a rabid possum."

"Who?"

"Tensia" he said. "Hortensia Calderon. Mother of two boys, the strongest woman I ever knew."

"Your secretary? She was killed?"

"That's just the start."

The sheriff tottered forward a half step as though his knees were giving out, and Thorn slung a steadying arm around Castillo's shoulders, turned him and guided him back to his padded chair and eased him into it. Castillo looked up at him, subdued, his mouth softening, eyes glassy.

"Diego Martinez and Maria, his wife. The doctor who patched you up. The couple who took Dulce in."

"Ex-military and a former state trooper. Those two?"

His looked down at his lap and nodded.

"And Dulce?"

"The girl got away. Don't ask me how. The scene's a bloody mess. The doc and Maria went down swinging hard."

"Why aren't you still at the crime scene?" Sugarman asked.

"FBI team from the Phoenix Field Office muscled me out. Along with those DOD hotshots, Perkins and Doyle. I'm not in the food chain anymore. I'll have to get my updates from the goddamn TV."

"Dulce escaped? You're sure of that?"

"It appears so. She wasn't there when I arrived. Neighbors heard the shooting, called it in. The couple we exchanged gunfire with at my sister's trailer, it was them again. When the shooting was done, those two just walked back out to their SUV, calm as you please. A young woman directly across the street got a video of them leaving. Muscled-up man, lanky woman, no masks, nothing. Carrying their weapons out into the afternoon sun. Got in the car, drove off."

"And Dulce wasn't with them?"

"No, she wasn't. Look, that's a close-knit neighborhood. Everyone had met Dulce, understood the situation, the doc and his wife were looking after her. So, no. Nobody saw the girl after the gunfire started. Neighbors on either side of the house ran inside after the killers left. Nothing they could do for Maria. Diego was still alive, but he didn't survive till the ambulance arrived. The neighbors searched the house for Dulce, top to bottom. Nowhere to be found.

"Then, Christ, just as I got to the Martinez place, I got a call from a young mechanic lives out in a trailer on the south of town. He was working around the house when his hound showed up with blood on its snout and paws, so he went looking to see what the dog had gotten into. Found Hortensia a half-mile away.

"Bled to death from a single shot to her upper leg. She'd tried to crawl out to the asphalt to wave down help, but no one much uses that little strip of road. So the dog found her, must've licked at her wound for a while. And that's the goddamn trouble you've brought with you, Thorn. Fifteen dead by my count. Eleven migrants, Tennyson, the doc and his wife and Tensy."

"How'd the shitheads find Dulce?"

"Must've been Tensia," he said and stared down at his desktop. "They tortured it from her and left her to bleed out."

"No masks," Sugarman said. "What do you make of that?"

"Sounds like they don't give a shit anymore."

"Yeah," Thorn said. "Like they weren't dangerous enough already."

"I was stuck in the morgue with you and Sofia when Tensy was taken hostage and tortured. In the damn morgue, for godsakes. If it hadn't been for you coming here and sticking your nose where it doesn't belong, I would've been sitting here in the office where I should've been and Tensia would still be alive."

"I'm sorry," Thorn said. "I'm truly sorry."

Castillo shook his head, no interest in forgiveness.

For another half hour Sugar and Thorn stayed with the sheriff digging for anything more, but Castillo had already told them everything relevant he knew or was willing to share.

It was after eight when they climbed back in the Tahoe and Sugarman drove them north out of Frontera. After a few minutes of silence Sugar had them back on the interstate heading toward the distant glow of Tucson. That's when her voice sounded from the darkness of the rear seat.

"Hello."

Thorn swung around.

Dulce's eyes flashed in the gloom.

"Can you help me? Please, mister Thorn, can you?"

EIGHTEEN

Jolted, Sugarman pumped the brakes, and an eighteen-wheeler buffeted the Tahoe as it blew past in the outside lane, its air horn blaring.

"My god, Dulce, how'd you get here?" Thorn said.

She said she'd escaped from the back door of the doctor's house while the gunfire was still going on, and she'd hid out in backyards and bushes till nightfall, then she found her way back to the sheriff's office and had been waiting in the darkness to see if it was safe when she saw Thorn drive up.

After he and Sugar went in the sheriff's office, she climbed into his car and lay down on the floor in the back. She believed she could trust him. He'd been kind to her.

When she'd finished her account, Thorn reached a hand out to the girl and after a moment's hesitation, she took it in both of hers and gripped it tightly.

After Thorn reclaimed his breath, he said, "Of course we'll help you, Dulce."

She thanked him, went silent, let go of his hand and settled back in the seat.

"I want to go to Phoenix, be with Sister Kathleen."

"Do you have an address, a number of any kind?"

"She is in Phoenix. That is what I know."

"We'll find her," Thorn said. "Don't worry. We'll track her down."

"Might be more than one nun named Kathleen," Sugar said.

"But yeah, we'll find her."

"Do you feel strong enough," Thorn asked the girl, "to tell us about your journey, whatever you can about the man who dropped the coin in the straw?"

"I'm strong, yes."

In choppy English peppered with Spanish phrases, Dulce described her father's death at the hands of the *Maras* gang in Honduras, a pack of predators who'd terrorized local citizens for years. Dulce's father had been saving money for the journey to America, and it was that money that Dulce's mother used to buy passage on the truck with a dozen others from her region. They had just crossed into America when the truck exploded and *el vajo* filled the truck.

"Vapor," Thorn said. "Gas."

"I figured," said Sugar.

Dulce believed she'd only survived the poison gas because her mother fell atop her and flattened Dulce's face to a rip in the floor of the truck, and protected her exposed flesh. *Aire fresco*, fresh air had saved her. *La suerte*, good luck, and her mother, and of course most of all, God had directed her fate.

The man who entered the van was wearing a rubber suit and a breathing mask like ocean divers. Dulce saw his face but it happened quickly and she had to feign death, and was frightened, so she didn't think she could recognize the man again. All she knew for sure that he was big and *musculoso*, brawny.

As she gave her account, Dulce's voice was shadowed by grief, but she told it in a clear-eyed and precise manner. If her trauma had scarred her or shaken her optimism, she hid it well. Considering she'd survived the truck bombing, watched her mother die and endured two attempts at abduction and murder, she was eerily calm, which suggested that the horrors she'd fled in her homeland must have been so monstrous that these American cruelties were mere trifles.

"Are you hungry?" Sugarman asked her.

"Yes," she said. "Can we eat McDonald's? I never know it. It is delicious, no?"

"Delicious?" Sugar said. "If you're hungry enough, I guess."

"McDonald's it is," Thorn said.

They found one on the southern outskirts of Tucson, got Dulce a cheeseburger, fries and a chocolate milkshake. Fish sandwiches for Sugar and Thorn. They ate inside, with Dulce closing her eyes for every bite to savor this ecstatic new sensation.

A group of teenage boys nearby kept staring at the three of them and whispering among themselves then breaking into cackles of laughter.

Thorn hadn't considered how the three of them might appear to outsiders.

"You want me to go have a talk with them?" Sugar said.

"We're almost done," said Thorn.

"He was making a movie," Dulce said.

"What? Who was making a movie?"

"The man in the truck, *el musculoso*."

"What kind of movie?"

"With his phone. A video of the dead ones and the coin he put in the straw."

"Did you tell the sheriff this? Or anyone else?"

"No one asked," Dulce said.

"A video," Sugarman said. "Now that's something."

"Terrorist porn?" Thorn said.

"Maybe. So why focus on the coin?"

"One of the DOD agents, the woman, Perkins, she called the medallion a calling card. An identifier, a way to take credit."

"Okay," Sugar said. "A movie that highlights a calling card, it would only be useful if it's broadcast."

"To taunt the authorities?"

"Maybe," Sugar said. "Or a promo to win hearts and minds. A recruitment tool. Look at us, see what we can do."

"We need to give this to Frank. This is too big."

"Starting to feel that way," Sugar said.

They finished their meal and on their way to the door, the redheaded teenager who'd been staring at them hissed at their backs: "Old enough to bleed, old enough to butcher."

Thorn turned, went back, picked up the redhead's half-finished shake and dumped it on his head. While the kid sputtered, his buddies rose in unison, but after a moment of sizing up Thorn, they decided to hold their fire.

"Some day, if you're lucky, kid," Thorn told the redhead, "you'll look back on this moment and realize what an ignorant little peckerhead you used to be."

When they were back in the Tahoe, doors shut, Sugar said, "You haven't had enough fun already today?"

"Yeah, you're right. I need to just let things go sometimes."

"Hope I'm around to witness that," Sugar said.

He turned onto the boulevard and Thorn spotted a shopping mall ahead.

"What do you think?" Thorn said. "New wardrobe for the lady? So she's presentable for the sister."

Sugarman agreed and Dulce smiled bashfully.

Inside the mall, wide-eyed at the abundance, Dulce resisted everything the two of them pointed out. Frowning, shaking her head.

"*Demasiado, demasiado*." Too much.

Unable to overcome her reluctance, Thorn found a Latina sales clerk, asked for her help, and the young woman spent half an hour guiding Dulce up and down the aisles then coaxed her into the changing room with a pile of clothes.

They left the store with two pairs of jeans, several bright frilly blouses, a denim jacket, belts, shoes, a backpack with an American flag embossed on the back, underwear and pajamas. They carried their haul back to the Tahoe, Dulce thanking them over and over and asking how she could ever repay their *generosidad*.

"These are gifts," Thorn told her. "Welcome to America."

As they left the parking lot, Sugar said he'd seen a Holiday Inn a mile back.

"Clean up, get some rest, sounds good to me," Thorn said. "It's a little late to be dropping in on Sister Kathleen."

Dulce said that sounded very good to her as well.

At the front desk, Thorn had to tap the bell several times before the night clerk emerged from the back room. He was a bald man in his sixties with a Marine Corps tattoo on his muscular forearm and a leery squint. Thorn got two rooms with a connecting door. As he was counting out the bills, Dulce appeared beside him.

"You okay? Something wrong?"

"I stay close," she said.

He gave her shoulder a soft squeeze.

To the clerk, he said, "I need toiletries, toothpaste, toothbrush, like that."

The clerk pointed out a kiosk on the other side of the lobby. With Dulce's help, Thorn selected a few items she needed, paid and the manager bagged them, his eyes even more prying than they'd been before, shifting between Thorn and Dulce.

The clerk gave Thorn the key cards, then followed them to the front door and stood watching the two climb back into the Tahoe.

"What's that guy's problem?" Sugar said.

"It pains me to imagine," said Thorn.

Sugar parked in front of the first floor rooms at the far end of the complex.

When Thorn got out, he saw the bald clerk standing beneath the front portico smoking a cigarette and openly observing them. Thorn waved jauntily at the man, but the old Marine didn't wave back.

A sleek black man, a scruffy white guy and a young Hispanic female in dirty clothes were sharing adjoining rooms at the fellow's motor lodge. Surely the clerk had seen more shady characters renting rooms there before. But apparently this combination of races and genders had lit the guy's bigotry fuse.

When they were inside the room, Thorn unlocked one side of the adjoining door, then went into the adjacent room and unbolted that side of the door.

"You see how this works, Dulce? You can lock your side or leave it open. It's up to you. Okay?"

"I like with no lock," she said. "I am sleeping better this way."

"Tomorrow we'll figure out our next step."

"Thank you, Mr. Thorn. Your friend too."

"His name is Sugarman," he said. "Similar to yours."

She pronounced his name in English then said, *"El hombre de azucar."*

"Yes," said Thorn. "I'm surrounded by sweetness."

Thorn handed her the bag of toiletries.

She walked over to Thorn, opened her arms and embraced him briefly, her right ear pressed to his chest as though appraising the thump of his heart.

When she stepped away, she smiled at Sugarman, then went to her room and shut the adjoining door and left it unbolted.

"We going to have trouble with that guy? Front desk clerk?"

"What? Call the police? Why would he do that?"

"He just had that look," Sugar said. "Kind I'm all too familiar with."

"I don't know," Thorn said. "I doubt it."

"Maybe he thought we were, I don't know, taking advantage of Dulce."

"Or he could have seen her picture on the news."

"What do you know about this Sister Kathleen?"

"Dulce mentioned her," Thorn said. "She was on a mission in Honduras, ran a school or something and took an interest in Dulce. That was their destination, Dulce and her mother. Phoenix, a couple of hours up the road. But how do we find her? Are nuns on the Internet?"

"Everything is," Sugar said.

"Maybe Sister Kathleen can find a home for her. Get her papers sorted out."

At the front window, Sugar fingered open a slit in the blinds and peered out.

Thorn stripped out of his shirt and checked the bandage on his wounded arm. A splotch of blood was showing through. He'd need to clean it tomorrow and apply a new bandage, but there was only a minor ache.

"You know, one thing that keeps bugging me," Sugar said.

"There's only one thing?"

"Those weapons are stolen in 1971. They disappear for decades. Why now? What set this off? What motivated these people?"

"Probably be one of those things we'll never know."

"Turning out to be a lot of those."

"Half the time," Thorn said, "I don't know what the hell my own motivations are."

"With you I'm surprised it's only half."

"There's one thing we can be sure of."

Sugarman turned from the window and settled his chestnut eyes on Thorn.

"Whoever these assholes are and whatever is inspiring them to kill, it makes perfect sense to them. They think they're the good guys. Their mission is just."

"But they're wrong," Sugarman said. "Dead wrong."

NINETEEN

Vegas was only nineteen when she was knocked up. By then she'd screwed so many local boys she couldn't identify the father. Or if she knew who it was, she refused to confide it to anyone, least of all her mother.

But Savannah didn't give a damn about the father, because it turned out her grandbaby was a girl with the same bottomless blue eyes as her gallant brother Marty.

Vegas named her daughter Nora Lee. A name the girl shortened to Nola when she turned seven. Whip-smart and drama-free, a happy girl who liked to pedal her bike into the summer fields outside of town and host pajama parties where her friends laughed and sang on the upstairs porch well past everyone's bedtime.

On gloomy winter afternoons, home from school, Nola devoted her free hours to drawing fanciful pictures in pen and ink. At fifteen she began to spend time in the big, open attic of the house on Taggart Road where she sectioned off a small room with walls of plywood that Judson helped her fit in place. It became her artist's studio, a room of her own. One with a view of the backyard, the barn, the shed, and the farm land beyond. A place to read, and muse and draw in privacy.

Nola's isolated hours in the attic gave Savannah a prickle of worry. For stored up there was a footlocker filled with family photo albums, and her daddy's wartime memorabilia, medals, brass, and ribbons, and there were bundles of letters Marty had written home during his time in the service, dark treasures that Savannah had long ago pushed into a corner and never returned to, but could not bring herself to abandon.

Nola became the bright, energetic unifier in the family. Even Judson, who'd shown no interest in parenting his own offspring, grew so fond of Nola that when she was only seven or eight, he started taking her along on weekends to his job sites. Business was thriving and he talked about grooming Nola as an apprentice.

Inheriting Judson's fluency in mechanics, Nola embraced the work with the same good-natured zeal as all her pursuits. By the time she was a senior in high school, she'd decided to skip college and was preparing to take her journeyman electrician's exam.

In early July that summer after high school graduation, one evening at dinner, Nola announced that she had changed her plans. She'd passed the journeyman exam but decided she wanted to see more of the world beyond the borders of Bad Axe.

"Damn right," Vegas said. "Go down to Detroit, have some fun. You earned it."

Nola drew a photograph from her pocket and handed it to her mother.

The black and white snapshot of Marty Snyder in full dress uniform passed from hand to hand around the silent table. Marty's eyes were still clear and he stood ramrod straight, a sly, almost cocky smile on his lips.

"He was a war hero," Nola said. "A Vietnam vet."

"You broke into that footlocker," Savannah said.

"Why?" she said. "Why'd you shut him away like that?"

"That guy was a drug addict," Judson said. "Hung himself. Some war hero."

"I'm going to follow in his footsteps," Nola said. "Carry on the family tradition. Like Uncle Marty and my great-granddaddy."

"You can't do it, Nola," Savannah said. "I forbid it."

"Too late," said Nola. "I enlisted already. End of the month I'm shipping out to Fort Carson, south of Colorado Springs. I'm going to learn to shoot the big guns, howitzers."

"Girls aren't allowed around those things," Judson said.

"Times have changed, Granddad."

"Hell, Nola. I was counting on you to join the business."

"I won't allow it," Savannah said.

"You don't have a say," said Vegas. "If that's what my girl wants, she gets it."

"Don't worry, Granny, I'll be safe, I promise. It's something I have to do. Fight for our country, our freedom. It's a good thing. I'll make you proud."

"It's not a good thing," Savannah said. "It'll contaminate your soul. It'll poison you."

"They won't let girls anywhere near those guns," Judson said.

But he was wrong. Women had been holding field artillery cannoneer positions for years. And by the following winter, Nola became a member of the Second Battalion, 12th *field artillery regiment of the First Stryker Brigade Combat Team. She was assigned to the M777, a quick-strike howitzer.*

Shipped off to the mountainous Uruzgan Province in Afghanistan, Nola wrote chatty letters home that Vegas read aloud at the kitchen table.

In her first few months in Afghanistan, Nola wrote that she'd distinguished herself to her commanding officer and was integrating well with the all-male gun crew.

"It's just like her," Judson said. "Keeping everybody in line."

"Shut up," Savannah said. "Keep reading, Vegas."

Half the time Nola's letters sounded like a field manual in the weapon she operated.

Because the M777 howitzer was lightweight, it was a rapidly-deployable artillery system combining strategic mobility with minimal radar and thermal signatures. It was towed quickly into place, usually at night, and had a rate of fire of five-rounds-per-minute. Which meant the entire team had to move as quickly and precisely as a NASCAR pit crew changing tires and gassing up.

Each howitzer had a crew of ten, each with an exacting role. When the big gun was in operation, those ten soldiers moved in a synchronized ballet with a perfectly timed artfulness.

As cannoneer number two, it fell to Nola to open the breech while two of the other crew members heaved a 95 pound shell into the gun, then Nola loaded charges and propellant and shut the breech tightly while the other members of the crew aligned the howitzer and drew down on the target.

Late in August of her first year on the ground, Nola was on a night time mission to an airfield at a forward operating base. The objective was terrain denial, lobbing heavy shells at a mountain pass twenty miles away to discourage Taliban forces from using that route, and redirect them to a path where NATO coalition forces had set up an ambush.

Four shells were fired, then five, the crew moving with quick efficiency as incoming small arms fire began to rake the hillside near their position. On the sixth shell, Nola slipped up. Probably distracted by the incoming fire, and trying to keep up with the breakneck pace, she made a rookie mistake. Nola failed to properly close the breech.

When the M777 fired its sixth round, the shell blew open the unsecured breech and Nola and two of her fellow soldiers were enveloped in an inferno of super-heated gases and molten steel fragments.

A week later, early September, what was left of Nola's body was returned stateside for burial. They drove to Dover Air Force base to meet her coffin, then drove the Dodge Ram back to Bad Axe with Nola's flag-draped casket in the bed of the truck. Eleven hours each way. Two days on the road, two in Dover.

That Dodge was brand new, meant to be a surprise gift to Nola on her first day of work when she partnered up with her granddad. Judson had tricked out the truck up with chrome bull bars covering the grill and a custom paint job that was an after-market add-on done in

Nola's favorite colors which had never varied since she was a toddler: powder blue and pink. Big beefy truck with girly colors and super dark tinted windows the way Nola liked them.

On that drive home, somewhere north of Pittsburgh, Judson was fueling up at a truck stop when the guy who'd pulled up to the pump just ahead of them, a fella with a big beard, long hair and driving a dinged up Chevy truck, made some smartass remark to Judson about the pussy-ass color of his truck. And when Judson finished topping up their tank, he got behind the wheel, buckled up, revved the Dodge Ram's V-8 and plowed into the back of that man's truck, spinning it halfway toward the next set of pumps.

It was late in the afternoon when they pulled in the drive after Nola's burial and Savannah saw the shed door swung open and the birdcage toppled to the gravel. She gently lay the folded flag on the seat, got out of the car, and walked to the open door.

Big Blue's head had been chopped off and tossed ten feet away.

And the shelves in the shed were empty. Not a single landmine left.

That's when she texted Ray Murphy to tell him what his goddamn son had done.

TWENTY

Thorn was sinking into the first warm downdrafts of sleep when Sugar shook his shoulder.

"Got to move. Border Patrol and five uniforms just entered the lobby."

Thorn scrambled out of bed, stepped into his shoes, slipped on his T-shirt.

"Get Dulce," he said.

"I'm here," she said. "I'm ready."

She was wearing one of her new outfits, black jeans, red ruffled blouse. She must have been sleeping in them.

Sugarman carried the shopping bag and his own luggage, ducked down at the doorway, then slipped out into the shadows and was inside the Tahoe in seconds. He gave an all-clear wave and Thorn took Dulce's hand and hustled to the driver's side back door, boosted her in and came in behind her.

Sugar started the Tahoe, lights off, backed slowly, did an efficient U-turn, then headed to the end of their wing of the motel.

"Buckle up, Dulce."

Twenty, thirty seconds later while Sugar searched for a side exit, the whoop of a siren sounded behind them, and Sugar swerved right, bumped across a drainage ditch, plowed through the field behind the motel.

"Those trees to the right," Thorn said. "Looks like a park, a playground."

Sugar blew past a stand of palms, flattened a chest-high bush and slewed onto a bike path that seemed to meander ahead of them through the park.

He flashed the headlights to get his bearings. Another siren whoop, the blue flash of a cop car, still back a few hundred yards.

"They bring a helicopter, we're screwed," Thorn said.

"I don't think we're big enough fish to warrant that."

"I'd rather not find out."

Sugarman clipped a swing set, bounced across a sand pile rimmed by railroad ties, and tore through the shadows of what looked like an apartment complex. He wove through the parking lots of the three-story buildings, saw a busy thoroughfare off to their south. Slipping into the stream of late night traffic, he went a block, made a right, then another right and one more, coming back down a dark side street to look out at the boulevard they'd just left.

Two cop cars blew by, followed by the Border Patrol SUV.

Sugar waited half a minute, turned right onto the boulevard, following the blue lights and sirens that sailed ahead into the night.

"Good driving," Thorn said.

"We're not done."

A few tense minutes later he took an entrance ramp onto I-10, signs for Red Rock and Phoenix.

"Interstate?" Thorn said. "You're sure?"

"More traffic, less chance of being spotted."

"All this because a desk clerk didn't like our little band of misfits?"

"Could be Perkins and Doyle had second thoughts, put a BOLO out on us. I don't know and I don't want to find out."

They drove for a half hour. Fighting to stay awake, Dulce rocked against Thorn's shoulder then jerked upright.

Thorn pulled some of her new clothes from the shopping bag, folded them into a makeshift pillow and lay it on his lap. He scooted over to the passenger side door and patted the pillow. After a moment of hesitation, she lay down, and in seconds was snuffling into sleep.

Sugar drove silently, eyes flicking to the rear view every few seconds. Thorn looked down at the girl's smooth skin that glowed like burnished copper and he found himself tracking back through the last few days, recalling snatches of conversations with Doyle and Perkins. Then saw again the gathering of migrants around the bonfire at Marjory Banfield's ranch. The Whitman brothers on their dune buggies terrifying the migrants into the shadows. The handsome doctor and his elegant wife who took Dulce in, Bobby Tennyson's last rambling speech recounting his time at Johnston Atoll.

It was like trying to fit together a puzzle with pieces from different boxes. Bobby had conned Thorn and Sugar into taking up his quest and made Sofia his willing accomplice. Bobby was not Bobby at all, but an ex-con with a son who'd become a domestic terrorist. Then there were the brazen killers who'd taken down Bobby and Hortensia and would have murdered Dulce if they'd been able. There were simply too many incompatible stories, too many mismatched people, too many jagged-edged puzzle pieces to arrange into a coherent whole.

Thorn rested his head against the window glass that buzzed with roadway noise. He wanted to talk to Sugarman, sort this out with his clear-headed friend, but he worried their voices would wake Dulce, so he said nothing and simply watched the dark miles fly by and finally closed his eyes and in time drifted into a dream of blue waters and a sunset streaked with veins of lavender and crimson, a squadron of pelicans heading home, skimming low across the Gulf, while miles away at sea distant pulses of lightning were muffled within a mass of darkening clouds, golden bursts, one then another, as if warring armies were out in the gloom exchanging cannon fire.

From the very start Marco was trouble.

When the boy was six, Savannah, in a moment of anger disclosed that Judson wasn't his father. His real dad was a man named Ray Murphy serving time in Leavenworth for thievery. Maybe that was too much for a six year old to digest, or maybe Marco's DNA was what made him the aggressive little shit he turned out to be. Savannah refused to take credit or blame for the boy's future. It was challenge enough raising Vegas without trying to nurture such a hardcore brat.

As a child she used to find Marco in the bathroom studying his face in the mirror. Through some tragic alchemy he'd inherited half of Savannah's features and half of Ray Murphy's, a Frankenstein's brew of the tough guy and the girlish. He had Ray's prominent cheekbones, his piercing blue eyes, perfectly straight nose, and Savannah's long dark lashes, tiny pink mouth, her rosy cheeks and receding chin. It was a freakish blend that instantly made him the target of schoolboy tormentors which so enraged Marco that he declared war on his male counterparts and devoted himself to building his body with obsessive farm chores and every other physical challenge he could invent, and by the fall of second grade, he easily outmatched his worst antagonists and turned himself into the king bully of the schoolyard.

It helped that he was big for his age and a natural intimidator. He began picking fights in school, suspended every other week. He cursed out his teachers, defaced textbooks, set fires in the playground, smuggled into class the squirrels and house cats he'd murdered, flaunting their carcasses until the girls screamed. Everyone was Marco's enemy.

By the time Marco was ten, Savannah had given up on the boy. She stopped punishing him for bad behavior. He seemed to enjoy his paddlings too much. So at fifteen when Marco struck up a bond with Ingrid Whitman, the skinny red-haired daughter of a neighbor family, a girl as reckless and cruel as Marco, Savannah didn't protest. Besides Ingrid there were two boys in that household, Mickey and Jackson, both older than Marco, no sign of a father, and a mother notorious around Bad Axe for her ugly temper.

At sixteen Marco left home for good and took up residence in the Whitman's barn three miles down the road. That was the year the

Whitmans tried to start a Christmas tree farm. Planting saplings of spruce, scotch pine, Eastern white pine, Douglas and Fraser fir. Not even realizing it took years before those trees could be harvested, years of discipline and focus. Two skills the Whitman family sorely lacked.

The Whitman brothers were arrested for a variety of punk ass crimes, assault, burglary, strong-armed robbery, though the only jail time they served was for the arson of the Assemblies of God church in a nearby town. Two of its black congregants were hurt in the blaze, but because the brothers were teenagers, they spent only six months in juvie.

Maybe the church fire and their hitch in jail was where it began, or maybe the family were fervent racists all along, but by the time Marco was seventeen he'd joined with Mickey and Jackson Whitman in adopting the shaved scalps, the heavy black boots and dark clothing of skinheads. Swastikas and Confederate flags began appearing on walls in the downtown shopping district, a cross was burned in the front yard of a Jewish merchant. Everyone knew who was behind this law-breaking and one afternoon a deputy paid Savannah a visit to speak about Marco's behavior.

"He hasn't been a member of this family for years. The one you need to talk to is Flora Whitman."

Shortly after that visit from the law, the Whitmans and Marco disappeared. Their ancient Suburban gone, all the shutters closed, no lights in the house, everything sealed tight.

A few weeks after they vanished, Vegas broke into the Whitman's place and came home with a handful of souvenirs. Silver disks that were etched on both sides with two pyramids overlapping at the base, a bolt of lightning intersecting their juncture. She'd found them in a saucer in the basement workroom where apparently they'd been custom made.

"The hell is this?" Judson said at the table as they passed the coins around.

"They're pewter stamping blanks," said Vegas. "Soft as aluminum but with the weight of a coin."

"I know they're stamping blanks," Judson said. "What's with the goddamn pyramids?"

"Some idiot hate group," she said. "I looked it up on the Web. They call themselves Abyss."

"Who do they hate?" Savannah said.

"From what I can tell, just about everybody."

"They leave anything of value?"

Vegas said she'd poked around but found nothing worth stealing except a toaster oven and a couple of clocks.

"Wonder where those dickheads went?" Judson said.

"I heard they had an uncle die out West, left them some land."

"Where'd you hear that, Vegas?"

"Dougie Trautman, bartender at Pete's Tavern. Mickey and Jackson were there a couple of weeks back bragging about all the land they inherited, some place in Arizona, down near the Mexican border."

Though she would never admit it, Savannah felt an ache of betrayal in Marco's departure without so much as a word of farewell. Her son. A demonic shithook, yes, but still her flesh and blood, her first born.

The next afternoon with a chilly autumn wind in her face, she walked the three miles to the Whitman's farmhouse and stood for a while outside the gate, then swallowed back her nerves and went down the walkway, climbed the steps and pushed open the door that Vegas had left ajar.

She was shocked to discover the house was immaculate. A military precision to the folded dish towels, the plates stacked in the cupboard, the array of cleaning products neatly arranged beneath the sink. A creepy orderliness. For the Whitmans' outward appearance was unruly and anarchic, their dress sloppy, their two-toned Suburban was dented and uncared for.

Savannah drifted through the house, finding the same fastidiousness throughout. From the mantelpiece knickknacks to the paperbacks organized on a shelf in alphabetical order. She searched out Marco's room, and found what was clearly his domain at the end of the narrow hallway. A mattress on a low frame, its sheets tucked with hospital corners, pillowcases showing barely a wrinkle.

In his closet his heavy winter parka was surrounded by flannel shirts and Carhartt overalls. The drawers in his chest were mostly empty, but the black sweater with red diamonds Savannah had knitted for him as a Christmas gift was still there, between a stack of long underwear and the insulated gloves he'd had for years.

Where Marco was headed, he was done with Michigan winters.

She lay down on the bed and inhaled the young man's scent. Recognizing it with such force the air clutched in her throat. His boyish aroma of freshly cut clover mixed with the bite of adult male musk.

Savannah was rising from the bed when she heard a crackling beneath her. Stooping alongside the bed, she probed between mattress and box springs, expecting to find a young man's stash of nudie mags.

The first one she drew out was ancient, its garish cover faded, the pages brittle. The rest were fresher, their photographs as lurid and explicit as the porn Marco brought home from Detroit. Except that these naked bodies were lacerated and bloody, the bare flesh despoiled by gunfire or instruments of torture. Faces slashed, private parts ravaged, jawbones gaping, men, women, children, old and young, all of them dark-skinned, some African, some Asian, some of mixed race, but all brown. The captions were succinct and laced with bitter irony.

"Winked at my little sister. Eyelids removed."

"Blew a kiss at Mama, no lips no more."

"Ordered a beer in a local joint. Last order he ever gave."

Savannah tipped up the mattress and slung it off the springs, exposing a trove of similar rags. Mixed among the death porn were half a dozen pamphlets with construction paper covers and Xeroxed pages.

It only took a minute to scan their contents, one rant echoing the next. The invasion of the mongrel races was a threat to the civilized world. The flood of beasts must be stopped. All god-fearing warriors were called to battle for the white man's primacy.

She returned the magazines, settled the mattress back in place, tucked the sheet again into its rigid formation.

As she hiked home through the frigid dusk, she tried to talk herself beyond the shame weighing on her. The Whitman family had turned her child into a monster, stolen whatever innocence and virtue he might have had. It was unthinkable that it was in any way Savannah's fault that Marco was nursing fantasies of mutilation and dismemberment.

Absolutely not. No way in hell.

PART THREE

TWENTY-ONE

It was a three-hour drive north on I-10 through Tucson and on to downtown Phoenix where Sister Kathleen's church, St. Mary's Basilica was located. When they arrived, with still two hours before sun-up, they decided to indulge in breakfast. Sugar found a twenty-four hour McDonald's a dozen blocks west of the church and Dulce yipped with delight.

While she went inside to wash up and choose their meals, Sugarman spent a few minutes scrolling through Bobby Tennyson's phone. Thorn waited as long as he could manage then asked if he'd found anything interesting.

Sugar mumbled in the affirmative and kept at it for a while longer.

Finally he said, "Okay, here's what I see. Lots of calls between Bobby and two numbers in the same area code."

"What area code?"

"989, which covers a few dozen counties in Michigan. Including Huron, where Bad Axe is."

"So he was calling Savannah?"

"No, it looks like she started it with that text. The one Bobby showed us. 'M23's stolen. Bad things are coming.'"

"And then?"

"After that Bobby called her in early September. Then after the first conversation, Bobby called a different 989 number. He called that one a half dozen times. Long calls, some of them as much as an hour. Then he called back to the first number in 989."

"So Savannah texts Bobby then Bobby calls the other number which is probably Marco. That's what Sofia claimed, that Bobby talked to Marco several times. Which means Marco's still using a number from when he lived in Michigan. Is that weird?"

"Not weird, but not very smart for a terrorist."

"Maybe he has burners for his criminal work. Just keeps the old number active as a cover."

"Still not smart."

Dulce came back to the car with a bag of McMuffins and two large coffees.

"I like McDonald's," she said. "It's so fast."

"City life is like that," Thorn said. "Everything's fast."

"Do you live in a city?"

"No, we live on an island. The opposite of fast."

"Are there mountains?"

"No mountains, but a lot of water. The ocean all around."

After a moment Dulce asked if there were gangs.

"Not that I know of," Thorn said.

"You are lucky," she said.

"I know," said Thorn. "Very lucky."

"Why are you helping me?"

Thorn fumbled for a moment, then said, "Because we care about you, Dulce."

"You do not know me, a few days only."

"We know enough," Thorn said.

Dulce was silent for a moment, then: "I told my story. I want yours. Both. You can maybe say why you leave your island and come to Arizona. And the years before that. Your story, the work you do, the important things."

"That's fair," Sugar said. "You want to start, Thorn?'

"Go ahead."

"Okay, so I have two beautiful daughters, twins, Janey and Jackie. I was a policeman for years, then I started my own business, helping others with their problems. Like a private policeman."

"You have daughters, so you have a wife?"

Sugarman sighed. Yes, he'd once had a wife. A problematic one. No way to sum up Jeannie in a sentence or two. Thorn would have called her a flake, an immature, terminally self-indulgent loon. She and Sugar had married right out of high school, never a good idea, and little by little Sugar realized what a terrible mistake they'd both made, but he'd held on for years out of a sense of duty, and an unshakable love for his twins.

"My wife and I don't live together anymore," Sugarman said. "We had problems."

"*Divorcio*," Dulce said.

"Exactly," Sugar said. "*Divorcio*."

"Thorn? What is your story? You have a wife?"

"No wife."

"I liked Sofia. Maybe marry her?"

"I liked her too. But no, that's over."

"I'm sorry."

"*Yo también*."

"You have work you do? A policeman too?"

"I don't have a job. I make fishing lures and sell them. *Señuelos de pesca.*"

"So you catch fish, eat them for your dinner."

"On good days, yes."

Dulce seemed satisfied with that abbreviated history and was eager to get started on her McMuffin.

An hour later they were standing beneath the massive pillars and soaring domes and stained glass of St. Mary's cathedral, waiting with an elderly nun who'd greeted them as they entered and had sent word to Sister Kathleen that she had visitors.

Thorn wasn't sure if the architecture was Mission or Colonial or what, but its effect was potent as they stood in reverential silence taking in the grandeur and grace of the sanctuary, inspiring in Thorn, if not exactly a worshipful mood, at least a moderate surge of awe.

Sister Kathleen was young and pretty with green eyes and an easy smile.

She was thrilled to see Dulce, scooping her up and holding her in a long embrace as Thorn gave the sister a sanitized summary of Dulce's last few days.

"Oh, I saw that on the news," Sister Kathleen said. "That was you in the truck that exploded? You escaped! God must have been protecting you."

"But he forgot about my mother," Dulce said.

Sister Kathleen released Dulce and said something to the girl about God's mysterious ways. Just the kind of pap that kept Thorn from being a believer. Though he often considered how much easier things might be in dealing with the losses, the deaths of friends and loved ones, the incessant suffering in the world, the hate, the evil, the injustice—to have such an all-purpose rationale that softened every blow, helped to file away the pain into the handy bin of 'mysterious ways.'

When the sister turned her attention back to Thorn, he explained that there were some dangerous people searching for Dulce, so it was best to keep her presence private. Even from the authorities. Could she manage that?

"Yes, of course. We shelter the undocumented all the time. She can stay in our women's refuge until I find the right family for her, a happy home with godly people to care for her."

Sugar jotted down his cell number.

"If you need anything, or just want to talk, call any time, day or night."

Thorn gave Dulce a questioning look. Was this what she wanted? Was she sure? Dulce nodded and showed him a smile tinged with gratitude and relief.

There were parting hugs and misty eyes, then he and Sugar were back in the Tahoe driving away from Dulce and Sister Kathleen and St. Mary's Basilica.

While Sugar concentrated on his phone, Thorn headed back to Tucson. Their plan was to return to the airfield where Bobby landed the Cessna. Since Thorn had no official ID, he couldn't fly commercial, so they either found someone to pilot the Cessna back to South Florida, or hitched a ride on another private plane. Both of which seemed unlikely. Next choice, Sugarman had an old pilot friend back in Minneapolis who might help. But since Sugar wasn't sure if his friend was still alive or still owned a plane, Thorn was starting to adjust to the idea of taking a Greyhound back to the Keys.

For a few miles, as Thorn guided them through the thickening morning rush, Sugar tapped on his phone and kept tapping.

"You going to tell me what you're doing?"

"Searching the dark web," Sugar said. "Looking for posts about Abyss, maybe a website."

"And the dark web is what?"

“It’s a sewer. A place where everyone’s anonymous and everything’s for sale. Heroin, crack, guns, body parts, child porn, snuff movies, murder-for-hire.”

“Jesus. A place like that, you know your way around?”

“Since I left the sheriff’s department, I’ve had to learn to speak a lot of different languages.”

“You can do that on your phone, surf the dark web?”

“With the right browser.”

“I don’t know what that is either, so I’ll just shut up.”

“Good idea.”

Thorn was quiet for a few more miles, then Sugar said, “Find somewhere to pull over. You need to see this.”

Thorn spotted a strip mall and slipped into a shady space.

“They didn’t try very hard to conceal it,” Sugar said. “Making it easy for their followers to find.”

“Find what?”

Without a word, Sugar tapped the screen and handed him the phone.

The video jiggled and jostled and the sound quality was poor, but the images were graphic and gut-wrenching. The bodies of the eleven migrants were flung about in a grisly tableau. Blood still oozing from wounds, thick white lather foamed out of mouths, splintered bones erupting through flesh. A thirty second pan around the gory interior of the truck and then back again, and finally moving in for a close-up of the Abyss medallion lying atop a layer of straw.

The only sound was the labored breathing of the photographer.

When the video ended in a solid black screen, a woman’s voice spoke with cold precision: “If you want in on this, you know how to connect.”

Thorn handed the phone back to Sugarman and they sat for a while watching the shop clerks arrive for work at the strip mall. A coffee shop, nail salon, insurance agency, sporting goods store.

Thorn was trying to imagine being one of them, a worker, a solid citizen playing by the rules, raising a family, home at night with the kids watching favorite sitcoms, putting money by for retirement or to send the kids to college, following the stations of the cross for ordinary folks. Averting their eyes from the bloody movie scenes. Living a measured, sensible life, insulated from the grisly and the gruesome.

"What're you thinking, Thorn?"

"I wish we'd never come."

"But we did come. We're here and in the middle of this."

"This isn't a recruitment video," Thorn said.

Sugarman rubbed his hands across his eyes as if to scour away the images.

"It's an ad," Thorn said, "a fucked-up commercial for nerve gas landmines. They're peddling these goddamn things."

"It appears they are," Sugar said with an undertone of sadness. Seen way too much of this, the shit people were capable of.

"I say we hand this off to Sheffield. This is his world."

"Sounds about right," Sugar said. "Can you do that, step away?"

"I'll call him."

"I'm going to get a coffee. Want anything?"

Thorn shook his head.

As Sugarman crossed the lot, Thorn took Bobby Tennyson's phone from the cup holder and instead of calling Frank Sheffield, on impulse he tapped in one of the numbers in Bad Axe, Michigan. A woman answered on the second ring.

"I told you, Ray, goddamn it, stop calling me."

Her voice had the rusty throatiness of one who had not spoken in days.

"Is this Savannah?"

"Who the fuck is this?"

"Ray's dead," Thorn said.

"I don't believe you."

"My name is Thorn. I was a friend of Ray's. Though I knew him only as Bobby Tennyson.

She was silent for several moments.

She cleared her throat and replied in a brusque manner that did not quite mask the quaver in her voice.

"Yeah, yeah, I know who you are," she said. "Bobby told me about you, how he was trying to get you to help him. You're the tough guy, the hero with the cape."

"Is that what he told you?"

"You're not a hero?"

"Not at the moment."

"Ray never was much of a judge of character."

"Ray was shot by a big muscular guy and a tall skinny woman."

"Marco and Ingrid Whitman," she said. "Those shit heads."

"Your son, Marco?"

"Yeah, isn't that perfect? Killed his own father. I warned him and warned him but Ray didn't believe what a monster the boy became. He thought he could reason with him. Thought he could trick him into believing Ray had converted to Marco's fucked up religion, pretend he'd become a true believer, just to get close to the boy, save his soul from that Abyss bullshit."

"It may have been an accident," Thorn said. "A stray shot. Marco and the woman were spraying lots of rounds, I got winged, Ray was gut-shot. I don't think Marco or Ingrid even knew who they were shooting at."

Savannah breathed into the receiver, slow, steady and deep.

"What do you want? Why're you calling me? Just to tell me a man I haven't seen for decades is dead. You looking for a reaction, want to hear me cry, what?"

"I'm not sure why I called. Maybe I just wanted to make sure you were real, hear your voice."

"Well, now you heard it."

She cut the connection.

☣☣☣

After Savannah ended the call with Thorn, she stared at the phone, then drew back her hand and flung it across the kitchen. It bounced off the refrigerator door and tumbled onto the rug. Not broken, not even its glass face. She set it on the counter and went to find Judson to tell him what she'd learned of Ray and Marco and talk it through.

She hollered for him and got no reply. She went upstairs, and found no sign of him there. Vegas was off somewhere in her car, so maybe he'd gone off with her on her errands. She went outside, called his name some more.

At the open doorway of the shed she stood for several moments blinking, and struggling to comprehend what she was seeing, then struggling just to breathe, staring at his body, at the noose taut at his neck, at the clothes he'd chosen for his big finale. Faded jeans, a clean white T-shirt, old running shoes, his favorite wardrobe.

He could have managed it other ways and lots of other places. He had guns which would've been easier, quicker, more dependable.

Maybe even less painful. Walk out in a back field and be done. But she realized that Judson had wanted this act to have meaning. To send a message. So he'd chosen the shed where the landmines were stored and where they languished all those years.

Even the rope he used was significant. It was one of the dock lines that for years was coiled and stored in the cabin of the *Flying Dragon*. The shed and the vessel were both linked to the aborted fantasies of their youth. And of course the *Flying Dragon* was where Marty botched his own hanging, forcing Savannah to finish it.

Savannah cut his body down. No need to finish Judson's job. He even left her a step ladder and a box-cutter nearby. Typical of his attention to detail, a workmanlike exercise in death. A skilled electrician and carpenter whose last task was perfectly carried out, from the neatly tied hangman's knot he'd fashioned, to the half hitch he'd fixed to the rafter. All measured and exact. He'd even factored in the stretch in the rope and the height of the oak barrel he'd climbed atop. His shoes missed the wood floor by inches.

It was no surprise he was grieving Nola's death. The whole family was. Vegas was mute and inconsolable, and Savannah was paralyzed, could barely perform her daily functions. Hardly eating, sitting long hours in the recliner staring at the blank screen of the TV. But Judson hid his pain. That was his way.

He'd always been the impassive one. Grew up as an Army brat, the only child of a master sergeant who for years made Judson endure silently the beatings he administered with a length of garden hose, thrashings done with such expertise they left no marks other than the invisible scars Judson lived with ever after.

The grown-up Judson was stoic and even-tempered, but his placid exterior was a lie. So thoroughly had he mastered his emotions that Savannah often forgot how the horrors of his childhood still churned below the surface.

Still, Judson was a decent father to Vegas, offering sound advice and support, never raising a hand to her despite her face-spitting contempt, her screaming tantrums, her years of slutty outrages and the string of derelicts and scum she brought home to her bed. Boys and men she had no interest in except to infuriate Savannah and Judson.

Unruffled in the face of every hardship the family endured, poverty, sickness, loss and disappointment, the bitterly cruel winters, Judson was the family's rock. Even Marco's years of brutish misconduct never roused Judson's ire. It sometimes seemed Judson was floating a thousand feet above his own existence.

But Nola changed him. From the moment he saw her in the hospital bassinet Judson was defenseless. Her happy smile, her raucous giggles stripped away his armor. Stirred sensations he never permitted himself before. Not even Savannah penetrated as deep inside Judson's heart as that child.

This was to be Savannah's revelation.

No one truly knew anyone else.

No one could see beyond another's skin. Everyone was a mystery.

Savannah's entire adult life was intertwined with Judson, but she hadn't recognized the depth of his desperation. In his last act he made it clear. She'd failed him, failed to console him, failed to tug him back from the precipice. So lost in the closed loops of her own sordid history and her forsaken dreams, she'd never truly known this man.

Savannah stood for a while looking at Judson's body. Then she sagged to her knees and wept.

TWENTY-TWO

In the long, slow days following Judson's suicide she was hollowed out. Her despair deepened and darkened. Normal enough, she supposed, predictable. What she didn't expect was the fear.

He'd always been there to protect her. Not an overpowering presence, not a badass brawler, but he was a big man, thick and sturdy, and until he was gone, she didn't realize how much she depended on him to feel safe.

Without him nearby, she found herself flinching at every creak of the floor, every twitch of wind, rattle of window shade, every car passing on the road, night or day. Sleep was impossible, she spent the dark hours listening to sounds she'd never noticed. Not sure why. But there it was. Fear festering in her bones.

She took a pistol from Judson's gun locker, kept it near, safety off. When that proved insufficient, she took down a shotgun, loaded it, leaned it against the wall beside her bed. That helped some, but didn't quell the tremble, the shallow breaths, the sickening dread.

Days after Judson's body was cremated, Vegas appeared beside Savannah's recliner.

"There's action down the road," Vegas said.

"Be specific, girl."

"The Whitmans are back."

"All of them?"

"Just Marco and Ingrid, I think."

"Oh, Jesus. Oh, Jesus God."

☣☣☣

Thorn and Sugarman flew home, a process complicated by Thorn's lack of ID. First, Sugar chatted up the owner of Total Air Service, the only charter company operating out of Glendale Municipal Airport in Phoenix where Bobby had landed the Cessna. Even smooth-talking Sugarman couldn't convince the hard-jaw owner to fly some stranger without even a driver's license back to Florida. But okay, the guy finally took pity on them and directed Sugar to an old gentleman across the field who operated out of a hanger with the paint peeling off. His name was Walter but everyone called him Duke. He'd do it for cash, no questions asked.

Turned out Duke no longer flew planes, something about a heart condition, but his daughter Romy had taken over the piloting side of the business. Romy said she'd always wanted to see South Beach and the Keys, so sure, she'd do it, then she'd find some way to deadhead back to Phoenix when the time came.

Romy was an inch or two taller than Thorn, her short blond hair styled with the same scruffy indifference he employed. She was lean and had flared cheekbones and large green eyes and a Roman nose that had probably bothered the hell out of her when she was growing up. No make-up, a small scar that intersected her left eyebrow. Taken separately the ingredients clashed, but somehow they blended into an alluring though somewhat daunting face.

She caught Thorn checking her out and returned the favor, stepping back to tick across his scuffed-up features, roving up and down his frame with brash amusement. A stand-off that caused Sugarman to sigh and say to no one in particular, "Oh, boy, here we go."

They'd been home four days, Sugarman getting back just in time to celebrate the birthdays of his twins. Thorn was catching up on his sunset watching. His wound had nearly healed and no longer throbbed. He'd fallen back into the quiet rhythms of his ordinary life, watching the shimmer of Blackwater Sound, the jet skis and boats roaring past, the occasional dolphin rolling near his dock, when a sound came from somewhere in his stilt house, a sound that took him half a minute to recognize.

Romy came out of the bedroom in cut-offs and Fly United T-shirt holding Bobby Tennyson's cell phone. Thorn took it from her and nodded his thanks.

The number showing on the screen was from Michigan.

"I didn't know who to call."

Her voice was even huskier than a few days earlier. Tighter now, under severe strain, the ragged pitch of one whose throat is nearly swollen shut.

"What is it, Savannah?"

"You were willing to help Ray, travel all the way out west and watch his back, I thought you might want to finish the job. Complete the thing Ray wanted, the thing he wanted you to help with."

"Get those landmines back, turn them over to the authorities and save his son. That what you mean?"

"There's no saving that boy. You can forget that part."

"What is it, Savannah?"

"Marco is here, him and the Whitman girl, Ingrid."

Thorn was silent, staring out at the silver ripples from a passing boat, the choppy wake slapping against the pilings of his dock.

"What do you mean 'here'?"

"Can't be any cops," she said. "No FBI, no feds, none of those people. If you don't agree to that, I hang up, that's the end of it. I'll manage on my own."

"Why no cops?"

"I don't mind spending the rest of my life in jail cause how's that any worse than how I'm living now? But I'll not put that on my daughter Vegas. And that's what would happen. She'd be an accessory, she'd get sent away sure as hell. So if you can't promise me that, we're done."

"I'll think about it."

Savannah was quiet. He could hear the creaking of wood as if she might be pacing heavily across some ancient floorboards.

"I'll call back in the morning then. Your last chance. You decide if Ray's mission is worth finishing. But no goddamn feds. Until I hear you say those words, I'm not telling you anything more."

He set the phone down on the teak dining table—another creation of the man who'd raised him. Like all the other furniture he'd made, that table was basic and unadorned yet quietly elegant. Thorn had studied it for years and never figured out how the old man had achieved such an outcome.

"Old girlfriend?" Romy asked. "Not that it matters."

"No, a woman I've never met. She wants my help with something."

"Is that what you do, help people?"

"Wasn't ever my intention, but yeah, it's turning out that way."

"So what, you and Sugar are a tag team, Sherlock and Watson, Starsky and Hutch?"

"Sugar is the detective. He's good at it."

"And you're the muscle? The wrecking ball?"

Thorn chuckled.

"You're a quick study."

"Got to be. A woman these days, if you can't size up a guy in five seconds and get it right a hundred percent of the time, you better be a Kung Fu master or heavily armed."

"It's that bad, is it? Men?"

"Like you say, I'm a quick study. You're proof of that. At least so far."

He smiled his thanks.

"Want to take a boat ride, get a grouper sandwich and a draft at a waterfront restaurant?"

"I was thinking more like a top shelf Margarita."

Romy was stepping into her flip-flops when Sugar appeared at the screen door and tapped.

"All clear," Thorn said.

Sugar greeted Romy, then tipped his head back and grimaced at the ceiling.

"Should I go outside?" she said. "This looks serious."

Thorn told her it was okay, her perspective might be useful.

"Give me the good news first," Thorn said.

Sugarman looked at him and shook his head.

"There's bad news and worse news. Which do you want to start with?"

"You choose."

"Frank Sheffield called."

Thorn explained to Romy, special agent in charge, Miami field office, a friend.

She lifted her eyebrows, impressed.

After Sugar passed the video of the truck bombing on to Sheffield, Frank sent it along to his colleagues in the Phoenix field office and they brought in the two DOD agents, Perkins and Doyle. In short order somebody on the fed's cyber team traced the provenance of the video. A day after the truck bombing, it had been uploaded to a site on the dark web using the Wi-Fi at the Hacienda del Sol Guest Ranch.

"Fancy ass resort in Tucson," Romy said.

The feds thought there might be a local connection so they got Sheriff Castillo to view the hotel's security footage from the twenty-four hour period around the time of the upload. Castillo matched a man and woman at the hotel with the couple who'd broken into the home of Dr. Diego Martinez and his wife and murdered them while searching for Dulce Mérida. Husky guy, tall skinny woman. They'd stayed one night at the hotel, paid with a stolen credit card. The Lincoln SUV they were driving was also stolen.

With the video images of the couple, it was only an hour later after running them through the national DMV facial recognition system that names on their driver's licenses were kicked out. Ingrid Whitman and Marco Murphy, AKA Marco Snyder and Marco Whitman.

"Using all the family names. Bright guy," Thorn said.

"Frank agreed the video looked like an advertisement. They're out for a score, and they don't care who the buyer is. After they posted the video it set off an avalanche of traffic on a few encrypted platforms the feds monitor for extremist activity. There's a severe limit to what FBI can see inside those messages. Location of sender and receiver are masked, sometimes they can grab snatches of the back and forth and decode some of it. Not enough to tell when and where these sales are going to take place.

"But good Christ, if those things get distributed, FBI estimate of the max casualties for two dozen M23 landmines is in the multiple thousands. Terrorists could set off a couple of those off in a rock concert or shopping mall or office building, the VX nerve agent sprays out in an aerosol form, it could take down hundreds in a matter of minutes. A lot of ugly dying, not to mention what could happen in the panic, stampedes and all that. And Frank said the worst case is the Whitmans sell them to multiple buyers, then it's ten times harder to know where they all end up. Or even where to start tracking. So they had to act fast, seal it down.

"The feds assembled their Phoenix SWAT unit. They added a bomb squad, and flew in several doctors with nerve gas specialty. They surround the Whitman ranch, go in at three in the morning, overwhelming force."

Sugarman halted for a moment, bracing himself.

"Is this the bad story or the worse one?" Thorn said.

"I'm afraid this is just the warm up," Sugarman said.

"Great."

"The Whitman place was booby-trapped up the yingyang. They had infrared cameras, tripwires, grenades, and automatic weapons of various kinds."

"No more play-by-play," Romy said. "Just give us the body count."

"I'm with her," said Thorn.

Sugarman drew a long breath as if he were going underwater for a while.

"Not including those in the mass graves, you have three dead feds, two dead Whitmans, Mickey and Jackson. No sign of Marco or Ingrid. And you also had five deceased migrants who were caged up on the property. The Whitmans were apparently using them for target practice or some other kind of amusement. Castillo said a few of the surviving migrants were among the folks you met at Marjory Banfield's house. He said the Whitmans came on ATV's that night, scared them off, then captured a few and kept them hostage on their ranch. Three of those survived the assault, including one newborn. Don't ask me how with all the bullets flying. Sounds like an unholy mess."

"And the mass graves?"

"They haven't finished excavating those. Looks like dozens, maybe more. The Whitmans had been living on that property going on twenty years. Seems they were catching and killing migrants all that time. A hundred acres, nearest neighbor was the Banfield woman, and house to house, that's five miles. Very isolated. If there was gunfire or people crying out for help, no one would ever hear."

Romy sat down heavily in one of the sculptured wood chairs.

"This is what you guys do? You deal with these kinds of people?"

"Not usually," Thorn said.

"I can't believe there's a worse story than that one," she said.

"Let's hear it," Thorn said.

"It's Dulce," said Sugar.

Thorn stifled a curse. He waited till the tremor in his chest subsided then gave Romy a quick recap of Dulce's role in recent events.

"It wasn't Sister Kathleen's fault," Sugar said.

"Just tell it."

"Some guy, he might be a priest, I don't know, I didn't get that part straight. Castillo called me, thought we should know. So this priest, or maybe he was in the congregation of the church, anyway he heard about Dulce, found out Sister Kathleen had taken her in, and that she was the sole survivor of the truck explosion. Well, he thought it would be a great fund-raising idea to promote..."

"It made the TV news," Thorn said.

Sugarman grimaced that it was true.

"And she was kidnapped right after."

Sugar nodded grimly and said, "Sister Kathleen has a broken jaw, two cracked ribs, lost some teeth. She tried to fight them off, Ingrid and Marco. But they got Dulce from her, drove off in black Cadillac Escalade similar to one reported stolen from Sky Harbor Airport in Phoenix. The Caddy was towing an oversized trailer. The Sister got a license plate. It's circulating, for all the good that will do. One more license number on the national BOLO, as if the state troopers don't have enough on their plates already."

"When was this?"

"I'm not sure. Sometime right after we left."

"And Castillo is just getting around to telling us."

"Apparently we're not high on his call list."

"So Dulce was taken four days ago. Long enough to drive cross country."

"What do you mean?"

"Bad Axe," Thorn said.

Romy said, "Bad Axe? Is that a place?"

TWENTY-THREE

Four days or maybe five, Dulce lost track during the journey. The trailer was dark, only a single air vent in the roof allowing so little light there was no difference between day and night. Again there was a plastic bucket for their waste, and again her companions mostly slept for the entire trip. Four times the door opened at the rear of the trailer and the muscular man threw in bags of fast food and gallon jugs of water. Fearing future scarcities, they hoarded the water, taking only measured sips, building up a stock of fifteen gallons that they stored in a corner of the trailer.

Five of them rode together on the hard metal floor, sharing the food and drink. No dangerous men rode with them this time. The only man was a grandfather with a white beard and purple bruises on his arms. He was barefoot and his clothes were tattered. He smiled most of the time and seemed to be dreaming while awake.

There was a mother and her son and daughter. The Flores family. The son was no more than five and he kept his eyes closed and his mouth wide open like one affected by a disorder of the mind. The daughter repeated stories aloud that had been read to her as a child, fairy tales. When she finished one she began another. The same five or six stories mile after mile.

Dulce spoke to the girl's mother, Alejandra Flores. A pretty woman with *mirada embrujada*. Dulce wasn't sure how to say it in English. Ghosts in her eyes, perhaps. Dark memories she would never be rid of.

"Do not worry," Dulce told the woman. "Everything will be all right."

"Why do you think this?"

"I know it will be. The good men will find us. They will set us free."

"I have not met any good men in this country."

"They are here. There are many of them. More than the bad ones. It is not so different than home. The gangs, yes, they are bad, and there are bad men and women here, but there are more who are good. The religious ones, the ones who care with their hearts."

"I do not believe this is the way in America. No one cares."

"The good men will come. I have met them. They are brave and smart and they will find us and they will set us free."

"Then you are a stupid girl. We will never get away from these two. I have seen what they do. My own husband, they filled him with bullets. They told him he was free to leave. As he ran he called out that he would send help, but they shot him as he climbed the fence. They were laughing and slapping each other on the back. It was sport to them."

Dulce said she was very sorry.

She waited until Alejandra had calmed and said, "The good ones will find where these two have taken us and they will come. They did it before and they will do it a second time. Have faith. They will come."

Aarushi Arrowsmith lived in a townhouse in Buttonwood Bay, a condo complex popular with Yankee snowbirds and Miami weekenders. The complex had been constructed a few decades earlier on the bay side of Key Largo and was laced with canals that had been dynamited into the limestone rock when such a practice was still legal.

Aarushi was born in Mumbai but her parents had immigrated to Miami twenty years earlier and were now the owners of a trendy Indian restaurant in Miami Beach. She was married to Billy Joe Arrowsmith, a fishing guide buddy of Thorn's. They had three girls, all with colorful first names.

Aarushi had a lucrative sideline in Mehndi, a form of body art. She applied a paste made from the powdered dry leaves of the henna plant which stained the skin. Aarushi's designs, which were usually drawn on hands and feet, were intricate and artful and within the Miami Indian community, her work was much in demand for weddings and other Hindu celebrations.

The tattoos were temporary, usually lasting no more than two or three weeks. She was also the go-to body artist for the multitude of aging hippies in Key Largo who were looking for something groovy for their third or fourth marriage, and she picked up a bit more income catering to the pranksters who wanted to teach a drunk spouse or boyfriend a lesson. She'd drawn more than one "I Am A Fucking Asshole" on the forehead of some jackass who was out cold.

Her name, Aarushi, meant 'first ray of the sun' which seemed to fit her perfectly because there was always a calm, deeply-rooted smile on her lips as there was that afternoon when she opened her door to Thorn's tapping.

He explained what he wanted, and handed her a piece of paper with the design he'd drawn.

Outside on the small patio in the bright sunlight, Aarushi used an eyedropper with a metal tip, and took less than half an hour to finish the two pyramids with overlapping bases and the lightning bolt intersecting them. After the drawing was done she spritzed his arm with lemon juice and dusted it with white sugar to darken the brownish red paste for a tint closer to the black of the tattoo on Sofia's neck.

"I won't ask what this means."

"That's probably best."

"Would you like another on the other forearm?"

"If one doesn't do the trick, two won't help."

Aarushi wrapped his forearm with tissue to lock in body heat, a way of creating a more intense color.

"You can take the wrap off in five or six hours. Overnight would be better. The design darkens through oxidation, 24 to 72 hours is usually enough."

He thanked her, offered her payment, but she closed her eyes and shook her head wearily.

"Billy Joe would kill me. He says at least half his business comes from the fishing grounds you've shown him. There are days his anglers wouldn't have a single catch if not for your spots."

"I'm glad they're still working."

She handed him back the paper with the drawing of the overlapping pyramids.

"Keep it," Thorn said. "Sugarman is coming over later and will want the same thing."

"Oh, Thorn I don't know what you two are up to, but try to stay safe. Please?"

"Always."

He met Sugar and Romy at mile marker 100, on a side street next to Waldorf Plaza. Operating inside the four small warehouse buildings lining the street were an auto glass repair shop, a plumbing supply outfit, a window shades wholesaler, and Stewy's Print Shop.

For the last twenty years Stewy Nance had been printing church programs, daily special menus, announcements for weddings, births and funerals. Stewy and Nancy, the owners, were longtime buddies of Sugarman, their kids playing soccer and singing together in the church choir.

When Thorn arrived at the T-Toons plant, Sugar and Romy were already toting stacks of printed paper out to Sugarman's Camry.

"How much did this set us back?" Thorn said.

"Stewy insisted it's all free. They're misprints, mainly, or extras. Some defect or another. But they'll suit our purpose."

"This is a silly idea, you know." Romy laughed as she loaded her stack of papers in the backseat. “But I marvel at the absurdity of it.”

“Absurdity is our specialty.”

“Thorn has been perfecting bizarre behavior for half a century.”

“If we’d had longer than fifteen minutes to come up with it,” Thorn said, “no telling how loony we might’ve been.”

“You realize, don’t you,” Romy said. “This won’t work with that Cessna. Doesn’t matter how low and slow I manage to take us, there’s no way we can pull this off. I can manually depressurize the cabin but to get the door open in the slipstream would be extremely difficult if not impossible. Good chance the hinges would fail, door would go flying off and hit the vertical stabilizer. Take us down.”

“Now you tell us,” Thorn said.

“I don’t think we can afford to take that kind of risk.”

“There’s a way,” Sugar said.

“What way is that?”

“Don’t worry, I’ll take care of it. Now let’s finish loading these things.”

“Always the optimist,” Thorn said.

Romy wanted to see Thorn’s new tattoo.

“Got to keep it covered overnight. I’ll show it off first thing tomorrow.”

“One more stop,” Sugar said. “Got to get moving before the bank closes.”

Though it was only last winter when Thorn had a brief and pleasurable fling with Darla Knopfler who was now the assistant manager of the Bank of America where Sugar kept his savings account, Darla wasn’t as obliging as Thorn had hoped. Apparently their romance hadn’t been as blissful for her.

She gave a petulant shake of the head and said, “Five minutes till closing, you want to cash out your entire college fund in ones and fives?”

Sugarman apologized, and Thorn said, “We have an emergency, Darla.”

Darla studied Romy for a few awkward seconds then said, “Are you doing this of your own free will?”

“Jesus,” Romy said. “You think I’m strong-arming these two?”

“It’s for a very good cause,” Sugar said. “If things go like we expect, I’ll put the money back in that account in a couple of days.”

“Another of your escapades, Thorn?”

“Is this some kind of Florida thing?” Romy said. “Banks give you shit when you withdraw your own damn funds?”

Darla shot Romy a stinging glare, then stalked away into the bank’s inner sanctum.

“You guys let a bank clerk push you around? How you going to stand up to the bad guys when the time comes?”

“She’s joking,” Thorn told Sugar. “It took me a while to catch on to her droll sense of humor.”

“Joking my ass,” she said.

“See,” said Thorn. “She’s doing it again.”

Romy snorted and fought back a smile.

In ten minutes Darla returned, holding a white cloth bag chunky with bricks of cash.

“Seventeen thousand five hundred and eighty-four dollars in ones and fives. You want to count it?”

Romy said, “I don’t think these two can go that high.”

“There she goes again,” Thorn said.

Outside the bank in the afternoon sun, Thorn said, "You think that's enough to get us in the door?"

"It better be," Sugar said. "Look, I need to go get my tattoo, then pack a couple of things. I'll drop you at your place and swing back in an hour. Bring a sweater or sweatshirt and long pants. It could be chilly up there this time of year. So we fly tonight?"

"We do," Romy said. "Off into the starry starry heavens."

"Sorry," Thorn said. "That margarita will have to wait."

"No worries," she said. "It'll just taste that much better."

Back at his stilt house, Thorn used Bobby Tennyson's cellphone to call Savannah again.

"You decide?"

"We're coming," he said. "Where's Marco located?"

"Down the road from me. It's a dead-end, only way in or out is past my house."

"Good. I'll need the closest private airport, your address, the address of where Marco is. And listen, before we get there, if you see anyone, a stranger in a truck or van going past your house, get their license number, a description of the vehicle."

"Why? What's going on down there?"

"Marco's selling those things. The landmines you stole."

"And I'm supposed to take down license plate numbers?"

"Don't try anything. These people will eat you alive."

She laughed grimly.

"I know all about that," she said. "I gave birth to the little shit. Whoever he turned out to be is my doing. I used to kid myself it wasn't. But it damn well was. Most of it."

"Just the license numbers. We should be there just after

daybreak tomorrow."

TWENTY-FOUR

They'd finished breakfast, canned tuna and crackers, and Ingrid was cleaning up, throwing shit in the old trash basket that was still under the sink. Marco was sitting at the kitchen table. The place stunk of mildew and mold and rat shit. He hadn't slept last night, just paced the house, thinking, picking at the plan, trying to see if he'd made any stupid errors. Around dawn he'd decided, no, none he could find anyway. It should work. They were going to be rich, free to do whatever they wanted for once in their lives.

Ingrid slept in her old room. He could hear her snore all the way across the house. Skinny woman could make some noise. So loud the rats and other vermin stayed in their holes.

"It's kind of sexy, don't you think," Ingrid said, "being here again. The house where we met, fell in love, made our lifelong pact."

Marco tilted his head to the side, peering at her. Was she joking or had she gone nuts?

"Sexy?"

"Romantic," she said. "All the happy memories from long ago when we were kids and full of dreams. Some of which are about to come true."

"Full of dreams? Really, that's how you remember it?"

"Man, you're such a downer. What's wrong with you? I'm just remembering how it was when you moved into the barn, how I'd come out and see you, spend all night rolling around, me trying not to scream. We were great, it was a great time."

"Except for Mickey and Jackson. Your wonderful brothers."

"Okay, yeah, they were rough on you, I know. But it made you tough, it made you the guy you are today."

"Probably gave me brain damage, all those beatings. And your mother slapping you around. Is that some of the happy shit you remember?"

"I survived. We both did. Look at us now."

"I don't have happy memories," he said.

"None? None at all? Not even us, how we were?"

He tried to find something to say that was true but that didn't crush her. But the words wouldn't come.

Ingrid gave him a pouty look and shook her head.

"Okay," he said. "That shrink I offed. I have happy memories of that."

"Oh, god help us."

"Come on, I'm just joking with you. We were hot together back then. We're still hot."

She squinted, not believing him, but wanting to so bad she finally sighed and said in a quiet, girlish voice, "You remember those magazines?"

It took him a minute to figure out what she was asking.

"You know, with the photos. The ones we used to look at together."

"I remember where I left them."

He got up and she followed him down the narrow hallway and into his old bedroom. Everything exactly how it was. Heavy metal posters, a dark-haired Playboy playmate tacked above his bed. On his chest of drawers was a bowling trophy he'd stolen from the trunk of somebody's car he'd ripped off at the Detroit airport, thinking it was funny at the time, Marco with a silly-ass bowling trophy.

He flipped the mattress off the bed, revealing his stash.

Ingrid stared at the treasures he'd collected, cast-offs from Mickey and Jackson when they'd tired of looking at gore and wanted to start making it.

"Still there," he said. "Kid stuff."

Ingrid moved close, reached up and scraped her nails lightly across the stubble on his cheek. Her lips spread slowly into a smile like a flag unfurling.

"You want to choke me, big man? A little strangulation for old time's sake."

"Right now?"

She kept smiling.

"Right here, right now."

"Got to make it quick. Our ten o'clock will be here soon."

☣ ☣ ☣

Waking in the dull morning light, Dulce was cold, very cold.

She wore the ruffled red blouse that Sugarman and Thorn had bought her and a pair of black jeans and silver jogging shoes. The blouse was short-sleeved and little help against the temperature. Not freezing, but colder than any she'd ever known. Like her traveling companions who shared the fenced pen, Dulce was shivering.

The ground was muddy and chopped into clumps as if by the hoofs of cows or pigs. There were puddles scattered about and it was difficult to find a dry place to sit or lie down. They had spent their first night in the open air, the other four finding small spots in the muddy earth to rest on, hugging themselves to keep warm. Dulce squatted in a corner, watchful and listening, staying awake most of the night.

In the sunlight, leaning against one of the fence posts, the old man continued to smile as he plucked at his eyelashes, a new habit he'd begun yesterday, pulling the lashes out one by one and flicking them away.

The Flores family was huddled at the far end of the pen, the young boy sitting in a squashy patch of mud while his sister, Rosa, hopping on one leg then the other, continued to repeat her five fairytales. Speaking faster now as if only by hurrying through them could she block her terror.

Their mother, Alejandra, had given up attempts to quiet Rosa or comfort her son. Her lips moved wordlessly as she fingered her rosary beads.

Dulce had tried several times to console them and had failed. She had stopped these efforts, though she still believed the good men would come. She wasn't certain how they would locate her in this place so distant from Arizona. Perhaps if she could think of a way of signaling them.

Once again Dulce surveyed the terrain beyond their cage. To her right was an open field dotted with patches of weeds where it appeared crops had once been planted. A dense forest spread beyond the field. To the left there was a barn with wood that was gray and warped with age and beside it a tractor with flat tires, and two old cars that were rusting and supported by concrete blocks. Rows of evergreen trees were planted in rows a few steps away from the holding pen. Deformed Christmas trees. Some too fat, others too tall and scraggly, all had lost the triangle shape. Planted too close and left untended, some had merged with one another and formed a wall of green, pine scented branches.

There was no road she could see. Straight ahead was a two-story house that once was painted yellow but now was nearly naked of color, its windows broken, TV antenna tilted to one side. A gravel driveway led to the house, but she could not see where the drive began, trees and bushes in the way.

She heard no machines, no passing cars on a nearby road, no voices, or barking dogs. Only the calls of crows and birds she couldn't name. The sky was dirty gray, the sun hidden behind an unmoving layer of clouds. The metal fence that surrounded the pen where they were imprisoned was twice Dulce's height. She had climbed such fences as a child, some even higher than this one, and she believed it was possible she could still accomplish such a thing. Perhaps when night came again, when their captors were asleep, the man with muscles, the tall, thin woman.

That might be her best chance. Escape the pen, run to a road, find a house with a telephone and call Sugarman and Thorn. She had memorized the number Sugarman wrote on the paper he gave Sister Kathleen. But Dulce realized she did not know how to describe her location. She could see no billboard signs, no stores, no street markers, nothing that she could use to show them the way.

To stay dry, Dulce continued to stand. But her legs ached, her back was sore and she was sleepy and her belly rumbled from hunger. Despite her difficulties, she had not given up hope. She had faith God would not abandon her. Sister Kathleen had taught her to have such trust. God was merciful, God was all-knowing and all-seeing, and benevolent. The trials she was enduring had a larger purpose that Dulce could not yet comprehend. But one day she would. She was certain of it.

A few minutes later she heard a motor and turned toward the sound.

A dark blue van was coming up the gravel drive. It pulled beside the house and two men got out. They wore khaki pants and blue shirts and dark V-neck sweaters. Each wore a red tie, neatly knotted at their throats. They looked like brothers, maybe twins. Both the same size, not tall, not short. Their haircuts were exactly the same. Neatly clipped. They had large jaws and though neither was smiling, Dulce could see their white teeth. One was redheaded, the other blond.

It was then her heart soared, for they looked like policemen. Saviors.

The red-haired driver walked to the side of the van, slid back a door and removed a leather briefcase. He opened it, looked inside and closed it again. Across the open yard the brawny man, their captor, came striding toward the two arrivals. She did not know that man well enough to tell what he was feeling. But his body seemed loose and light-footed like he was confident. He wore jeans and a dark T-shirt and in his right hand, Dulce saw the dark gleam of metal.

A pistol.

Heart speeding, she watched intently, expecting the two men to draw their own weapons and take the brawny man into custody as such men did on television.

But that is not what happened.

☣ ☣ ☣

"You know these two?" Ingrid said.

They were watching from the dining room window.

Marco didn't answer her, but kept eyeing the arrivals. One of the young men opened the van door and withdrew a briefcase.

"They're our ten o'clock," he said. "That's all I know."

"Twenty thousand for each," she said. "That's what you told them?"

"That's what I told them."

"They look like boy scouts, that clean cut bullshit. Where'd they get that kind of money, from Daddy Warbucks?"

"Who cares?"

"Maybe we should've screened these dickwads better, know exactly who was showing up in our front yard."

"Enough," Marco said. "Go set up behind the barn. Get going."

"I know my job. Don't get bossy."

"So do it. Take the AR and don't forget the .38, just one round in the cylinder."

"Jesus, how many times we been over this?"

"Do it, Ingrid."

"We could scrap the plan, just kill them all, one by one. Take their money."

He turned and fixed her with a hard look.

"Think about it. What could happen if we did that?"

"Yeah, yeah. Word spreads, assholes like these two would be looking for us the rest of our lives. Never be safe again. It was just a fantasy. Forget I said it."

Sometime in the last few days, Marco had felt the power shift between him and Ingrid. This whole deal was Marco's idea, shooting the video then posting it on their site, selling the landmines to their followers, let somebody else take the risks. No more hate rants, no more manifestos, churning up their people. It was time to cash in, walk away with a mountain of greenbacks. Ingrid had seen the beauty of it, though she'd tried to pick at it, find flaws.

Flaws like the Honduran girl who'd gotten away. Ingrid beat up on him about that fuck-up for days. But now that they had her back, everything was on track.

The online clamor for the VX landmines had been huge. Just shy of two hundred requests. Everybody wanting to know how much they were going for. Marco figured out the price, a sweet spot between a number that nobody but millionaires could afford, and a number so low the whole venture wouldn't be worth the effort. Twenty thousand per mine was what he settled on.

Almost half a million by Saturday. Of course there'd be some risk. His biggest worry: vans coming and going to the old Whitman place. Which was why Marco made each buyer settle on an appointed hour, two a day at ten and three, spreading them far enough apart there wouldn't be a goddamn traffic jam on Taggart Road. Though Taggart was so far from town, nobody was likely to notice any extra traffic anyway. The closest house was Savannah's a couple of miles away. But her place was empty, no sign of cars, no lights at night. He'd pounded on the front door yesterday, peeked in all the windows. Saw no one. Apparently she and Vegas had left town. Good fucking riddance.

Still, Marco was playing safe. Telling each customer to drive a rented van, preferably white or blue. Something non-descript, unmemorable. Don't speed or draw attention.

His list of guidelines went out to the five buyers, five landmines each to the first four, and the leftover three to the last guy. Four hundred thousand by Friday and the final sixty Saturday morning. The buyers had to agree to everything. All of it Marco double-checked, made certain each of the crazy fucks knew exactly what was expected. Check each box, check it again. No weapons, dress decent, get a haircut, rented van, small bills, nothing larger than a fifty, be on time. Ten minutes late, you were fucked, no sale. He and Ingrid could afford to get top dollar and set strict rules because VX nerve gas didn't come onto the market every day.

During the long drive from Arizona to Michigan, Ingrid started looking at him different. Showing a whiff of respect for the first time he could remember. It gave him such a rush he struggled to keep from pushing his advantage and begin to lord it over her. Kept reminding himself he just wanted things to be equal. Nothing more than that. No more brains versus brawn. He never wanted to hear that drill sergeant voice of hers turning him into a ten year old ever again.

"So go," he said. "Get set."

"I know, I know. 'If they don't pull the trigger, I pull mine.'"

Marco waited till Ingrid was out the back door and headed to the rear of the barn, her path shielded from the buyers by a shed, the rusty cars, and the old John Deere tractor.

When he saw she was positioned, he went out the front door.

The two eagle scouts watched him cross the front yard. They seemed to come to attention as he closed in, shoulders going back, chins tucking in.

The redhead holding the briefcase stepped forward and extended his hand.

Marco stared at the kid's wimpy paw and said, "What are you smiling about?"

"I'm not smiling."

"You're smiling, both of you are smiling."

The blond said, "It's just the way our mouths are. People think we're smiling, but we're not. It's the shape of our mouths, sorry."

The redhead still had his hand out.

"Show me," Marco said.

The guy lowered his hand and started to open the briefcase and Marco said, "Not the fucking money. You know what I want to see."

Blondie said, "He means the tat."

Red reached up to his collar and pulled it away from his throat to display the Abyss symbol.

Marco wet his pointing finger, leaned in and rubbed at the Valknot.

It didn't smudge.

"Now you, kid."

The blond tugged his collar down and tilted his head to the side, trying to be helpful. Marco scrubbed his wet finger over the tat. No smudge there either.

"We're with you all the way," redhead said. "We've been followers for years. You're an inspiration. Some of the shit we've pulled, we would never have done it without your encouragement."

Blondie said, "When do we get to see them, the items we're buying?"

Marco grunted and gave the two a sleepy sneer, then turned his back on them and marched to the barn. He rolled open the big door and stepped into the dusky interior. The crates were stacked four high along the left wall.

The briefcase guy walked over and leaned in to get a better look. He drew out a mini-mag flashlight and trained the beam on the landmines.

"These work, right? You're not selling us duds. I'm sorry, but I have to ask."

"You saw the video. Damn right they work. You don't want to be anywhere around when one of those sweethearts goes off."

"How can we be a hundred percent sure you're not scamming us?"

"If you're dissatisfied in any way," Marco said, "I'll be right here waiting. Money back guarantee."

"I think he's joking."

"Now we've got one more step before the deal is done. Got to make sure about you guys."

Marco led them back outside then across the yard to the holding pen.

"First come, first served," he said. "You got your pick."

The two of them peered through the chain-link, appraising the five migrants. The old man was tugging at his eyelashes, the little boy was lying on his side in the mud moaning softly, the woman was fingering her prayer beads and her daughter was repeating the same damn stories she'd been reciting for days. Dulce, the girl who'd given them such trouble, was glaring at Marco as though she was daring him to come into the pen, like she might leap on him, try to claw out his eyes.

"What'll it be, boys?"

"The MILF is cute," the redhead said.

"I'd rather have the girl."

"Which girl?"

"The little one. The other one's homely."

Blondie hummed a tuneless jingle, getting excited, trying to cover it.

"Okay," the redhead said. "The little girl then. Does she ever stop talking?"

"I don't mind the talking," the blond said.

"Behind the barn," said Marco.

"What are the rules?"

"One rule. When you're done, put her down."

"You've got nothing to worry about from us."

The redhead extended the briefcase and after letting a few seconds pass, just to show these punks they couldn't rush him, Marco took it from his hand.

"You want to hear how we're going to use the weapons? It's really cool."

"I don't want to know."

"You'll read about it in the papers. You'll know it's us. Movie theater in San Francisco, packed house, pick the right movie and it'll be a few hundred snowflake libs choking to death all over the place, killing each other to get out of there."

"I don't give a shit," Marco said. "Take the girl, and get it done."

Marco opened the padlock.

"Until the girl's history, you don't get the goods. Understood?"

"A loyalty test, sure. To weed out feds, covert infiltrators. Sure, we expected that."

"My assistant behind the barn will give you a handgun. It's

loaded with one round. That's all you get. She'll be supervising the two of you while I count the cash, make sure it's all there."

"Very well thought out arrangement," the redhead said.

"Yeah, I know," said Marco. "So get it done, and get the hell out of here."

☣☣☣

Dulce stood out of range as the thick-chested man entered the gate. He stared at her like she was a coiled rattler. While she kept still, he began a slow circle of the pen, acting like some of the boys she had known back home, the boasting boys, the cocky ones who taunted and ridiculed girls and weaker children, showing off their smirking superiority.

Dulce knew something about evil. At home in San Pedro Sula the *Maras* gang were ruffians and thieves who stole whatever they wanted and murdered any man or woman or child who stood in their way. She and her mother fled their homeland mainly to escape them. Twice Dulce had been face to face with one of them in the street and had looked into their eyes, and for all their cruelty she thought she'd seen a hint of guilt and maybe even a trace of dignity. These men were committing brutal acts to survive in a land of turmoil and scarcity.

But the eyes of the muscular man who stood before her were different. They were empty and soulless like one who had long ago abandoned all human beliefs. Nowhere in the pretty photographs of America in Sister Kathleen's magazines would such a man be at home. Not in the beautiful kitchens, not on the green lawns or the perfect blue swimming pools where children splashed and played. For reasons she did not comprehend, Dulce was being held in a godless zone where commandments had no force. A dark realm with no connection to the land of freedom and opportunity she and her mother had been seeking.

Dulce wanted to fling herself on the man but knew it was useless. He was far too sturdy and she had no weapon, nothing to give her advantage. And she had to save her strength for later, for climbing the fence, escaping. She smothered her anger and stepped away but didn't turn her back to him to demonstrate she was unafraid.

The red-haired man followed the muscular one into the pen and walked over to Rosa. The girl was almost done with the story of Hansel and Gretel and the gingerbread house, the part where Gretel pushes the witch into the oven so she and her brother can flee.

The man reached his hand out to Rosa but the girl turned her head away and shook it hard as she continued with the fairytale.

"Go on," the brawny man said. "You're not asking her out for a dinner date."

Alejandra was on her feet. She screamed at the red-haired man who loomed over her daughter then flew across the muddy ground to defend the child, but the brawny man stepped in her path and with a single blow to her chest, he slammed her backwards to the ground.

As the red-haired man led Rosa from the pen, the girl was silent, her final fairytale finished, whatever magic she'd expected to summon from those ancient tales had failed her. Her eyes were turned down, looking at the ground at her feet while her mother wailed.

When they were all gathered outside the pen, the muscular man snapped the padlock shut, smiled at Dulce and walked back to the house carrying the briefcase.

The two men disappeared with Rosa behind the barn.

Sobbing, Alejandra fell to her knees in the mud, hands clutching her face. Dulce went to her and slung her arm over the woman's shoulder, embracing the woman while her body shook with anguish.

High above Dulce a vast flock of crows filled the wintry sky, passing overhead like a tattered mass of windblown smoke from a thousand bonfires. As they flowed across the sky, their shrieks and cries trailed away, then finally the commotion faded into silence when the birds settled into the treetops of the neighboring forest as if they meant to observe the unfolding events from a safe distance.

TWENTY-FIVE

"Take down license plates? Why?" Vegas raked her fingers through her hair.

"Marco is selling the landmines. When they stole them in September, they must've moved them down the road, probably stored them in that old barn. That blue van that went by after breakfast, that's one of his clients."

"So?"

"What do you mean? This is serious."

Vegas made a slow circle around the living room, not looking at Savannah, then she halted at the front window, looking out at the road. Taking deep breaths, building up to something, her body stiffening.

"Those landmines, isn't that what their purpose is? To kill people."

"Yes, of course, but..."

"Isn't that why you ripped them off in the first place, to get even for losing your precious brother, Marty? Attack the military industrial complex. Isn't that why they've been sitting out there all my goddamn life, out there in the shed, hovering over us, this black fucking cloud of nerve gas. Just a few yards away hovering and hovering, more important to you than anything else. A reminder of all the shit you meant to do but didn't have the guts for. Isn't this their purpose all along?"

"Vegas? Are you all right?"

She swung around from the window, eyes blazing.

"Hell, no, I'm not all right. I've never been all right. You made sure of that. You, Mother. I might as well have grown up on another planet or the goddamn moon, for all the attention you paid me. Every fucking day, there you are, rain or snow, ice or whatever, I'm eating breakfast with Judson, my Wheaties, my Cheerios, and where are you? You're walking to the shed to feed Big Blue, make sure nothing was leaking, make sure your precious landmines are okay. Never checking if I'm okay. But your goddamn landmines, they're always out there, on your mind, first thing in the morning. Every morning.

"And the *Flying Dragon*, that boat sitting in its crib, decaying away plank by plank. I used to play inside it, me and Marco, we'd climb up there and explore and make up stories. Sail to some island out in the Pacific, monsters and pirates and crazy things we invented. Until Judson told us not to go into it anymore, saying it was rotting and wasn't safe. But we knew that wasn't true. It was safe. He just didn't want us in it for some mystery reason.

"We kept doing it, climbing up into it and making up our stories. You didn't know that, did you? You didn't know about all the hours Marco and I spent inside that boat fantasizing. You were off at work or in your room staring at the wall. Until finally Judson had enough of us disobeying him, and he told us what happened on Johnston Atoll with the boat, it was to scare us off, to make us quit. He told us the whole story. Every detail, how you got pregnant with that man's baby and the man got sent to prison and you went on and had his baby, Marco. Judson told us the story. You didn't know that, did you?"

Savannah said no, she didn't know that.

"That's the kind of life I had. My mother, the big bad revolutionary who didn't have the guts to pull it off, the one important thing in her life, the one thing she risked everything for, fucked a complete stranger so she could steal those things and sail away, raised the stranger's kid, for christsakes. And she didn't have the guts to tell it straight to her own daughter, what she did.

"So now all of a sudden you're upset someone else is going to use them? Why is that? Someone else has the nerve you didn't have. Marco is making a buck, unloading the goddamn things and we're supposed to care. Christ, they're more Marco's than yours. All that he's gone through, the fucked up way you treated him. Pushed him away, ignored him. Those are his landmines. He's earned them.

"And now I'm supposed to go out there and write down the license plate of some half-assed terrorist. Really, Mother? Did I hear that right? Now all of a sudden you don't want those things used?

"And while we're at it, let's not forget my sweet perfect girl, Nola. If you hadn't kept those goddamn pictures of Marty, and those letters and all that fucking bullshit paraphernalia from his days in Vietnam, the great war hero. If you hadn't kept those in a footlocker where Nola could get to them, she'd still be alive. It's your fault, Mother, your fault what happened to her. Joining the Army, inspired by your fucked-up brother, the great, tragic war hero, the reason you went sailing off for those landmines in the first place. It's all a great big fucked-up circle. With you smack in the middle. Do you see that, Mother? Do you understand what I'm saying? This is all your fucked-up fault. Do you see that? You orchestrated all of it. And now I'm supposed to get a license plate number and then what, sic the police on some poor lunatic who's got the nerve you never had? Really? Do you hear yourself?"

Savannah pushed her body up from the recliner. Her head was swimming.

She staggered across the room to her daughter, reached out a hand, but Vegas slapped it away.

"It was me that called Marco," Vegas said. "I told him we'd be out of town. He was free to help himself to the landmines."

"You did what?"

"You stupid, stupid woman. You left my little girl alone with that footlocker, day after day, up there in the attic alone with all that shit about Marty a few feet away. What did you think was going to happen? Nola's dead because of you, you stupid bitch. You stupid, worthless woman.

"I'm leaving. I'm packed. I'm going away. I don't know where. But I'm not coming back. Not ever. I'm done with you, I'm done with all this. All of it."

"Vegas, no. Listen to me. I'm sorry, I'm sorry."

She pushed past Savannah and marched out the front door. Savannah watched her cross the yard, climb into her old Ford, start it, and spin her wheels in the sloppy dirt and speed off down Taggart Road toward town and all that lay beyond.

☣☣☣

Savannah had never driven Nola's truck. It still smelled new, only three thousand miles on the odometer, most of that from the trip to Dover and back. Savannah fired up the big V-8 and eased the Dodge out of the back shed they used as a second garage. She turned onto Taggart and headed north in the direction Vegas had taken. Her hands were trembling, her jaw was sore from grinding her teeth.

She drove another mile, then coasted to a stop at the entrance to the Lawrence farm. Savannah looked down their long maple-lined drive, her vision smeared with tears.

Last week Mary and Joseph Lawrence had left for their yearly sojourn in Boca Raton. Like always, they'd checked with Savannah before pulling out, and as usual Savannah promised to keep an eye on the place through the coming frigid months, make sure the snow didn't cave in the roof or topple a tree.

Mary was a retired orthopedist and Joseph ran a Buick dealership over on Sand Beach Road. Nice people, plenty of money but they didn't act like it.

Savannah backed into their driveway, facing out to Taggart Road, forty, fifty feet away, getting the truck set just right so she had a clear view back the way she'd come—the direction the blue van would have to travel as it exited the area. Judson's shotgun was braced against the passenger door, and two of his handguns lay on the seat.

She didn't have a plan, but she'd decided she was going to do more than take down the van's license plate. Thorn said he'd be here by now and since he hadn't arrived, she had no alternative but to handle this herself.

Directly across Taggart, the Lawrence family had scooped out a few acres of earth and lined the depression with plastic so their kids would have a pond to swim and fish in when they were growing up. For several summers all the kids from surrounding farms played there, until one afternoon Marco tried to drown one of the Lawrence boys. Even as kind as Mary Lawrence was, after that incident she put a stop to all contact between Savannah's kids and her own.

Savannah sat with the truck idling, her cheeks still enflamed from Vegas's speech, an agonizing roar in her ears.

It was true, all her daughter said. Those landmines had governed her family's entire life. She'd been cowardly in never using them as she'd intended and even more spineless in storing them for all those years, never able to let them go. They'd poisoned every corner of her existence, poisoned her kids, infected her marriage. Those goddamn landmines were a bloodstain on her soul.

The hate she'd once harbored for the American war machine had simmered for decades until it almost flickered out, then suddenly flared to life again with Nola's death, but this time the rage was no longer directed at the Pentagon or the nameless lawmakers who ordered the nation's children into pointless battles, this time her hatred was directed inward.

The footlocker in the attic, that part of Vegas's rant was true as well. Though Savannah had never admitted it openly to herself, she'd invited Nola's contact with that trove of memories. Secretly she'd wished the girl to be so enthralled by Marty's history that she would come to Savannah for a fuller understanding, then Savannah could flesh out the lost love who'd shaped the tragic course of her life and perhaps forge a more intimate bond with Nola.

She'd lost Marty. She'd lost Nola. She'd lost Judson, and now Vegas.

When Savannah's phone trilled in the truck's cup holder, she looked down at the screen, praying it was Vegas, she'd changed her mind, was coming home, willing to give Savannah another chance.

But no, it was Ray Murphy's number. Thorn.

"We ran into some issues on the flight up," Thorn said. "Just arrived at the airport, Engler Field, you know where that is?"

"A few miles east of here, four, five."

"You okay? You sound strange."

"You don't know me. Don't pretend you do."

"All right."

"I'm okay. I'm fine."

"Give me your address, and the address where Marco is, any details about the layout of the area."

When Savannah answered, her voice was not her own, but a ghostly replica speaking through her body, giving Thorn her address on Taggart Road, describing the three houses on the road, each one a few miles apart, a pond across from the first one, the second house, her own, and the last one, where Taggart dead-ended, that's where Marco and Ingrid were, and the landmines. The Whitman place consisted of a two-story house, a barn, a couple of sheds, some animal pens. An empty field where long ago the Whitman's grew corn, the remnants of a failed Christmas tree farm. And a forest west of that.

"I'm on my way," Thorn said. "Green Ford pick-up."

"Good-bye, Thorn." Savannah broke the connection.

Nothing left to say, only one thing left to do, some come-from-behind justice.

The blue van was approaching, driving slow.

She put Nola's Dodge in gear, engaged the four wheel drive and waited till the van was so close she could make out the red-haired driver, close-cropped hair, toothy smile.

She flattened the accelerator, kicking up a flurry of gravel and roared from zero to forty in a few head-snapping seconds.

The driver must have heard the rumble of the engine or caught a flash of Savannah's approach because he swung his head around to stare at her, his eyes bulging as she aimed the chrome bull bars into the side of the panel van and rammed, skidding it sideways, where it caught the shoulder of the road, tumbled onto its side, and began to somersault down the bank toward the lip of the Lawrence's pond, making it almost to the water's edge before the first explosion blew apart the vehicle, then a second landmine detonated as the shattered van sank beneath the pond's surface which muffled the next blasts and fired geysers of pond water fifty feet in the air leaving a hazy mist aloft, a cloud that must have been tainted with VX because a pair of low-flying geese veered away from the explosions, fought for altitude, but their wings failed and for a few moments they thrashed drunkenly before spiraling back to earth.

Savannah pulled forward to the shoulder of the road, slipped the shifter into neutral, revved the engine, revved it higher and higher and took a moment to plead for forgiveness from all the loved ones whose lives she'd ruined.

☣☣☣

"Did you hear that?"

"Hear what?" Marco was shoulder-deep in the mucky earth, digging a grave for the talkative little girl who was talkative no more. "I'm down here in a fucking hole, shoveling, what am I supposed to hear?"

"Sounded like an explosion."

Marco stopped digging, back-handed the sweat from his forehead.

"I don't hear anything."

"It was an explosion, three or four of them."

"Next asshole is going to dig the grave himself. This was stupid, leaving the work to me. Bad planning."

"I'm serious, Marco. I heard something."

"Which direction?"

"I'm not sure. It's windy, it could've been anywhere. Miles away, I don't know."

"Go get me a Bud Light, Ingrid."

"Those boy scouts could've smashed into a tree, set those things off."

"Jesus Christ. You're so worried about it, get the car, drive around and see."

"And what, drive into a cloud of VX? You trying to kill me?"

"Get the beer, would you? I got to finish this goddamn hole."

TWENTY-SIX

For the entire first leg of the journey, Thorn felt a knot tightening in his gut, made more acute by the unexpected headwinds that shaved a healthy chunk off their cruising speed, then an aggravating stop at a private airport north of Chattanooga where they'd arranged to be refueled, but found the fuel depot unoccupied.

Romy had to make several calls to locate the attendant, all of which tacked an additional hour on to the trip, most of that spent tracking down and rousting the twenty year old out of his one room shack a mile's hike from the airport.

While the kid dressed, Thorn asked in the most laid-back voice he could muster, if the kid wasn't supposed to be on-duty at the airport itself.

"Whatever," the kid said.

"Whatever?"

"You heard me."

Sugarman grabbed Thorn's shoulder and steered him out of the room.

"He's not the enemy," Sugar said. "We'll be there soon. Save your energy."

Romy said, "What're you so worked up about, Thorn?"

He shook his head, didn't want to discuss it.

"He's worried about Dulce," Sugar said. "What she's going through."

"If she's even still alive."

"Look, we're hustling as fast as we can." Sugarman patted him on the back. "Unless you want me to call Sheffield and have him express some field agents from Detroit or wherever."

"Leave Frank out of it. I'll be all right."

When the fuel tank was full, Romy gave the kid a credit card and shot Thorn a cool-it look.

Back in the Cessna, she said, "I know it's hard for you to accept, Thorn, but as long as I'm piloting this crate, you're outranked, and you'll do exactly what I say at all times. This is no joke. Like the Captain on his ship. Got it?"

Thorn considered a salute, thought better of it and nodded.

"I'm sorry if I was being an asshole."

"No ifs about it," Romy said.

"The woman's honest," Sugar said. "Got to love that."

"Now that we're topped up," Romy said, "I'll push this beauty as fast as it'll go. We should be there before lunch."

"I was hoping for breakfast."

"We all were."

☣ ☣ ☣

At eleven when they touched down in Bad Axe, the green pick-up Sugarman had rented from the local Chevy dealership was waiting on the edge of the runway. A plump white-haired lady had the paperwork ready to sign. While Sugar handled the forms, Thorn called Savannah to let her know they'd landed and were on their way. She provided some sketchy details about her location and Marco's whereabouts, then ended the call with an abrupt and ominous good-bye.

Maybe there'd been a time when Thorn was angrier. But he couldn't remember it. On the final leg of the flight while Sugarman dozed and Romy was locked in on the details of flying, Thorn found himself tapping a knuckle on the window, looking out through his reflection into the bleak darkness. He tapped until tapping was not enough, then he drew back his hand and clubbed the window with the side of his fist, harder and harder until Sugarman jerked awake.

"You okay, hombre?"

"Fine and dandy."

"We're getting there fast and we have a decent plan. Putting a hole in the fuselage isn't going to help. Try some deep breaths."

"Ah, yes. The universal cure-all."

Sugarman shrugged and settled back into his seat and was soon asleep.

Thorn held himself in check but couldn't stop the flood of images. For the next few hours he combed through his time with Dulce Mérida. From the first moment he'd seen her wedged into a storage compartment in that rundown mobile home outside Frontera and held her hand and calmed her, to the last words they'd shared as he left her in the care of Sister Kathleen. The girl's resolute smile, her astonishment at the excess in the Tucson shopping mall, her instant affection for McDonald's food. And swirled together with that was all Thorn had learned of Abyss and their loathing for migrants. Chasing them down like jack rabbits, capturing them, imprisoning them, using them for target practice or worse, the mass graves on the Whitman's ranch, the macabre video of the gassed Hondurans.

For several minutes he tried taking Sugarman's advice to ease the pressure in his chest: breathing in and out, going slow, following the breath into his lungs, holding it for a second then letting it go in an easy stream, but the technique failed. Nothing was going to smooth him out, nothing except putting his hands on Marco.

He felt every heartbeat in his throat, dry and constricted, a fire alarm clanging in his chest. He didn't want to kill these vermin, he wanted to lock himself in a cell with the guy and gouge and rip and stomp, inflict as much agony and humiliation as he could bring about.

Which of course would solve nothing. There were countless Marcos scattered in rat holes across the globe. Their numbers seemed to be multiplying every year. Not just the fanatics who donned fatigues and camo gear and played warrior in the woods and nursed their rage, passing it on like some precious flame from one loser to another, but also Marco's silent allies, the decent church-goers who only let their true beliefs slip in winks and nods and sly off-color jokes like a secret code spoken between other polite, god-fearing folks.

Thorn knew some of those, his neighbors in Key Largo, masquerading as virtuous and patriotic, hiding their resentments against those with the wrong accent or shade of skin or land of origin behind affable smiles, courteous manners, while their bloodstream was fouled with the same dark acid as Marco and his cohorts. Of course, these folks would never commit outright violence, but their silence, their passivity, their quiet contempt for refugees and exiles made them, at the very least, Marco's witless accomplices.

When Thorn was a kid growing up on the island, he believed Key Largo was a tolerant paradise where locals welcomed all newcomers, including those with strange customs or foreign tongues. The Keys had always been a mecca for grifters and romantics and outcasts, Cubans, Haitians, Jamaicans, Yankees and Midwesterners, a wild assortment of misfits who shared common appetites: the saltwater life, hard liquor, a simmering carnality in the palm-shaded heat, endless stretches of sea in all directions, gaudy sunsets, and spice-scented breezes. Maybe Thorn's memory was too rosy. Maybe the island had always been littered with the same racial animus he saw today. He wasn't sure. Perhaps his exposure to Marco and his ilk had soured his outlook beyond repair.

Thorn watched Sugarman use the map on his phone, locating Taggart Road and choosing the best route from the airport. When he was done, Sugar retrieved the money bag from the Cessna while Bill Duffy briefed Romy on the operation of the crop duster parked on the runway. Thorn drifted over to listen to the quick, efficient exchange between the two pilots, after which both seemed satisfied with the competence of the other.

Duffy had flown the plane in from his home near Minneapolis. He was a retired Baptist pastor whose congregation had once included most of the African American community in Key Largo and Tavernier. In those years, decades ago, Duffy had wooed one of the church ladies who'd adopted Sugarman, and for the duration of that courtship the reverend was the closest thing to a father figure Sugarman had.

He was a tall lean man, unstooped by age, with the decorous manner of one who has lived a full and proper life. That he and Sugar had stayed in touch after all these years came as a surprise to Thorn, further evidence that despite his long-standing bond with Sugarman, there would always be parts of Sugar's life story Thorn would never be privy to.

"Ah, the famous Mister Thorn," Duffy said.

"Some say infamous."

"So I've heard. Though the two are not always mutually exclusive."

"Look, I'd like to stay and chat," Thorn said. "Maybe we can do that later, but right now we need to get moving, sir. Thanks for your help."

"You two are not doing anything unlawful with my plane, are you?"

"It's a noble cause," Sugar said. "One you'd fully approve of. We'll give you the whole story when we get back."

"And when will that be?"

"A few hours. If all goes as planned."

"And if it doesn't?" Duffy asked.

"It will," Thorn said.

Agnes Sheeran, the car rental agent, suggested she take Mr. Duffy into Bad Axe and treat him to lunch at Rachel's, the best local restaurant. She was sure he'd love the Philly cheese steak flatbread.

Thorn asked Sheeran to hold on a second, then Sugar, Romy and Thorn huddled near the crop duster.

"You sure you can fly this thing?"

"Pretty basic. Duffy keeps it in good shape."

"Would it be better if Duffy flew and you were the bombardier?"

"Thorn, don't worry, I can handle it. Might need to make a couple of passes to unload everything one-handed. But other than that, I'm fine."

Thorn ran through the plan one more time. When he and Sugar located Marco's place, Sugar would call to let Romy know it was time to get airborne. Then she would allow them ten more minutes before the fly-over, fifteen max.

Thorn climbed into the pickup and settled behind the wheel and Sugarman lay the money bag on the seat between them and dug out a .357 Smith.

"Is that it? Our total firepower?"

"Unless you brought something," Sugar said.

"Actually, at this point I don't believe I need a weapon."

"You're that mad?"

"Madder."

"But you can keep that under control, right? Until we find out what's what."

"I can try," Thorn said.

A half hour later, they found Taggart Road, and passed by the pond Savannah had described, noted the pretty house down a tree-lined drive.

After another mile on Taggart, Sugar said, "Well, I'll be damned."

Thorn slowed as they passed a two story wood house with a

shed out back, a small barn with a powder blue pickup truck parked beside it. And on a wooden cradle east of the house was a Chinese junk maybe forty feet long with a wide beam and a boxy hull and twin masts.

"The *Flying Dragon*," Sugar said. "From Bobby's story."

"At least some of it was true."

Thorn pulled to the side of the road.

"What're you doing?"

Thorn nodded toward the *Flying Dragon*. Stepping from the ship's shadow, a willowy woman looked out at them. Her right hand was touching the hull. Its red and gold paint had faded and the figure of the golden dragon had been weathered for so many seasons its details had been nearly smoothed away.

Thorn got out of the pickup, walked over, Sugar hanging back a few paces.

Her long mane hung to the middle of her back, silvery white with a few tenacious strands of black. Her face was gaunt and her eyes so fatigued she seemed to be laboring to keep them open. Though Bobby Tennyson's seductress had lost her lush radiance, and her hypnotic charm had clearly faded, Thorn saw a lingering luster in her eyes, a last trace of the mystique that caused Bobby to betray his oath and abandon his duties.

"Savannah?"

She blinked hard as though waking from a melancholy trance.

"I'm Thorn."

"I know."

Her hand had flattened against the sleek wood hull as if she was drawing voltage from its core.

"Marco's down there, down the road," she said. "At the dead end. He and the girl, Ingrid, they've got the landmines, selling them to people, revolutionaries or terrorists, or whatever they call themselves.

But it's not any revolution I recognize. What Marco believes, and his followers, it's got nothing to do with me or Judson, our cause. We had ideals, we were goddamned dreamers, we hungered for a better world, fair and just, that's all we wanted, and peaceful. We didn't believe in some noble, utopia bullshit, but we had hope we could make a difference. We had a rotten war to stop, thousands of innocent boys being destroyed. But these people today. They're bullies, full of spite and contempt. All they want to do is crush, mutilate, to tear down."

"I don't know," Thorn said. "Sounds like a family business disagreement. When it comes to blowing up people with landmines, I don't see a lot of difference between one cause and another."

She looked at him sharply and shook her head.

"You don't understand. You weren't there. You don't know how it was."

"No, I don't."

"It's all changed," she said. "It's gone rotten. A virus eating away at decency and human dignity."

Thorn glanced at Sugar and he shook his head, let it go. And yeah, as usual, Sugar was right. Arguing with Savannah was pointless. Like Bobby Tennyson, she had never truly left behind Johnston Atoll, that poisoned island, and that raging war.

Thorn said, "We're going to do what we can to stop these people. How many are there besides Marco and Ingrid?"

"Don't know. Could be dozens, or it could be just the two. I'm not sure."

Savannah turned away from them and reached both arms as high as she could stretch and pressed her palms against the hull of the *Flying Dragon* as if she meant to claw her way up the side and climb aboard and sail back half a century when revolutionaries had flowers in their hair and the best of intentions

"Go on, get out of here. Go, I'm done with you. I'm done with all of it."

Sugar gripped Thorn's shoulder and steered him back to the truck.

When they caught sight of the last house on the road off in the distance, Thorn pulled to the shoulder and cut the engine.

"What's up?"

Thorn sighed.

"Maybe you should get out here, work your way to the house through those trees. Take the Smith. Get the drop on them."

"That wasn't the plan. We're going in together. I got this damn tat for the occasion." Sugar patted his forearm.

Thorn tried to find the words, but nothing came for a few awkward seconds.

"I don't know, Sugar. Given who these assholes are, you might set them off."

Sugarman looked away at the bare trees, nodding, absorbing the remark.

"Hadn't thought of that."

"Just occurred to me. Mexicans, Hondurans, African Americans, to these assholes what's the difference?"

"Yeah, yeah, good catch, Thorn." But there was nothing upbeat in his tone. "Sometimes I forget."

"I forget all the time."

"Except just now," Sugar said. "Just now you remembered."

Thorn stared out the windshield. In the stretch of silence, he felt a gulf widen between them, one that never existed before or else until now had gone unspoken.

"Look, I'm sorry."

Sugar waved him off.

"Not your fault. Like I said, it's good you caught it. We could have walked in there together, the blond WASP dude and the darkie, they wouldn't think twice before mowing us down."

Thorn lay a hand on Sugarman's shoulder, trying to find something to say to bridge the divide, bring them back. Sugar reached up and patted his hand.

"It's okay, man," Sugar said. "Really, don't sweat it. You go through the front door, hit 'em in the face and I'll sneak in the back and shoot 'em in the ass, between the two of us we'll take down these jamokes. Make the world a safer place. That's what we do, right?"

"That's what we do," Thorn said.

Sugar got out of the truck, closed the door quietly and without a backward glance wandered away into the woods.

"Okay, what the fuck is going on? This asshole is way too early."

Marco stood at the front window fingering open a slit in the curtains.

"And he's driving a pickup not a van," Ingrid said.

"I don't like the looks of this. Not even a little bit."

When Thorn stepped out of the pickup truck and strolled into the center of the big yard, Dulce wanted to scream with joy and relief. He glanced over at the pen, stopped, met her eyes and though his face remained empty, she believed he was telling her to stay quiet and still, to let him do whatever it was he'd come to do.

Thorn dallied in the yard for several minutes, not moving, not looking her way again, just staring off at the forest where the giant flock of crows had landed.

It seemed like a long time before the muscular man threw open the front door of the house and came down the steps in jeans and a tight black T-shirt. The pistol was in his hand again. He walked slower than last time, something different about him, tensed and cautious like a street dog approaching a menacing trespasser.

Dulce's fellow prisoners were also watching intently. Now that they'd seen what was in store for them, they were alert to every unfolding event. If their captor repeated the process he'd used before, it would only be a minute or two before he brought Thorn over to the pen and directed him to select the next victim.

With a quiver of suspicion rising inside her, Dulce found herself considering the thought that Thorn had not come to rescue her at all. Was it possible he was an accomplice of her captor? No, no. Everything Thorn had done on behalf of Dulce seemed evidence of his goodness. Every single thing.

But as the tremors in her chest grew with the growing doubt, she began to imagine each step Thorn had taken on her behalf was actually a deception. What if it was all done to move Dulce closer to being taken hostage and brought to this remote place? A scheme to betray her. It seemed incredible, but as she went over each step, recalled how he coaxed her from her hiding place, won her trust, tempted her with food and lavished her with new clothes, then left her with Sister Kathleen, so exposed and defenseless, she was no longer certain if she could trust this man.

Why would anyone, especially a stranger, be so kind? When she asked him that, why he was helping her, his answer was *torpe*. Clumsy, awkward. He said he cared about her, and when she challenged him that he had only known her for a few days, Thorn replied that was enough time. But was it? Was it really?

Thorn and her captor were talking in the yard, the muscular one had his back to the pen where Dulce and the others were trapped. A cloth bag was in Thorn's hand, much like the briefcase the red-headed man held. Thorn glanced over at her again and his face was empty. Nothing to reassure her.

All she'd believed was a lie. Dulce had been tricked. She saw that now. She was certain of it. She was on her own. Any hope of survival was in her hands alone.

She turned to the fence at the rear of the pen, hesitated a moment, gathering herself, picturing her run toward the chain-link fence, leaping as high as she could, grabbing hold and climbing.

TWENTY-SEVEN

Thorn had no idea what Marco's protocol was, his specific arrangements with the buyers. There had to be numerous tripwires with a transaction as lethal as this. He and Sugar had discussed it on the flight and they'd run a few possible scenarios. Though there was simply no way to predict how the deal was supposed to unfold, the one common element in all their versions was weapons. Marco and Ingrid would be heavily armed. These two wouldn't dare peddle nerve agents otherwise.

There was also a possibility Marco would have a crew to back him up. It seemed unlikely that he and Ingrid would risk trying to pull this off alone. The Whitman brothers had been killed in the assault on their ranch, but surely Marco had other allies in Abyss.

"On the other hand," Sugar had said, "far as we can tell, they've done everything on their own, just the two of them, Bonnie and Clyde."

"We have to assume there'll be more than just those two."

"To be on the safe side, yeah."

"As if there's a safe side to this," Thorn said.

They also suspected there'd be some other requirements. No way to predict that either. The only one they were sure of was the Abyss tattoo. They had that covered, otherwise, Thorn's best chance of grabbing Dulce and making it out of this alive was to stay flexible, improvise, adapt to whatever wild cards were played.

But as soon as he'd climbed out of the pickup truck, he was already tensed and off balance. Seeing Dulce caged nearby had spiked his anger.

Maintaining a poker face wasn't in Thorn's skill set, neither was throttling back his fury, but for Dulce's sake, he tried to keep his expression neutral, trying to let her know as best he could that she shouldn't expose any hint of their connection.

Thorn scanned the surroundings, an eye out for Sugar or any of Marco's crew but saw no sign of either. He surveyed the layout, the barn, a sagging two-story house, the pen, an abandoned tractor and two cars on blocks, a field where crops had once grown and a distant forest. Ragged rows of evergreens rimmed the property and more firs and pines were sprinkled randomly around the edges as though this place had briefly been a Christmas tree farm before it went to seed.

The nearest neighbor was Savannah Snyder, two or three miles back on Taggart Road. Like the Whitman's ranch in Arizona, this place was so isolated, any gunfire or explosions or screams would go undetected. Perfect spot for whatever butchery these monsters had in mind.

There was no obvious sign of the landmines, but storing them inside the house was unlikely. If leakage or any mishap occurred it would pose a high risk to anyone lodged there. If they were stashed on-site, they had to be in the dilapidated barn adjacent to the pen where the migrants were caged.

Assuming he was being watched, Thorn stayed stock-still in the open yard, staring off at the distant forest where batches of crows left their perches, fluttered into the air then resettled back into the limbs in an edgy dance whose music only they could hear.

He didn't fidget, did nothing that might give away the thump of anger in his chest, and as much as he wanted to, he didn't take another sideways glance at Dulce.

An agonizing five minutes passed before he heard the screech of rusty hinges and turned to see the front door of the house open and a big man come warily down the steps.

Thorn had only a single glimpse of Marco during the shootout when he'd been grazed and Castillo hit twice, a blurred image of a bulky man clambering into the front seat of a van while gunfire sprayed. But from all Thorn had learned about Marco and his hateful creed and ruthless acts, Thorn formed an image of the man, a picture that took such vivid root that he'd begun to believe he might be able to spot Marco in a crowd. He'd be the man with the warped smile, the ugly laugh and the acid twist of flame in his eyes.

But as Marco crossed the yard, Thorn saw he'd got it very wrong. This was a melancholy specimen, a guy who Thorn would wager was adrift in an ocean of pain and humiliation.

His face was so malformed that he'd probably attracted waves of bullies and drawn taunts and cheap shots since he was a kid, which had no doubt pushed Marco past the usual adolescent insecurity into full blown self-loathing. If a person's face alone could set the moral trajectory of one's life, this was one that could do it.

It was a face at war with itself, composed of hard cheekbones, chilly blue eyes frilled by lashes so long they might have been a movie starlet's, and a nose that had been broken and reset inexpertly more than once, features that together might have given him a certain masculine authority were it not for a tiny, puckered mouth that belonged on a five year old girl or a Barbie doll, and below those pink lips was a chin that was hardly there at all.

What his face lacked in menace, his body made up for. He was a few inches taller than Thorn, twenty pounds meatier with upper arms that strained the short sleeves of his black T-shirt. He had the rubbery hardness a man can't build with gym equipment. This was work-muscle, the sort earned by decades of digging postholes or slinging hay bales into the beds of pick-ups. Wrists so thick there was no ordinary cuff that would button around them.

"Who the fuck is this asshole standing in my yard?"

The Glock in his right hand was pointing down, finger touching the trigger.

Thorn allowed himself a faint, reassuring smile, then drew back the sleeve of his black sweatshirt, presented his right forearm. With a dubious frown, Marco came close, examined the symbol, then he wet a finger and scrubbed it across the Mehndi image.

Thorn's gut clenched and he sketched out an escape route, figuring a sprint toward the far corner of the barn was his best chance.

But bless Aarushi's skill, the drawing of the interlocking pyramids didn't smear.

Marco wiped his finger dry on the front of his shirt.

"I said three o'clock. It's not even noon."

"I was eager," Thorn said. "I couldn't wait. I'm ready to do this."

"It's a breach," said Marco. "Means you can't follow instructions. I made it clear. Any fuck-ups, the deal is off."

Marco stepped back a half-step as if to bring Thorn into better pistol range.

Thorn shrugged a half-hearted apology.

"Okay, so I fucked up. Not the first time. Probably won't be the last."

"What's your race?"

"What?"

"You heard me. What's your genetic stock?"

Thorn was baffled.

"You can't tell just looking at me?"

"You're too dark for Caucasian. Looks like there's jigaboo blood pumping around in there."

"Fuck you, Jack."

"Pakistan, India, one of the third worlds. Where you from, your parents?"

"I believe my great grandfather was a drunk in County Cork. That's Ireland."

"I'm not joking around, smart guy. You want some of my inventory, answer the question. You don't look like any white man I've seen."

"I spend a lot of time in the sun, maybe that's what you're seeing, it's called a tan."

"Oh, yeah? Where's that place, all this sun you been lying around in?"

"Florida," Thorn said.

Innocent enough answer, and true, but it triggered something in his face. A twitch around the eyes, a hardening in the jowls as if Marco felt a wasp tickling across his cheek and wanted to send it off with the least chance of being stung.

"Is that a problem, being from Florida?"

"It fucking well could be," Marco said.

"Why?"

"Where in Florida?"

It was clear to Thorn the time for truth-telling was past.

"Ft. Lauderdale, ever hear of it? Big with spring breakers."

"How close is that to Key Largo?"

A swallow of air clogged in Thorn's throat like a chunk of raw meat.

"What's wrong, I say something you didn't see coming?"

"I'm not following you."

"See, here's how it is. Out in Arizona last week, I hear the name of a guy, some kind of secret agent or some bullshit. He was sticking his nose way up my ass, looking to fuck with me. I was informed he was from Key Largo, Florida."

"Florida's a big place. Lots of people. The Keys are hours from where I live in Lauderdale. I don't know anybody down there, and I'm not here to fuck with you. I'm here to make a deal, hand over a shit ton of money in exchange for items to use for our shared goals. Yours and mine, and the goals of Abyss. Bringing fire and fury down on our mutual foes. You've been an inspiration to me and my people. We're going to show our appreciation by using these babies for our common interests."

"Your name wouldn't be Thorn, would it?"

By slow degrees the pistol was rising, aiming now at Thorn's knees, inching upward to his crotch.

"Man, I don't know where you're getting this shit. But my name is Lucas. Never heard of anybody named Thorn. What kind of dumbass name is that?"

Marco's eyes worked over Thorn's face as if trying to pry beneath his neutral mask. It took him half a minute before he made his judgment, then he backhanded the moisture off his tiny mouth. The deadly gleam in his eye waned and the pistol sagged.

Thorn allowed himself a sigh that he tried to conceal, though he wondered if Marco might notice the veins bulging in his temple from the throb of his pulse.

Marco knew his name, knew Thorn had been tracking him in Arizona. The only person with that information was Castillo who as far as he knew had never had face to face contact with Marco. So it had to be Tensia, his secretary, who Marco and Ingrid tortured to learn Dulce's whereabouts.

"Give me the cash," Marco said.

Thorn handed him the bag, making another quick scan of the surroundings for signs of a sniper. He was beginning to worry about Sugar, if he'd gotten lost or fallen into the hands of one of Marco's goons or maybe worse.

Romy in the crop-duster was another problem. Dropping hundreds of leaflets was meant to create a distraction, give Thorn a chance to do whatever was necessary at that moment. Instead, now that Key Largo was on the five-alarm watch list, if Marco spotted those words on a random page, things could move fast and fatal.

Marco lifted the cloth bag and said, "Feels light."

"It's what you asked for."

"We'll see about that."

"I need to have a look at what I'm buying."

"In the barn. Lead the way."

And yes, the landmines from Bobby Tennyson's long ago story were inside the shadowy building stacked three high and arranged in orderly rows. Marco stood close behind him, a tempting target.

But Thorn stifled the impulse to take him on, unsure who might be hiding in the gloomy corners of the barn or worse, sighting their weapons on Dulce and the others in the pen. He was willing to risk his own skin but not the innocents outside.

"Impressive," Thorn said. "We'll put these to good use."

"I give a shit. Take them home, blow them up in your backyard for all I care."

"What about the cause?"

"You're on your own. Our connection stops here. From today on, I don't know you, you don't know me."

"You don't want any credit for what we're going to do?"

"I'm retiring. I'm out of the game."

"Lost interest?"

Marco waved for Thorn to get moving, then followed him into the open yard.

"So tell me, Lucas. Why're you so concerned about my welfare?"

"If a leader retires, it creates a vacuum. Someone else will need to step up, assume the mantle."

"You applying for a job?"

"It might interest me, yeah, I've been looking for something with impact."

"My advice, go home, work on your tan."

Thorn had been making systematic sweeps of the grounds, ticking across every possible hiding spot and he'd seen no sign of any back-up. Marco said Ingrid was set up behind the barn, waiting.

Though he still wasn't sure where Sugarman was or how soon Romy would do her fly-over, it was time to take his shot.

"What's next?" Thorn said.

"Behind the barn, dig a grave, come back and choose who's getting buried."

He waved at Dulce and the others huddled in the far corner of the pen.

"I'm supposed to kill one of them?"

"While I'm inside with the cash, making sure it's all there, you prove you're one of us."

"Oh, shit, wait. I left my phone in the bag."

Thorn held out his hand. Marco drew back, puzzled.

"My cell phone, it's in the bag."

"Jesus Christ, what a total fuck-up."

As Marco extended the money bag, Thorn braced his feet to get his full weight behind the blow, picturing a hard right to the chin followed by a knee to the groin, a street-fighter's one-two, but before he could uncoil, a white van slewed into the yard, engine roaring, and braked to a hard stop about ten feet away.

The side door slid open and Sugarman came tumbling out, rolling twice across the lawn before he caught himself and began a slow struggle to his feet. There was a wash of blood on his forehead, a gash on his left cheek.

Two heavyset women in matching black jump suits dropped down from the van, the one in the lead holding a revolver that looked a lot like Sugarman's.

"You must be Marco."

Marco didn't answer.

"Saw this eggplant skulking around in the woods on our way in. Didn't look right, so we grabbed him. Thought he might be a cop or fed and you might want to grill him or kill him."

"Who the fuck am I talking to?" Marco's Glock was focused on the larger of the two women, the one holding Sugar's pistol.

The women's identical pixie cuts looked like they'd been styled with garden shears and whisk brooms. The leader's hair was dyed purple, her partner's pink. In the center of both their foreheads, inked in scarlet, were Abyss tattoos.

With a submissive shrug, Purple held Sugar's .357 by the barrel and leaned down and set it in the scraggly grass and stepped away. Marco kept his Glock steady on her, inching forward to less than ten feet, a can't-miss shot.

"I asked you a question. Who the hell are you?"

"Hey, look, we're sorry. We got here faster than we thought, killed some time in Bad Axe, but ran out of things to do. I'm Joany and this is Jilly, we're your three o'clock."

TWENTY-EIGHT

The gathering arranged itself into an untidy ring. Sugarman stood six feet away from the two women, while they kept a buffer of two long paces between them, then spaced a bit farther apart were Thorn and Marco. Like some kind of unholy assembly encircling Sugar's revolver as though it was an object of adoration.

Thorn weighed the odds of diving for the pistol, rolling to a shooting position and getting off a decent shot or two at Marco. But the geometry didn't favor him. Buying a Powerball ticket might be a safer bet. The other alternative was not much more attractive, crossing the six-foot span between him and Marco and tackling him before he could unload.

Or if somehow Sugar and Thorn managed to coordinate a pincer attack, chances were excellent that one of them would be dead instantly and if Marco's reaction time and shooting skills were simply average, both of them could go down together. From the look on Sugarman's face, he'd arrived at the same conclusion: wait for a better opening.

Such lethal calculations had lately become so routine out in Arizona and now in Michigan, Thorn had begun to wonder if he'd ever find his way back to those sun-stunned afternoons on his skiff tracking the ghost shadows of bonefish across the flats or the silver flash of tarpon. For an instant Thorn felt the twitch of muscle memory in his hands, a light tug on his line that a second later became a weighty lurch then a lightening zing of eight-pound test burning off his reel. A tarpon running at scorching speed for a hundred yards, then heaving its enormity to the surface, bursting through a white churn of water into the air, spinning, twisting in an acrobatic display to free itself of the hook, hanging forever five feet up against the blue sky then slamming onto its back against the waters where it lived and longed more than all else to return.

Marco's voice was gruff, impatient: "Where's your money, Joany and Jilly?"

"In the van, you want it now?"

"How much you bring?"

"Exactly what you said, what we agreed on. A hundred thousand for five landmines with VX nerve gas. Small bills like you want."

"You're good obedient girls, aren't you?"

"Obedient, yes, good not so much. You want it now, the money, or anything else maybe?"

"What else?"

Joany gave Marco a sly smile, a single flutter of eyelashes.

For a second his eyes dulled, deliberating the offer, then abruptly his face hardened like a dreamer roused by the hiss of a snake.

"The money will do."

"If you change your mind," Jilly said. "We're pretty gifted with certain things most men love. A double team like you won't believe."

"Just stay put until I finish up with these people."

Marco fixed his gaze on Thorn's face, his pistol fixed there too.

Without so much as a jiggle in his aim, he bellowed Ingrid's name, bellowed a second time before she appeared, rounding the barn in a trot, an assault rifle in her hands, a Kalashnikov with a long curved magazine. More than enough rounds to kill everybody arrayed before her. Kill them twice if need be.

She was long-legged and sinewy with a spiky thatch of dark red hair and eyes that flicked across the faces of each of these strangers and registered nothing that troubled her in the least. She wore blue jeans, heavy boots and a crudely knitted black sweater rimmed with red diamonds.

"What is this?" she asked Marco. "All these people."

"That's what we're about to find out."

Thorn shot a searching look at Sugar. Since climbing to his feet, he seemed to be swaying unsteadily, his eyes dreamy like he might pass out at any moment. Thorn read it as an act for Marco's benefit, playing an easy target till the moment came to strike.

But any scheme Sugar and he might have tried was derailed when Ingrid swung around and yelled, "The bitch is escaping."

On the far side of the pen, Dulce was three-quarters up the chain-link fence, toiling hand over hand toward the top rail.

"Shoot her, Ingrid," Marco said. "Shoot the twat."

Ingrid raised the AK and sighted on Dulce who'd frozen with her chin at the brim of the fence. Thorn took two quick steps and blocked her aim.

"I'll do it," he said. "Chance to prove myself."

"Get out of the way," Ingrid said. "Now."

"That's what those scum are for, right? Let me show my allegiance."

"You think we're idiots?" Marco said. "Nobody's handing you a weapon."

"Then I'll do her barehanded."

Marco's tiny pink mouth widened ever so slightly into a grin.

"Knock yourself out, dude."

Dulce had stalled at the top of the fence, exhausted from the climb or rigid with terror.

"Follow him," he told Ingrid, digging a key from his pocket and handing it to her. "If he twitches, shoot. I'll deal with our African guest."

Thorn glanced at Sugar who gave him a quick go-ahead nod,

he'd find a way to manage on his own. As Thorn loped over to the pen, near as he could tell Ingrid stayed at least two or three long strides behind him. Too far back for Thorn to try a fancy move, too close for Ingrid to miss with that AK-47.

Last week Marco and Ingrid had taken down Dr. Diego Martinez and his wife, an ex-Marine and a veteran State Trooper when they'd been on high alert guarding Dulce, and for years Ingrid and Marco had also been slaughtering migrants as sport. Not a couple of amateurs. No hesitation to fire.

At the gate Ingrid told him to step back. She unlocked the padlock and swung the door open. An elderly man and a bedraggled Hispanic woman in her thirties and a boy of five or six were bunched in one corner of the pen, the boy shivering behind the woman's mud-stained skirt.

Thorn edged across the pen and stood beneath Dulce.

"No te preocupes estoy aqui para ayudarte."

Don't worry I'm here to help you.

"No te creo."

She didn't believe him.

"Speak English, asshole." Ingrid prodded him in the back with the AK.

"Come on down, sweetheart. It's going to be okay. I promise."

"Why should I trust you?"

"No one's going to hurt you."

"You said that before but it wasn't true."

"Wait," Ingrid said. "The hell's she talking about? You two know each other?"

Thorn heard the distant drone of a plane. Romy coming in low and slow.

As the crop-duster's growl became a deafening rumble, Ingrid turned toward the plane's approach and lifted the AK to fire at its belly. Thorn seized the stock of the AK, but his fingers slipped and Ingrid wrenched it from his grasp, swiveled hard and slammed the rifle butt into his jaw.

Head whirling, Thorn stumbled back against the chain-link while hundreds of pages fluttered down. Through his blurry vision, Thorn watched Ingrid take point blank aim at his chest. He tried to spin away to safety and might have made it, when Dulce screamed a war-cry and hurtled from her perch, landing with a staggering thump on Ingrid's back, her forearm locking across Ingrid's throat.

Dulce's shriek changed to the deep-throated growl of an animal that has finally turned on its master after years of abuse. So much fury, sadness and pain stored in the girl's heart gave her arms such strength Ingrid couldn't shake her loose. Dulce was choking Ingrid for the sake of her lost mother, the migrants in the truck who'd been fleeing with her from Honduras, for all the adults who'd tried to protect her and lost their lives doing so.

Thorn tore the AK from Ingrid's grip.

"Let her go, Dulce. Let her go and step away."

Dulce hesitated, peering at Thorn's face, searching his eyes for the man she'd believed he was, a trace of reassurance. She must have found what she was hoping for, because she gave one final tightening of her stranglehold on Ingrid's throat and jumped free.

Ingrid gasped and tottered and her back slid down the chain-link fence and her butt thumped into the muddy ground.

"We need to help Sugarman," Dulce said.

"I'll come back for him. First we need to get you out of here."

"And them, they go with us, no?" She waved at the three migrants.

"Of course."

"And this one, what do we do?"

Thorn stared at Ingrid, feeling the weight of the Kalashnikov in his hand.

"You want to kill her?" Dulce said. "Don't you?"

He didn't answer but knew his face revealed the truth.

"But you know it is wrong. The woman is evil, but she is helpless. It would be *asesinato*. That is not who you are. Not who God wants you to be."

No way to explain to Dulce that Thorn had long ago moved beyond the help of God's grace. But to preserve hope for Dulce's salvation, he drew the belt from his jeans and lashed Ingrid's wrists tight and yanked her upright and fixed her wrists high above her head to the chain-link.

"Now we need to move."

☣ ☣ ☣

Savannah was finished. There was nothing more for her. She'd failed at everything, even failed at suicide, ramming the blue van with its cargo of nerve gas, destroying it and the drivers, but somehow managing to survive. Not even Nola's blue and pink pickup had suffered major damage.

After Thorn left, she climbed into Nola's truck, and stared at the shack where the landmines had been stored, where Judson hung himself, where that damn bird, Big Blue, badgered her daily with its mindless taunts.

During the collision with the van, Judson's shotgun was thrown to the floor. If it still worked, it could end her misery in a half-second. She leaned over and grabbed it up and planted the cold barrel against her chin. A simple pull and it would be done.

She stared at the shed, held the shotgun hard against her flesh and thought the thoughts of one's last seconds, of all the empty hours of her existence that added up to this final emptiness. Only one set of memories stood apart, the moments of optimism and resolve she'd felt during the long voyage on the *Flying Dragon* across eight hundred miles of Pacific, the days of seduction on Johnston Atoll, and carting those crates through the midnight breezes to the boat and sailing away. It had been glorious. It had been the peak of all her years. So much passion burning, such righteous anger at the loss of her brother Marty, such fury for those spineless politicians who sold young men patriotic fairy tales, so much heat in her heart, so much vitality and quickness of spirit.

All of it lost, grain by grain, drop by drop, tick by tick, all gone until only the emptiness prevailed, the hollow heart, the helpless mind, the lost soul.

She stared at the shed for a moment or two more. She started the truck, gunned the accelerator and felt the V-8 rumble, Nola's car, a gift to the bright young hope that would send their bloodline into the future, live the life they had failed to achieve. Nola was to be her consolation, her final chance at value. But she managed to sabotage even that innocent child, leaving the footlocker of woeful keepsakes unlatched and unguarded.

She sat and sat until a flicker of an idea aroused her and slowly took shape. A last chance, a small renewal of her youthful principles, not the triumph she once imagined, but at least a worthy finish.

Savannah set the shotgun aside and slipped the shifter into gear, U-turned in the drive, and headed off to do the one thing she should have done years and years and years ago.

TWENTY-NINE

As Thorn and Ingrid crossed the yard toward the pen, Marco said, "Now talk, colored boy. Make it fast. I'm half a twitch from ending your stay on earth."

Sugarman's ad lib skills weren't in Thorn's league, but staring at Marco's pistol gave him a jolt of inspiration

"I'm a friend of Savannah's."

"What?"

"We go way back," Sugar said. "Even before Johnston Atoll. The *Flying Dragon*, I taught her how to sail that thing."

Marco shook his head and blinked as if trying to weigh the likelihood of Sugar's claim. The man had a face like a kindergartner's first Play Doh project. The eyes and nose might even be considered handsome but it all went wrong with his pinched little mouth and an impish after-thought of a chin.

"Savannah said you were selling some items I'd find appealing. If it's what she described, then I'm your man. Willing to pay double the going rate. I'll take your whole stock, right here, right now. I got a mountain of cash fifteen minutes from here."

"Whoa, Nelly," the pink-haired one said. "We were here first."

"I can't believe you're even talking to this pickaninny," purple-hair said.

Sugarman eyed his .357 lying in the grass a tempting few feet away.

Sugar heard the low growl of the crop-duster heading their way. Romy, Romy, Romy. Bless Thorn's cockeyed scheme. The growl became a drone became a rumble then a painful roar as it passed less than a hundred feet overhead, fifty, sixty miles an hour, barely above stall speed.

As dozens of sheets rained down, Marco snatched at a passing page, missed it, batted away another, danced back, unsure what the hell was happening. The two women inched toward their van, losing their nerve in the chaos.

When an oversized funeral program fluttered down and settled on Marco's shoulder, he turned to brush it away, and Sugar made his move, scooped up his pistol, and sprinted toward the pen where Thorn, Dulce and the others were heading into a stand of evergreens. Ingrid lashed to the chain-link.

Fifty yards of open ground, imagining a phantom slug tearing into his back. No time for panic or existential thoughts, those would come later, if there was a later. Afraid, hell yes. But as Sugar knew from other brushes with lethal risk, these moments gave him a triple espresso boost.

He raced halfway across the open space before two pistol shots hissed near his head, a sobering sound. Another round kicked up dirt a yard to his right. At such a distance, handguns had poor accuracy and every stride he took made them even less so, but the fact gave him no comfort as he cut left, then did a shoulder roll on a grassy patch to his right. As he was coming back to his feet, a lucky shot struck the back of his right running shoe and kicked it off, stinging his heel bone.

He struggled to his feet, hobbled another yard or two before a hand grabbed his collar and slung him sideways to the ground.

He looked up at Marco, the .38 inches from his nose.

"Lose the gun," Marco said. "Now."

Sugar let it drop into the tall yellow grass. Marco whisked it up, held it in his left hand, the .38 in his right like some Saturday matinee cowboy.

Across the yard, the van roared to life and with wheels spinning, it skidded a half-circle and swung back toward Taggart Road.

"You just cost me a hundred grand, boy."

"Like I said, I'll give you double that."

"Stop with the bullshit. Now, what's your deal, darkie?"

Sugar was about to embellish the *Flying Dragon* story when Marco's phone trilled. He stepped back, tucked Sugar's .357 in his waistband, dug out the phone, looked at the screen then answered.

"What the fuck do you want, old woman?"

"I'm in the barn," Savannah said. "Your barn."

"What the hell are you saying?"

The bad reception made Marco's voice thin and scratchy. She was parked less than a hundred yards away but the closest cell tower was miles distant, voices bouncing around in the heavens, losing traction all the way.

She held the mouthpiece close and raised her voice.

"I said I'm in the barn. I'm waiting for you."

"What're you talking about?"

It was an easy guess for Savannah. Where else could he have stashed them?

"Just walk over here and meet me. I've got something critical to show you. It could save your ass. I'm back in the haystacks on the left."

"Fuck you."

"All right, don't come. But that's where I'll be if you work up the nerve."

"I got nerve. I got more fuckloads of nerve than you ever dreamed of."

"In the barn, Marco. Now. I'm not waiting much longer. Bad shit is coming down. This is your two minute warning."

"You're crazy."

She watched the bi-plane circling over the forest, banking hard, then turning to make another pass over the Whitman's farm. She'd heard the gunfire, seen the cascade of papers flung from the plane. Had no idea what was going on. Something Thorn cooked up, she supposed. It didn't matter. Nothing mattered. Nothing except luring that son of a bitch Marco into the barn. Do the world a service to make up for all she'd unleashed.

"I'm counting down, Marco. One minute and it's all over for you."

"You're batshit. You've always been batshit. Since I was a kid. Everybody knew it, how fucking nuts you were."

"I fucked you up, didn't I? I pushed you over the dark edge of the world."

"You didn't do shit. You get no credit. I'm who I am because I want to be."

"Thirty seconds, Marco. Meet me in the barn."

She cut the connection, tossed the phone out the window of Nola's truck.

At this point whether Marco went into the barn or not hardly mattered. If he did, fine, it might nudge the scales a bit closer to balance, that's all. A fitting closure. Cherry on top. The cornsilk angel on the tip of the Christmas tree.

But necessary? No, nothing was necessary any more. Except the one last thing, the one final goddamn act she'd left undone all these years.

Almost there.

When Savannah saw the white van hurtling toward her, she didn't hesitate. She flattened the accelerator, cut hard left to T-bone the van, kept the pedal to the floor, driving the van sideways into a ditch.

It took the occupants only seconds to recover and scramble out, armed with handguns, one had a pink pixie haircut, the other purple, both of them hefty. As they inched closer to Nola's truck, trying to peer through the tinted windshield, she saw the red overlapping pyramids emblazoned on their foreheads. The image from those stamping blanks Vegas had found in the basement of the abandoned Whitman house. The insignia for Marco's cult. Abyss.

That's all the evidence she needed. She powered the seat back to give herself room, then raised Judson's shotgun, chose her target and fired through Nola's windshield, took down purple hair, then fired a second time. Pink hair was spun around and thrown backwards by the blast and her body piled on top of her partner.

Two down.

Savannah climbed from Nola's truck and walked to the overturned van and dragged the side door open. The van was empty, the deal with Marco unconsummated. She felt a pang of guilt, but it passed quick.

Hell, it didn't matter if they'd scored the landmines or not. These two carried Marco's virus in their bloodstream. They would have spread it one way or another. If not the landmines, then some other instrument of carnage later on.

Savannah climbed back in Nola's truck, sitting on shards of window glass. Feeling no pain, she eased past the toppled van and idled down Taggart Road.

☣☣☣

"Get up, dark meat. Go untie my lady."

Marco motioned with the .38.

"Do it."

Sugar figured that by now Thorn and Dulce and the others had a decent head start, but the old man and the child would be slowing down their escape. If it had been Sugar leading the group, he would've found them a hiding spot in the woods, and circled back with the AK to do battle with Marco, Ingrid and the two ladies in the van. Though it was nearly impossible to predict Thorn's conduct, Sugar was trying to stall the best he could, string this out long enough to at least give Thorn time to stash Dulce and the others somewhere safe.

Sugarman led the way to the pen, Marco's heavy tread close behind him, Sugar looking for his chance. Hearing Romy's plane in the distance, but not likely that more leaflets would distract a second time.

Sugar slowed his pace, slowed it more, narrowing the distance between Marco and him, then as the throb of the crop-duster's engine approached, he took his shot. A sweeping leg kick, swiveling, aiming low—ankles, knees, either would do. Sugar hooked Marco's leg, ankle high, and pivoted hard to snatch it from under him, crumple the knee, take him down.

As a cop he'd honed the technique for years, breaking up bar brawls and taking down drunken husbands during domestic disputes.

Marco didn't try to block the move and didn't need to. His legs were so stocky and unyielding it was like trying to uproot a tree stump with chopsticks.

Sugarman stumbled, caught himself and was about to take another shot when Marco backhanded him in the face, an impact as crushing as a sock full of marbles. Sugarman found himself on his back, dazed, nose numb and gushing. Marco stood over him and shook his head as if saddened by Sugar's futile attempt. He drew back his boot and executed a short, savage rib-kick, and before Sugar could roll away, he stomped his gut, exploding the air from his lungs, then tried a second kick that missed Sugar's testicles by inches.

Marco leaned over him grinning.

"Go another round, Kunta Kinte?"

Sugar fought for breath. Tried to worm away, get out of range, appear more disabled than he was, lull the big man into dropping his guard. Though if he took another run at the guy he'd need more than a half-assed judo move.

"Huh? Can't hear you, ghetto boy. Want any more of that?"

"No, but thanks for asking."

"Who's the slave, who's the master?"

It should have cost him nothing to answer as Marco wanted, but when he spoke the words, they scalded his throat, left a sour, abiding taste.

"It's clear. You're the master."

"Which makes you what?"

"Slave."

"Very good, darkie. Look, I'd finish you off right here, but I'm curious who the fuck you are and why you're pretending to be something you're not. Now get up, and no more tricks. Go untie my girl. She looks to be in distress."

THIRTY

Thorn was a decent marksman, but had limited practice with an AK-47.

He was hidden behind a stand of evergreens, fir or spruce, not sure, but too bulky and misshapen for Christmas trees, short and squat, excellent cover and easy enough to spread the scratchy limbs aside to poke the muzzle through and take aim.

Marco was only twenty yards away, so close Thorn could hear him speaking, but with Ingrid and Sugar and him clustered nearby, Thorn held his fire. Too risky he'd clip his buddy.

Then there was Dulce. Ignoring his repeated pleas, she and the others had refused to stay in the thicket he'd found, unwilling to let Thorn out of their sight. At the moment they were hanging back a dozen feet behind him. Their torturous journey had taught them the urgency of latching on to anyone they deemed trustworthy or reliable. Making a bad decision could be the end for them.

Dulce continued to reassure them that Thorn was that man, though she kept peering up at him, her dark eyes tinged with lingering suspicion. He'd let her down. Left her with Sister Kathleen without proper defenses, a choice that led to her abduction and this current nightmare.

He didn't blame her. What she'd seen, what she'd lived through in recent days, her exposure to a dark, poisonous stratum of America had shaken her bedrock beliefs, her optimism, her sunny views of this land that she and her mother had risked their lives for. Given all that, Thorn was surprised he inspired any confidence in her at all.

He watched Sugar untie Ingrid's wrists. When she was loose, she staggered against the chain-link, rubbing the circulation back into her arms.

It took a minute or two but when she'd finally recovered, she swung around, cocked her arm and slapped Marco hard in the face.

"You fucker. You left me hanging there. You're chatting away like everything's fine, I'm strangling on my own spit."

Marco smoothed a palm over his reddened cheek, and slid the hand down to his throat, massaging it like he had something stuck in his windpipe. Giving Ingrid a smoky, lustful look.

"Savannah's in the barn," he said.

"What?"

"She called my cell, said she was waiting in the barn. Warned we're in danger. Told me to meet her inside."

"She called?"

He patted his pocket where he'd tucked his cell phone.

"No way she's in there. No way in hell she could've sneaked past us. Got to be some kind of fake out."

"We need to check."

"Where'd the fat chicks go?"

"Jumped ship."

"Jesus, and you're okay with that? Acting all Mr. Blasé."

"Plenty of people willing to pay for what we've got. Next time round, we'll bump up the price. Maybe even double it."

"Are you crazy? Planes flying over throwing shit out, strangers showing up, that guy tying me up and making off with our wetbacks. We're blown, Marco. We need to pack up what's left and get the hell out of here right now."

"The plane, these pussies, those aren't the law, they're greenhorns trying to burn us, they saw the video online and tracked us here. When we finish taking care of them, we're cool."

He prodded Sugarman in the sternum with his pistol.

"Isn't that right, pussy?"

Sugarman mumbled something Thorn couldn't hear.

"Yeah?" Ingrid raked a hand through her red hair. "What's Savannah want?"

"My guess, a piece of the action. She figured out what's going down. Wants to bargain with us, cut herself in, gotta be something like that."

"She'll be armed, try to strong arm us."

"Time she was dead," Marco said. "Long past time."

"Oh, come on, kill your own mother? Not even you are that far gone."

"She wasn't any kind of mother, not to me anyway. And damn right, if she's trying to steal what's ours, fucking-a, she's a dead old cunt. On the phone, Christ, she sounded batshit we didn't include her."

"And this negro?"

"Guy gave me a load of bullshit, says he taught Savannah how to sail the *Flying Dragon*."

"This guy? Get out."

"It's what he says."

"In Honolulu, 1971," Sugar said. "I was dockmaster at Diamond Head marina. Met Savannah, hit it off, I showed her how to handle the boat. A little tricky, not your average vessel."

Thorn had to smile. Sugar doing some ballsy improv.

Though they were still bunched up as they approached the barn, Thorn raised the AK, settled it against his shoulder, looking for a clear shot. He seemed to recall the sights on the AK were usually zeroed a foot high at a mid-range distance like this, so he aimed at Marco's belt and his finger was a feather's weight from squeezing off a round when Sugar rotated alongside Marco, putting his back to Thorn, blocking the sightline.

"What will you do?" Dulce whispered close behind him. The others were grouped ten feet away, standing in jittery silence behind an oak tree.

"Damn it, Dulce. Stay here, don't move again. I'm going after them."

"So you can shoot them. Kill them."

He looked at her, said nothing, but she read it in his eyes and she nodded.

"I think the Lord will forgive you this time. The man is evil, the woman too."

"Stay here, whatever happens, stay put."

As the three of them reached the barn door, Romy made her second pass, buzzing at the treetops, tossing a few hundred sheets of paper that swirled in the plane's wake and swarmed down like a flock of gulls homing in on a tidbit of food.

As a neon orange page sailed by Marco's head, he snapped out his hand and snagged it and read the print, crumpled it into a ball and pitched it away.

Then spun around and yelled, "Hey, Key Largo. You fuckhead. It's you, isn't it? I knew it was you, out in Arizona, now here. Come on, show yourself, Thorn. You want a piece of my ass, come get it. Come on, you chickenshit pussy face."

When he took another step forward, separating from Sugar, Thorn fired two quick shots, missed with both, blowing fist-sized gouges in the side of the barn. Ingrid squealed, pushed past Marco and ducked inside the door and slammed it behind her.

Marco fired several rounds in Thorn's direction, splintered the trunk of an evergreen to Thorn's right, tearing off a branch and spraying pine needles.

Thorn flattened to the ground, waved to Dulce and the others to do the same. He squirmed to his left beneath the lower branches of another fir tree, elbowing forward across the damp earth. He stopped at another narrow slot in the branches, scooched around to aim the AK just as Sugar broke away from Marco's side.

Sugarman lurched left, limped a few yards toward the end of the row of evergreens. Missing a shoe, his white sock clotted with blood.

Again Thorn's angle was off. Sugar blocking a clear shot. Trying to shake things up, rattle their formation, Thorn fired high, a quick burst of five or six, blew holes in the rotten siding.

Marco jogged a few yards, caught up with Sugar, collared him and wrenched him upright, hugged him against his chest, face-forward, using Sugar as his shield.

"You asshole," he screamed. "You motherfucker. What do you want?"

With his pistol pressed to Sugar's temple, he backed up, backed and backed till he was at the door, then slipped inside the barn, dragging Sugar with him.

Thorn wriggled through the pine branches, taking the shortest distance to the barn door. He climbed to his feet, holding the AK at port arms, and sprinted across the open yard, made it ten feet from the barn door when his left leg went numb and Thorn toppled to the earth.

The slug had torn a long divot on the outside of his jeans and made an inch or two groove into his thigh. Quadriceps. Four muscle strands woven together. He remembered that from high school, Coral Shores anatomy class, taught by the football coach who mostly read from the textbook. All that flashed through Thorn's head as he wormed closer to the barn, hauling the AK with him. Femoral artery. That was in there too. Large vessel, carried a ton of blood to a lot of important zones. If it was severed, well, he'd find out soon enough, things would simply darken and disappear.

He spotted the rotten gap two feet left of the door where Marco had set up his sniper nest. A hole in the wall no bigger than a golf ball. Hardly enough space to squeeze a muzzle through and still be able to see.

Thorn writhed closer to the barn, counter-intuitive, but it made crazy sense, removed him from the limited angle Marco could manage with that small cavity. The leg was numb, still in the golden moments when adrenaline and nerve damage combine to deaden the flesh. It wouldn't last long. The shock was already telescoping his vision in and out and in again, wide-angle to pinhole, the focus dial spinning, bringing a sickening rush of digested food up from his gut. He didn't puke. Tasted it in his throat, swallowed it back down.

He managed to swivel onto his back, aim the AK at the golf ball hole and spray a half dozen rounds. It chewed the wood apart, made the golf ball into a pie plate. Thorn realized his mistake, giving Marco a larger view of the surroundings.

He bulled his body up, willing himself to stand and gimped around the corner of the barn. Steering himself like a car on an icy pond. He was on the side of the barn now, safer there. He could see down the length of the barn and detected no spy holes. Though the boards had warped and shrunk and split, so there were plenty of ways for Marco to see a human shape passing by.

Ahead of him an ancient wood ladder lay in the weeds. As old as the barn itself and in bad shape. He hobbled to it, levered it up from the snarl of grass, lost his balance and went down on his side. What good would a ladder do? He wasn't thinking straight. Thinking had never been his strong suit. He was the impulse guy, the flailer, the monkey wrencher.

From the ground he looked up to the roof of the barn. A single air vent near the apex. Two by two, smaller than an average window. The ladder might reach it. Maybe not. The ladder looked frail, a couple of rungs missing.

Rushing through the front door of the barn would be suicidal. If he had a chance to take Marco down, it looked like that vent might be the only way.

He staggered to his feet, felt the aching hollowness where his leg had been. Managed to balance on one foot as he lifted the ladder, used it as a crutch to get closer to the wall and prop the ladder against the barn. Its top rung was a foot shy of the vent.

Close enough.

He rubbed at the bloody wound, regretted it immediately, though the pain gave him a burst of juice. He counted twelve rungs. One at a time, carry the AK, don't drop it, don't fall, try not to groan when he put weight on the spoiled leg.

He mounted the first rung with his good leg, pulled the dead leg up. Fit his foot on the rung and added weight, pound by pound until the wobbly limb held but the stab of pain almost knocked him out. That wouldn't work.

He used his free hand to chin himself up to the next rung, brought his good leg up, chinned up to the next one and the next. To hell with the bad leg. Let it dangle as he mounted the ancient contraption.

In the far field, he caught a glimpse of Romy coming in for a landing, making a brutal touchdown that bounced the plane ten feet back into the air, but she got control and after a vicious series of bumps she coasted to a standstill on the rugged ground.

He heard another motor behind him and below. Couldn't let himself look down. Knew he'd lose his balance. Was it someone come to save them? Had Romy called Frank Sheffield? Was it the cavalry? He wouldn't let himself look. He climbed past the missing rungs. Out of breath, panting. Almost at the top. One more chin up. The motor coming closer. A big V-8. He recognized that throaty sound, the heavy throb of American engineering, the gas-wasting, clean-air-be-damned way over-powered workhorse.

He was at the vent, the damn ladder had held. He'd overcome his useless leg. He brought his head over the lip of the vent, standing one-legged on the next to last rung, brought the AK up to aim down into the barn.

And the V-8 was closing in behind him.

He wouldn't look, couldn't look or he'd fall, he'd swoon and go down. He knew that. Couldn't look.

But he did.

With high beams blazing, a powder blue and pink pickup truck crossed Marco's yard at forty miles an hour or more, no hesitation, heading directly for the front door of the barn, speeding up.

It hurtled through the front wall, jolting the entire structure, almost tipping Thorn backwards into the air. He grabbed a cedar shingle and held on, then drew back to the vent.

Through the opening, Thorn watched Ingrid and Marco leap out of the way of the truck and he saw Sugarman still standing off to one side. Saw the truck slam to a stop, put its gearbox in neutral, engine revving higher and higher to redline, 5000, 6000 RPMs.

In one corner of the barn the crated landmines were stacked neatly. The truck's high beams lit them up, engine racing, then slammed into gear, roaring toward them, crashing dead center. Dead center.

Pitching crates and landmines into the air. They tumbled and rolled until five or six of the crates came to a quiet stop in the layer of hay on the floor.

Marco raised his pistol and fired at the truck. Passenger window exploded. A woman's howl of pain and rage. Had to be Savannah.

Thorn aimed the AK down and let loose a dozen rounds, hit Marco with a couple of them, making him hop and jerk and dance like a convulsive puppet. Thrown backwards, staying on his feet, managing somehow to track the incoming fire upward to the vent and aim his pistol up at Thorn.

The truck started up again, backed halfway across the barn and lurched forward, Savannah adjusting the steering wheel, then halting and revving like a dragster at the starting line, as Sugar gimped toward the door, stumbled over something in the straw, went to his knees, but kept crawling toward the demolished front wall of the barn.

Thorn could see the side of Savannah's face. A bloody wound at her throat, her mouth set grimly. She gunned the engine, gunned it again, jammed it into gear and once again the truck raced towards the remaining crates of landmines filled with VX nerve gas, the M23's, stolen long ago from a Pacific Island, one of America's grotesque and unforgiveable weapons of war, and Savannah smashed the stack of crates head-on and this time one of them detonated and that first blast set off a chain reaction.

In a blaze of white light the barn erupted.

Thorn's ladder was blown backwards, slinging him into the branches of a spruce or a pine or a fir. Something he'd have to learn one day, the difference between evergreens, not information a Florida boy usually needed to know. But this one had saved his ass, so he had to discover its name.

Shingles flew around him, boards went spinning, hardware sailed past his face like shrapnel, and the stinging, choking fumes began to blossom from the wreckage, invisible and deadly.

THIRTY-ONE

Thorn woke sweating and cold, his arms and legs were twitching as if zapped with low voltage batteries. He lifted his head a few inches and saw the barn had collapsed into a mass of planks, rafters and beams. Flames were erupting in spots with gray smoke spiraling up. The roof of the pickup truck jutted through the debris, headlights still blazing, windshield washers ticking back and forth.

Warm water splashed over his face, more water poured on the front of his shirt. He tried to wipe his eyes clear but someone blocked his hand. He blinked several times and caught a glimpse of a plastic gallon jug. Dulce was holding it and tipping it onto his face. He sputtered, managed a breath.

"What're you doing?"

"The poison, washing it off to save you."

The white-haired man he'd seen in the pen was sloshing water onto Thorn's hands and his exposed ankles. Very focused on his efforts, peering down at his handiwork with a blissful smile as though this moment was the culmination of years of striving. Emptying one jug, and turning to pick up another that the young boy was delivering from somewhere.

"Sugarman? Did he make it?"

Dulce waved to Thorn's right where Sugar was laid out, the weary Latin woman was pouring water over him. Methodically working from his face to his feet.

"In Honduras Alejandra was a nurse. She tells us what to do with poison gas. She never see it before, but read about it in her studies. Must wash away quickly. There is hope you will survive, but you must continue with breathing, taking much into your lungs, the fresh air.

"Alejandra bandage your leg. It has stopped bleeding. I say that right?"

"Exactly right."

Though it hadn't stopped throbbing. A troubling lack of sensation was creeping up to his abdomen.

Thorn called out to Sugar, asked if he was okay.

He sputtered something as the woman poured more water on his face and hair. Raising his hand, giving Thorn a thumbs-up.

Dulce said, "I took Mr. Sugar's phone to call *emergencia*. They're coming."

Thorn lay his head back down and rested, relishing the bath, the first he could remember taking fully dressed. He eased the breaths down his sore throat, forcing himself to go slow and steady.

Behind Dulce the boy who'd been hauling water stopped and gasped and muttered something in a squeaky voice, turned his back on them and ran towards the road.

"What is it? What's wrong?" Thorn sat halfway up, propped on his elbows.

Twenty yards away Marco was pushing aside planks and twisting up from the rubble. He got to his feet, the pistol in his hand, his shirt ripped away, exposing a wound in his shoulder and another in his left biceps. From the corner of his tiny mouth a trickle of white foam was running to his chin and dribbling onto his bare chest.

Alejandra backed away from Sugarman, muttering in Spanish what sounded like exhortations to her lord.

Marco staggered across the grass, aiming his pistol at Thorn. Dulce angled in front of him, but Thorn told her no, step back, he'd handle this. Marco continued his lurching march, stiff-legged and as clumsy as a mummy recently reawakened.

He stood at Thorn's side, looking down at him, his nose was running, his pupils were pinpoints.

"The man with the tan."

"Yes."

"You're Thorn, aren't you?"

"I am."

"What do you want with me?"

"Nothing anymore," he said. "I think it's all done."

"Why did you do this?"

"To help a friend."

"What fucking friend?"

Thorn watched the .38 wavering, insecure in his hand.

"My friend was the man you killed in Arizona."

"What man?"

"He called himself Bobby Tennyson, but his real name was Ray Murphy. Your old man."

"Fuck my old man."

"Yes, you accomplished that."

"Why? What do you care about any of this?"

"It's what I do," Thorn said. "It's just what I do."

"Not anymore it's not."

Thorn only saw a fleeting shadow creeping behind Marco. He was woozy and his eyesight was a ghostly blur, clouded, muddled as if he was staring through cheesecloth at a hazy world.

Dulce screamed her war-cry again and leapt at Marco and he

turned his pistol towards her, hand shaking, but before he could fire, his knees gave out and he crumpled to the ground and sprawled face down alongside Thorn, a black length of steel buried between his shoulder blades, a tire iron Thorn would later discover, the one thing Romy had found in the plane's toolbox that might be used as a weapon.

A week later it was raining off and on in Key Largo, a gloomy sky that seemed to hover so low you could reach up and scoop some of the foamy air and use it as shaving cream. The three of them were assembled in Thorn's living room, Dulce with a new red backpack at her feet, Romy with the leather satchel she came with. Standing awkwardly, time to say good-bye but nobody ready for it. Sugarman was waiting in his car downstairs, giving them some privacy to say their final words.

"You understand, don't you?" Romy said

"Sure I do," said Thorn. "I would stay a few thousand miles away from me too if I could manage it. I'm trouble. I'm the worst luck you can have."

"I wouldn't go that far. You've brought some good luck too."

"The two of you will fly off, that's it, we'll never see each other again. We promise to stay in touch but it won't happen. Drift away into new adventures."

"You're getting maudlin," Romy said. "People come and they go. Nothing profound about it. No reason to get sappy. I gave you a lift back east and now it's time I go home, get back to work. You crossed paths with Dulce, it was an accident. You helped each other out. Great, say thank you and get on with it."

"You saved my life, Romy."

"I don't know about that. Dulce was about to chew off Marco's arm. She wasn't going to let anything happen to you. And Marco died from the VX not the tire iron. Don't hang that on me."

"What I did," Dulce said, "it was nothing you wouldn't have done for me."

"You'll be okay with Sister Kathleen? You're sure?"

"I'll be fine," she said. "I like her. She's simple and true."

"Frank Sheffield called Sugarman this morning. He's working to get your citizenship papers in order, and make sure they're expedited."

"He can do that?"

"He says he can. He knows people, important ones. He's never failed us yet."

"The feds should give Dulce a damn gold medal," Romy said, "or whatever they hand out for above-and-beyond-the-call-of-duty."

"Frank will come through. Count on it."

Thorn limped over to his fly-tying table and chose one of his favorites. A puff of fur that a raccoon had left behind on the prickly trunk of a floss silk tree that grew down by the shoreline. He'd paired that sprig of fur with a white tuft of an osprey's feather, the ocean eagle that roosted in a nest atop a channel marker a half mile offshore. A lure composed of elements from the land and from the air.

Before he gave it to her, he snipped off the point of the hook and used a file to smooth away the jagged edges. Taking his time, not wanting this to end.

When he was satisfied it wouldn't hurt her or anyone else, he handed the saltwater fly to Dulce. She examined it, turning it this way and that, holding it up to the window and the gray sunlight, looking through its filmy surface. Seeing what a fish might see, its quiet color, its exotic blend of ingredients, a shape that resembled nothing they'd ever seen.

"It's beautiful. But I don't fish. What can I use it for?"

"Nothing. Absolutely nothing. Like a lot of beautiful things."

Romy picked up her satchel, stepped over and gave Thorn a

moist kiss on the lips. A long one, though not long enough.

"It's been a blast," she said.

Dulce shouldered her backpack and opened her arms and embraced Thorn, holding him firmly, then with quiet resolve she stepped back and gave him a smile he would savor on the many nights to come when sleep eluded him.

"I'll be back to check on you, Thorn. Make sure you're staying out of trouble."

"I'll count the seconds."

ABOUT THE AUTHOR

James W. Hall has published 21 novels, two non-fiction works, two collections of short stories and five volumes of poetry. He lives in the mountains of North Carolina with his wife, Evelyn, and their Cavalier King Charles spaniels. To find out more and stay in touch, check out:

www.jameswhall.com

CPSIA information can be obtained
at www.ICGtesting.com
Printed in the USA
LVHW021458280921
698930LV00002B/332

9 798655 823051